THE COUPLE IN THE PHOTOGRAPH

VALERIE KEOGH

ALSO BY VALERIE KEOGH
BOOKS PUBLISHED BY BLOODHOUND BOOKS

THE DUBLIN MURDER MYSTERIES

No Simple Death

No Obvious Cause

No Past Forgiven

No Memory Lost

No Crime Forgotten

No Easy Answer

PSYCHOLOGICAL THRILLERS

The Three Women

The Perfect Life

The Deadly Truth

The Little Lies

The Lies He Told

In memory of my brother-in-law, Tony Lonergan.
Never forgotten.

1

Keri and Nathan Metcalfe were standing on the platform of a train station in Italy. Tracks stretched into the distance behind them and two rather battered suitcases stood at their feet. They were on their honeymoon. Young and in love. At six two, Nathan was eight inches taller than Keri and her head was tilted slightly upward, his a little down as they stared into one another's eyes. Her arms were around his neck, his around her waist. The warmth of his hands came through the thin cotton of her dress. Almost flesh on flesh. The erotic thought curved her lips into a sensuous smile that made his brown eyes narrow in echoing lust.

How long had they stood like that – her copper curls dancing in the slight breeze that blew through the station, his shoulder-length black hair falling forward so that he had to keep taking his hand away to push it behind his ears – perhaps a minute, maybe only seconds. But time enough for a stranger to have captured the shot. She and Nathan had separated before the photographer hurried over. 'I caught that pose,' he said, sounding as pleased as if he'd photographed a rare sighting of a wild bird. 'If you give me your address, I'll send it to you.'

Keri remembered staring at the man's prominent, crooked yellowish teeth and shaking her head, ready to say, *no thanks,* but even as she prepared the polite words of refusal, Nathan was spilling their name and address, repeating it slowly, spelling out the name of the street, and their surname.

'What harm could it do?' Nathan had said later when the train was chugging through the countryside to their destination. 'If he sends it to us, we'll have a nice photo, if he doesn't, we're no worse off, are we?'

Nathan was right, of course.

The photograph arrived a couple of weeks later. The stranger might have been dentally challenged but he had managed, by skill or luck, to have captured the magic of that moment in the train station.

But Nathan was also wrong. *What harm could it do?*

What possible harm could a photograph of the newly wed and very much in love couple cause?

2

K eri Metcalfe rocked gently back and forth on her office chair. There were contracts that needed to be looked over but she couldn't stir up any enthusiasm. It was Friday, there was nothing urgent that couldn't wait till Monday.

She'd promised their children, twins Abbie and Daniel, to be home on time for a change and they'd also made her promise to bring Nathan with her. They were up to something, something more to mark their twenty-fifth wedding anniversary than the dinner Keri had organised in their favourite restaurant. She squeezed her eyes shut and hoped to whatever gods there may be that they'd not organised a surprise party.

It had been an exhausting week. Once again, she wondered if it wasn't time to take a step back from her role as partner in the conservation and restoration company she and Nathan had founded shortly after they married. Metcalfe Conservation was regarded as one of the best in the UK but with that came commitments and responsibilities.

Their success had been hard won. They'd taken an enormous risk in the beginning. The banks refused their initial loan application so they'd borrowed money from both sets of parents to start up. Keri was convinced that Nathan's passion for the restoration of historic buildings combined with his skill as a stonemason was a winning combination. He was equally convinced that her organisational skills would make it work. And it did. But the early days were tough.

They rented a small premises and took on a couple of craftsmen, paying a higher hourly rate to get the best. Keri and Nathan worked long hours, and in the first year took any job that was offered. If Nathan considered some of this work beneath him, if he worried that a couple of the companies had less than ethical practices, Keri waved the sheaf of unpaid bills and lifted an eyebrow. She didn't need to say a word. All the money they made went to pay the wages and bills. Nathan worked seven days a week, and when the ends still refused to meet Keri took a part-time job in a local pub.

They were always tired but neither ever considered giving up, convinced success was a stretch of a finger away. Plans, hopes and wishes kept them going and despite the exhaustion, they were happy.

A little over a year later, they'd built a small client base and gained a reputation for excellent work and reliability. Capitalising on this, they moved to bigger offices and took on additional staff. With more work coming in, extra quotations to give out, contracts to sign and staff to organise, Keri finally gave up her job in the pub.

Shortly after they'd moved into their new office, she insisted that she and Nathan start taking Sundays off. 'We need time to relax,' she said to him. 'You've been looking tired recently.' She cupped her hands around his face. He did look tired and those dark circles under his eyes were new. She always slept like she'd been knocked unconscious, maybe he'd not been sleeping so well. 'Is everything okay, Nate?'

'Fine,' he said placing his hands over hers. He took them away and drew her closer.

Fine. Keri knew that word. She used it herself often enough when she was pissed off about something she didn't want to talk about. She started watching Nathan more closely. He was drinking more, eating less. He was a handsome man with the dark hair and olive complexion he'd inherited from a Greek grandmother who had died when he was a baby. His hair, long when Keri had met him, was now kept for convenience almost militarily short. It suited him, or at least it had until he'd lost weight. Now with his full cheeks slightly sunken, he could pass for an extra in a movie about a concentration camp.

They'd always talked about everything but now, when she asked if there was anything worrying him, his eyes slid away from hers and he laughed dismissively. She knew there wasn't another woman... not because she was so convinced he'd always be faithful, although she was, but because she knew where he was for every minute of every day.

She kept a closer watch, assigned him easier jobs, asked subtle questions of the other craftsmen but discovered nothing out of the ordinary. Eventually, she decided it had been stress, and when he'd said he'd work on the Sunday of a particularly busy week, she shook her head. 'You need a rest. Anyway, I want us to sit down and discuss the details of that business philosophy we've been talking about forever.'

It was still work, but she took him to a local pub for Sunday lunch, and over the food, with a couple of pints for him and glasses of wine for her, they drew up a company philosophy that promised to adhere to the highest work practices and health and safety standards.

Keri picked up the A4 pad and read over what she'd written. She looked at Nathan with a smile and lifted her glass to tip it gently against his. 'Here's to Metcalfe Conservation. We're getting there, Nate.'

He took the notes from her and read them over. 'This is where I wanted us to be. Professional and ethical.' He put the pad down on the table, laid his hand flat on top and looked at her with an unusually serious light in his eyes. 'I'd like to start turning down work that doesn't meet these standards.'

She pointed to his hand. 'It looks almost as if you're making an oath!'

'Maybe I am.' Then he pulled his hand away and laughed. 'No harm, is there, in making an oath to be the best we can be.'

'No.' She reached for his hand and clasped it between hers. 'No harm at all. We're going to be a great success, I know it.'

3

The slightly worrying dip in their income following their decision to turn down work that didn't meet their standards only lasted weeks. Keri had cleverly used their newly devised company philosophy in a marketing campaign and posted a copy to every contact in their database. She also persuaded a journalist in a local popular newspaper that they were worth a full-page article. It helped that Keri and Nathan were photogenic, he with his slightly exotic good looks and she with her pale skin and thick mane of shoulder-length copper curls.

She would have preferred that the journalist concentrate on the company, their new philosophy, their skill and expertise, but Keri wasn't a fool – if their smiling faces were what the journalist wanted, that's what she'd get, but Keri made sure that the background to each shot had the Metcalfe Conservation logo in view.

Either the marketing campaign or the newspaper article, or a combination of both, brought them more work. Two months later, as they walked home hand in hand one evening, they weighed up their options. They discussed the contracts they'd bid for... the ones that would guarantee work for months... and talked about expanding.

'*Qui audet, vincit.*' Keri laughed at Nathan's surprise. 'It's the only Latin I can remember. *Who dares, wins.* I think we should take the risk and go for it.'

So they did.

In their new spacious and more salubrious office with more staff on their payroll, they were back to counting pennies and eating cheap meals. They took turns to bolster each other's spirits when exhaustion weighed them down, piercing the gloom with talk of their future and the success that was waiting for them.

Slowly, the risk and their hard work began to pay off.

'We should get a bigger apartment,' Nathan said, when they'd signed a contract with a company that would guarantee work for a minimum of three years.

Keri looked around their tiny cluttered home. A bigger apartment? It was so tempting, but she was the practical one and shook her head. 'How much time do we spend here, really? I'd be happier to stay put for the moment, pour all the profits back into the business, and pay our parents back what we borrowed.'

It took another year to repay the loans by which time they'd moved into yet bigger offices, taken on more staff and won several more contracts for restoration of historical buildings.

'Now we can move into a bigger apartment,' Keri said waving the latest signed contract. 'We're on our way, Nate!'

By the time their twins Abbie and Daniel were born two years later, they'd made their first million. The following year, Keri and Nathan bought their first home together, a Victorian three-storey house on Northampton Park, one of the nicer areas of Islington, North London.

'It'll be our forever home,' she'd said when he questioned why they needed to move from a two-bedroomed apartment into a six-bedroomed house. 'And look–' She pushed open the bifold doors. '–tad dah!'

The one-hundred-foot back garden, with tall trees at the boundaries blurring the edges to give the impression of the house being set in the countryside rather than the middle of London, was certainly impressive.

It was enough to persuade Nathan. 'It's fabulous.' He turned back to the house. 'Not sure what we're going to do with all the rooms though.'

Keri laughed and hugged him. 'We'll have lots more children to fill them.'

She wanted to wait until Abbie and Daniel were older. In a year or two the business would be on a secure enough footing that she could step back from it and concentrate on her family.

But the years passed too quickly and despite their energetic attempts, more children never materialised. Keri and Nathan had grown into the house, not with the bigger family they'd hoped for, but with staff to free them to concentrate on the business.

Leigh, their live-in nanny, Freda who kept the house clean and Sarah who cooked nutritional if not very exciting meals five days out of seven.

Sometimes, Keri felt like a stranger in her own home and she swallowed the irrational resentment when she came in from work to find these women enjoying the beautiful house that she spent little time in. But all three adored Abbie and Daniel which made leaving the twins every day a little easier. Now and then, she'd think about reducing her days in the office, maybe doing a four or even a three-day week, but then another big contract would come in and she'd be swallowed by the work.

Success had its own problems. With so much work coming their way from the north of England and Scotland, Nathan had suggested they open a branch of Metcalfe Conservation in Glasgow. It made sense.

It also meant that she and Nathan were spending more nights apart.

4

Keri rocked back and forth on her chair again before pushing to her feet. She couldn't remember the last time she and Nathan had left work at the same time. He was often away overnight, either in Glasgow or to be near where one of their teams was working. She'd given up arguing that he didn't need to attend every site. He was convinced that the personal touch was one of the reasons for their success.

Recently, she couldn't be bothered arguing the point.

She left her office and crossed the broad stretch of the reception area to Nathan's door. The two offices, separated by a short corridor, were arranged in a semicircle around the reception desk. Both had glass walls – it was supposed to indicate their complete belief in transparency and had seemed like a good idea when they'd had an architect design their new headquarters several years before.

The idea had looked great on paper, but there were days when Keri wanted to shut the door and hide away. Hard to do in a goldfish bowl. It meant that she could see immediately that Nathan was on the phone to someone. Instead of interrupting him, she went to speak to their receptionist, Roy, nodding along as he filled her in on the latest in his long line of hobbies.

'Mixology! Sounds good. Maybe we'll put you in charge of the Xmas party this year. You can mix cocktails for us all.'

Roy, a slight, dapper man who was never seen, winter or summer, without a colourful waistcoat, stuck a thumb up. 'You're on. I might come up with a Metcalfe Special.'

'I'll look forward to that.' She turned to look towards Nathan's office and saw him put his phone down. She gave Roy's upper arm an affectionate squeeze. 'Don't put any more calls through to Nathan, please. I'm dragging him away.'

She hurried over and opened the door before he had a chance to pick up the phone and make one of his interminable calls. He could blend business and gossip like nobody she'd ever met. 'You haven't forgotten we're going out to dinner, have you?'

'Forgotten our wedding anniversary? Are you mad, woman, how could I? He got to his feet and slipped around the desk to grab her before she could escape. 'Twenty-five years!'

'Let me go, you idiot. People can see, thanks to those daft walls.'

'People? There's only Roy. He doesn't care. Shouldn't a man hug his wife especially on such a momentous occasion?'

She pushed Nathan's hands away. 'Are you ready to leave?'

'Sure.'

'Right, I'll get my stuff.' She punched his arm gently. 'Don't sit down again, I know you'd be tempted to make one more call.' His laugh followed her back to her office.

It wasn't a long walk from the office to Walthamstow Central where they'd catch the Victoria line to Highbury and Islington.

Since they'd moved to the new offices they'd only done the journey home together a handful of times.

'Remember when we used to walk home together every night?'

She saw him shoot her a curious look.

'Now the twins had to ask me to make sure we came home together.'

He sighed. 'You head off early. I have meetings, clients and suppliers who want to meet for a drink. It's an important part of the job, you know that. I've stopped asking you to come along 'cos you always say you can't be bothered.'

She lifted a hand. 'Yes, I know. I was just saying…'

'What?' He turned to look at her, surprised when she stopped, her hand over her mouth. He reached for her in quick concern. 'Keri, what's wrong?'

She kept one hand over her mouth and pointed to something behind him. 'Look!'

5

Keri heard Nathan's gasp, then his laugh rolling out as she continued to stand, her hand pressing so hard against her mouth it hurt.

She recognised the photograph, of course, how could she not, but what she couldn't understand was what it was doing blown up and filling the side of a bus shelter.

'It's that photograph of us at the train station in Italy,' Nathan was saying.

'The twins. This is why they wanted us to come home together, so we could see it.'

'We look good.'

They did. It was a beautiful shot of a couple gazing into one another's eyes, obviously in love. Blown up as it was, the image was slightly blurred, but it was still recognisable as Keri and Nathan, the blurring making it look as if they hadn't aged a day since it was taken. She ran a hand over her smooth chignon. Back then, when she was so much younger, she'd worn her hair loose. Now, it was almost always tied back, and the copper colour came courtesy of her excellent hairdresser rather than Mother Nature.

If they'd simply left it as a visual image it wouldn't have been too bad, mightn't have attracted much attention but no, their darling children had gilded the damn lily. Across the top of the black-and-white shot, written in large red print, *Keri and Nathan Metcalfe, still as much in love after 25 years.*

'Must have cost them a fortune,' she said. Not the reaction Abbie or Daniel would have wanted, and one that made Nathan raise an eyebrow in surprise.

'It was a lovely thing to do.' He put his arm around her shoulder and pulled her close.

'Lovely.' Keri tried to smile. *Maybe Barry won't notice, maybe he'll pass by without seeing it.*

They were almost at the station when her phone buzzed. Nathan was a step ahead, pushing through the mass of commuters heading in the same direction. She took the chance and pulled out her mobile and saw immediately her hope had been in vain. Barry's message dripped with sarcasm.

So, you're still as much in love, are you?

There was no time to tap out an answer or explanation. She'd ring him when she had a chance. She saw Nathan stop a little ahead of her. He was staring up at a large billboard plastered with another photograph of them. Obviously a recent one, she didn't remember it being taken. She was looking at him, he at her. They were laughing, looking happy. And, once again, in case it wasn't clear enough from the photograph that this was a couple in love, it was written in bold writing across the top. *Keri and Nathan Metcalfe... still in love after 25 years!*

Barry hadn't missed the photograph at the bus stop. There was no way he was going to miss this.

'We look fabulous,' Nathan said, still staring upward.

'Yes, but I hope that's it.'

Keri's voice was sharp and he turned to her with a frown. 'They must have planned this for a long time, don't spoil their excitement.'

She hooked her arm into his and tugged. 'Come on handsome, let's go home.' She squeezed his arm. 'I'll say I was thrilled, okay? They meant well.' *After all, the twins don't know it's a lie. Neither does Nathan.*

At home, Abbie and Daniel greeted them with glasses of champagne and grins of delight at the success of their plan.

'Did you like it?' Abbie asked, unable to control her excitement.

'It was an amazing surprise.' Keri was able to be honest in this at least. 'It must have cost a fortune.'

'One of my uni friends, her father is in the business, so I got mate's rates. They'll be there for a month too.' Abbie clapped her hands together, her eyes shining. 'We wanted to do something special for twenty-five years.'

A month! Bloody marvellous. Keri finished the champagne, wishing she could put a straw in the bottle and drain the lot. 'Right, I'm going to have a shower and change for dinner.' She left Nathan talking to Abbie and Daniel about the success of their plan and headed up the stairs.

In the en suite, she shut and locked the door before sitting on the toilet seat and ringing Barry, the man she'd been having an affair with for the last month.

6

Keri had bumped into Barry Morgan as she'd rushed from the office one evening, too busy tapping out a message on her mobile to see the man who'd stepped out of the building next door looking in the opposite direction. Only his quick reaction in grabbing her had prevented her from falling. Cue profuse apologies on both sides, at the end of which he'd introduced himself.

'Barry Morgan, solicitor, I work in there.' He waved to the building behind.

'Keri Metcalfe, general dogsbody,' she had replied with a laugh, enjoying the admiring looks the man was giving her. She pointed to the next-door building. 'I work in there.'

'Metcalfe Conservation.' He raised an eyebrow. 'More than a dogsbody, I'm guessing.'

Keri had had a hellish week with one thing after the other causing her headaches. 'Officially, I'm a partner. Believe me, general dogsbody is often more appropriate and it certainly was today.'

'It sounds like you need a drink.' He tilted his head to a pub further along the street. 'I've time for one, if you do.'

Nathan was away in the Glasgow office for a few days. The twins, if they came home, wouldn't arrive till late. Keri wasn't looking forward to watching TV with a Waitrose ready meal and glass of wine. She gave the stranger an assessing look, taking in the expensive suit, the startlingly white shirt and conservative tie. Only slightly taller than she, his build was almost weedy thin and, in complete contrast to the swarthy Nathan, everything about him, skin, hair, and eyes, was pale. He wouldn't be her type, but it was hard not to be swayed by his obvious admiration.

'Why not,' she said, throwing caution and everything she'd ever promised herself she'd never do to the wind.

Over a drink, Barry told her he was divorced. 'It didn't work out,' he said simply. 'We tried but we weren't making each other happy anymore. We divorced a year ago. She's met someone else and is talking about getting married next year.' He lifted his glass in a toast to the idea. 'She's happy. We made the right decision.'

'And now you're looking for happiness?'

'Not actively. If I find it, great, if I don't...' He shrugged. 'I have a good life, I'm not complaining.'

The one drink led to another, the conversation free and friendly. When Barry suggested dinner, she didn't hesitate. 'That sounds like a good idea. Saves me having to take something from the freezer when I get home.'

Freezer food. When Sarah retired the year after Daniel and Abbie started university, Keri had made the decision not to employ anyone else. But her plans to take over didn't get further than the purchase of several expensive cookery books and an internet search for local classes. Ready meals, from Waitrose and a local delicatessen, were her saviour, and once she discovered how good they were, all thoughts of cooking faded.

But there was something sad and lonely about freezer meals for one.

She hadn't meant to sound so pathetic, hadn't meant to give the impression she was unhappy. Because she wasn't. There was nothing to be unhappy about. She had a good life, a successful business, a loving husband, two great children, but for the last few months she always seemed to be tired, her mood low. Unsettled. *Menopausal.* She was forty-seven, it was possible. That thought depressed her even more.

Metcalfe Conservation was a huge success. But recently she'd wondered at what cost.

Barry's attention was flattering. A balm to whatever was causing her ache. When he suggested meeting again, she agreed without thinking of the consequences.

Nathan was away so often... maybe he'd found solace elsewhere too.

So it was she justified her infidelity.

She shuffled her position on the toilet seat as her call was answered. 'Hi, you saw it then?'

'Half of London saw it, Keri! How could you miss it? And those wonderful words, how you're so in love after all these years.'

'It was the children, Barry. They thought it would be a nice surprise.'

'Children! They're twenty-two, seems to me that they'd know the truth.'

'They see what they want to. Nate and I don't argue very much so they probably assume everything is hunky-dory.'

'You said you loved me.'

Had she said that? She couldn't remember. *He made her feel good. It was exciting to have someone so attentive. Excitement. Was that all it was really?*

'Meet me tonight.'

What? 'I can't, it's our wedding anniversary, we're going out for a family dinner.'

'Fine, then meet me afterwards.'

'Afterwards! Are you crazy? It's our anniversary, our children are here. What excuse could I possibly give?' She could feel her voice rising and took a deep breath.

'You'll think of something. Tell them you'd forgotten you arranged to meet a friend or something.'

On their wedding anniversary? 'I can't. Not tonight.'

'You can't or you don't want to? I think you've been playing me for a fool.' There was bitterness in his voice when he spoke again. 'You were never really going to leave him, were you?'

Leave Nathan? Keri swallowed. 'I didn't–'

'Stop lying! So now you're back-pedalling, are you? You said it last week when you were lying naked in my arms. You said you loved me, that you wanted to be with me.'

She shut her eyes as the memory washed over her. Barry was a remarkably good lover. She *had* said she loved him, and wanted to be with him. But she'd meant at that moment... not forever.

'Meet me tonight. Or we're done.'

'I can't...' She lifted her head when she heard the bedroom door open. 'I have to go, I'll ring you tomorrow.'

'No, don't bother. I mean it, we're done. I don't want to hear from you again.'

7

Keri put on a good show over dinner. It was easy, Abbie and Daniel were fun to be with and did most of the talking.

They told entertaining stories about their university courses, their professors, other students. Abbie, for a change, was between boyfriends, a situation so unusual as to cause ribbing from her twin.

'Have you dated every guy in your year already?'

'All the good-looking ones.' She smiled sweetly. 'I'm going to go for the intelligent ones next, do some hands-on research into looks versus brains.'

Daniel and Nathan laughed, but Keri looked across the table at her beautiful daughter and realised she was serious. Nathan often commented that their daughter looked exactly like Keri when she was that age. She could see a certain resemblance: the same pale skin, auburn curls, blue eyes, high cheekbones. And like Keri, Abbie was tall and slim. But her daughter's good looks were enhanced by something Keri hadn't had at her age – supreme self-confidence in her abilities and her looks.

Keri lifted her glass and took a sip of the chilled wine. Abbie

VALERIE KEOGH

was twenty-two. The same age as Keri was when she married the only man she'd ever been with... until Barry. Laughter rang out again as Abbie told another of her hilarious dating anecdotes. She'd never been embarrassed about talking about her sex life. Keri, who was still uncomfortable speaking about anything of a sexual nature, and who cringed when TV programmes included graphic scenes, looked on and listened in envy.

Envy.

Her fingers tightened on the stem of the wine glass. Was that what this was all about? Dread pressed her into her chair as the idea took root. *She envied her daughter.* Her freedom. The wonderful wide-open future that lay before her. The way men looked at her, entranced.

Had Nathan once looked at Keri like that? They'd met when she was sixteen, he a year older. Instant attraction, almost love at first sight. She let her eyes drift over him. He was a handsome man, she loved him, but their relationship was old and worn, comfortable rather than exciting. Was that what she'd been searching for when she'd embarked on that stupid affair... excitement. A chance to turn the clock back. To be twenty-two again and have a man entranced by her.

How pathetic.

She didn't think anyone noticed that she wasn't her usual bubbly self, that her contribution to the various conversations was reduced to agreeing with what anyone happened to be saying, a smile, a laugh when required. She acted her way through the evening. *She deserved a damn Oscar.*

By the time they got home, after more alcohol than she'd drunk in a long time, she was exhausted.

Too weary for Nathan's half-hearted amorous approach, she was relieved when he didn't take umbrage at her brush-off.

'I probably had too much to drink anyway,' he said and rolled over onto his side.

Keri lay with a hand resting on her forehead. Her head ached. Champagne or stress, or a combination of both.

When Nathan started to snore, she nudged him to silence with her foot. But the alcohol had a stronger grip on him and a minute later the stertorous rumbling started again. She threw back the duvet and swung her feet from the bed. One of the spare bedrooms was always made up for the occasional unexpected guest – usually friends of either Abbie or Daniel's. That night the room was empty. Keri crawled between the cool cotton sheets and shut her eyes.

But still sleep wouldn't come. She'd brought her mobile with her. There was no message from Barry. She tapped one out for him asking to meet the following day but deleted it without sending.

Maybe it was time to end it. She didn't love Barry. He was a nice guy but she'd never had any intention of leaving Nathan. She'd risked her marriage because she wanted a little excitement. What a fool she'd been.

Perhaps, this realisation was all she needed to acknowledge because a moment later, she was asleep.

The sound of laughter woke her the next morning. She lay with her eyes shut and listened to it, then the loud *hush* as one of the twins was trying to silence the other. Vaguely, she wondered where they were off to so early, then she was asleep again.

When she woke she guessed it was mid-morning and reached for her mobile to confirm she was right, her eyes widening to see it was almost eleven.

She opened the bedroom door and listened before hurrying across the landing to hers and slipping inside. Nathan was still asleep, flat on his stomach, his face buried in the pillow.

A wave of love washed over her, followed by one of self-disgust. What an idiot she had been to have risked losing all she had for a cheap thrill.

Nathan would never know, but she'd make it up to him anyway. She'd be a better wife.

She sat on the bed beside him and ran a hand over his shoulders.

'Hey,' he mumbled.

'Hey, yourself. Stay there, I'll get you a coffee.'

'And a pint of water.'

'Coffee and a pint of water. On its way.' She brushed her hand over his shoulders again then leaned to place a kiss between his shoulder blades. 'Back in a minute.'

Downstairs, while she waited for the kettle to boil, she sent Barry a message.

It's better this way. I'm sorry.

Later, she and Nathan headed out for a late lunch in their favourite pub. She made more of an effort than she would normally have done for such a casual meal, wearing a dress rather than jeans, and tying her hair back in a loose ponytail at the nape of her neck.

'You look nice,' Nathan said when she joined him in the hallway.

'Still celebrating my twenty-fifth anniversary to the man I love.' She hoped she wasn't overdoing it but she saw his smile and guessed everything was okay.

Outside, the sun was shining. The pub was only a short walk away. Keri slipped her hand into Nathan's and ignored his look of surprise. They always used to hold hands, when did they stop? When his fingers tightened around hers, she looked at him. 'Happy?'

'How could I not be?'

A twinge of guilt dimmed Keri's pleasure in his response. *How could he not be? Perhaps, if he knew the truth about his loving wife.*

He was never going to know. And she'd make it up to him.

The pub was, as usual, busy but they were in luck and found a table free near the window.

'Perfect,' Keri said, sitting on one side. 'I'm glad it's just us.'

'Me too. Abbie and Dan are great but they're exhausting.' He jerked his thumb towards the bar. 'Glass of wine?'

'No, I'd enough last night to do me for a while. I'll have a sparkling mineral water, please.'

While Nathan was gone, she pulled out her phone wondering if Barry had replied. He had, and with a quick look to the bar where Nathan was placing his order, she opened it to read.

You used me, you bitch, you'll regret this.

It was so unexpected it drew a gasp from her. Her thumb hovered as she tried to think of a suitable reply but she could see Nathan was on his way back. She put her mobile away and pasted a smile in place as he arrived with a drink in each hand.

'I thought I'd have hair of the dog,' he said sitting and taking a mouthful of beer. 'I ordered your usual food, that okay?'

Keri always had the same when they ate there; beer-battered haddock, chips, and mushy peas. The thought of eating that now made her want to heave. 'Yes, that's fine, although I'm not really that hungry after the huge meal last night.' She thought Nathan hadn't noticed that she'd eaten little so was surprised when he put a hand on her arm and looked at her in concern.

'You didn't eat much of your dinner, Keri. Is everything okay? You're not feeling sick, or anything.'

She put her hand over his. 'No, I'm fine. If you must know, I'm trying to lose some weight. My clothes have become a little tight recently.' She was horrified how easily the lie slipped from her mouth but it worked, Nathan relaxed.

'You're being daft, you're perfect.'

Perfect. If only he knew. Keri's heart twisted, her stomach churned. What had she done? *You used me, you bitch, you'll regret this.*

You'll regret this.

She already did.

8

After lunch, Nathan wanted to go for a walk but Keri pleaded tiredness.

'You sure you're okay?' His voice was laced with concern.

If she could confess, offload the guilt, she'd feel much better. How selfish that would be, to destroy him for her own ends. 'I'm fine, honestly, maybe I'm not up to the late nights and excess alcohol anymore.' She reached for his hand as they left the pub, keeping hold of it as they walked home.

Abbie and Daniel hadn't returned to fill the rooms with their individual brand of noise so the house was quiet. Peaceful and soothing, a balm for Keri's unsettled mind.

'I might do a little work if you don't mind,' Nathan said.

'No, that's okay. I think I'll find a movie and relax.' She changed into jersey trousers and T-shirt, switched on the TV, and found a movie she'd never seen before. It might keep her mind off things. She swung her legs up onto the sofa and rested her head against a cushion. The perfect position for relaxation but her hands were clenched into fists, her lips pressed together. A line of tension pulled her feet down, her chin up. Every time she tried to forget it, Barry's message would leap into her head and wind that line tighter.

She knew it wasn't really his words that had put her on the rack, it was her guilt.

What if Nathan found out?

Was that what Barry had meant by you'll regret this? Would he do such a terrible thing as to tell Nathan?

How much did she really know about him? She gave a self-accusatory snort. As much as she'd wanted to, which wasn't much. Had he been right, had she merely used him for some exciting extramarital sex?

She hadn't yet replied to his message, unable to think of anything suitable. High-pitched screams came from the TV. Dinosaurs were chasing people, biting their heads off. It was probably supposed to be terrifying but it didn't come close to the terror she felt as Barry's message flashed before her eyes at regular intervals.

She needed to do something. First, she had to make sure it was safe. She went out to the hallway. *Silence.* Nathan was probably still working. Shutting the door firmly behind her, she returned to the sofa and picked up her phone. There was no point in putting it off. Without considering what she was going to say, she dialled Barry's number.

To her surprise, it was answered almost immediately. He had to have known it was her, but his usual pleasant *hello* was absent. Instead, he gave a grunted, 'Yes.'

'Hi.' As a conversation starter it wasn't her best opening line.

Barry seemed to agree. 'I thought I'd made myself clear. I don't want to hear from you.'

'But–'

'No, no buts. You made your choice. Not that there was ever a choice really, was there? You never had any intention of leaving your husband. You used me, Keri, it's not a very pleasant sensation.'

It didn't seem the right moment to argue that she'd never said she was going to leave Nathan, that her relationship with Barry was supposed to be fun. *He was her bit on the side.* How tawdry it sounded. 'You said that I'd regret not meeting you. What did you mean by that?'

'Just what I said. That you'd regret it... that's why you're ringing me, isn't it? Because you do, but it's too late. I don't like being messed around. Women like you, desperately trying to hang onto the idea that they're beautiful and desirable, are two a penny. Well, you're still beautiful but I no longer find you desirable. I don't like being messed around, remember that.' He hung up without waiting for her response.

Shocked by the cold hard anger and the sneering contempt she'd heard in his voice, she dropped the phone and collapsed back against the cushions.

She'd brought this on herself. Now her guilt was fringed with fear.

Anger made people do terrible things. How far was Barry willing to go in retaliation?

9

Keri didn't sleep well that night. A dinosaur had escaped from that daft movie she'd been watching and it chased through her dreams, biting her head off when she tried to talk to it. It didn't take a knowledge of psychoanalysis to understand that she'd turned Barry into a larger-than-life monster ready to destroy her.

It was a Sunday morning tradition in their house that she would cook a big breakfast for whoever was home. Burying herself in the mundanity of its preparation kept her occupied. Abbie and Daniel had come home in the early hours, separately, each attempting to get to their rooms without making too much noise, taking off their shoes and tiptoeing up the stairs. She heard every muffled footstep, the soft click as they shut their doors.

It wasn't unusual for her to stay awake until they returned home. Then, knowing they were safe, she'd fall asleep. Not that night. It wasn't worrying about her two children that kept her awake, it wasn't them who'd done something stupid.

She took out two frying pans and began the breakfast ritual. Within ten minutes, Abbie and Daniel had joined her. They sat on stools at the broad, granite-topped breakfast bar that separated the kitchen from the living room and chatted about where they'd been the night before.

Keri was lucky. Her son and daughter were happy to talk about their lives. No moody, stroppy young adults to cause her angst. They were open and honest, and she knew all about their dynamic, exciting full-of-possibilities world.

Didn't she?

She flipped over the eggs and wondered if her children had secrets... as she had.

The formal dining room, accessed through a doorway from the kitchen, was rarely used. The family sat around the breakfast bar and helped themselves from the trays of food Keri placed in the middle.

'This is great, Ma.' Daniel waved the fork he was holding, a trio of sausage, bacon and black pudding impaled on the end.

'The perfect start to a Sunday,' Abbie agreed.

Keri smiled at them. Her plate held one piece of bacon and an egg, neither of which she wanted but she was unwilling to cause concern by taking nothing. Neither of the twins noticed her restraint, focused as they were on their own breakfasts.

Nathan did, of course, and raised an eyebrow. She speared a piece of bacon and waved it at him in reply, smiling when he shook his head.

If she could have pushed Barry from her mind as easily as she appeared to have put him from her life, Keri would have been able to relax. She wanted to believe his words were simply those of an angry, scorned man, that he meant nothing more by what he'd said. That she'd got off that lightly.

'Do you want a hand to clean up?' Abbie asked when they were finished. She or Daniel always asked, Keri always refused and sent them on their way. One of these days, she'd stop playing superwoman and shock them by accepting. Nathan helped, munching on the last remaining sausage as he cleared away the dirty plates and stacked them neatly in the dishwasher.

They'd barely finished before the twins appeared in the doorway. 'We're off to meet friends, see you later this afternoon,' Abbie said, Daniel adding a wave as his contribution.

Keri dropped the cloth she'd been using to clean the breakfast bar and walked with them to the front door. 'Have a good time, whatever you're up to.' She didn't remind them to let her know if they weren't coming home. As parents, she and Nathan were fairly laid-back but that was one rule they insisted on.

Daniel gave her a hug, opened the front door and stepped outside.

'Bye, Mum.' Abbie pressed a kiss to Keri's cheek. 'We'll be back in a few hours in time for dinner.' She grinned as Keri shook her head. 'It's a mother's duty to feed her young.'

'Young!' Keri laughed and gave her a gentle shove. 'Go, I'll go to a lot of trouble and defrost something exciting for later.'

'Sounds good to me.'

'Hey, what's this?'

Keri and Abbie turned to look out the doorway to where Daniel was standing with a wreath in his hands.

He held it up. 'It was resting against the step.'

Keri stared in surprise at the arrangement of plum-coloured carnations and dusky leaves. 'Is there a card?'

'Yes.' He pulled a small envelope from the edge of the wreath.

A shiver of foreboding slithered down Keri's back. She wanted to grab the envelope from him and open it in secret, her breath catching as Daniel fumbled with the flap of the envelope to pull the card out.

'It says RIP.' He flicked the card to see the reverse. 'That's it. RIP. No name.' He slipped the card back. 'Must have been delivered here by mistake. I wonder why they didn't ring the doorbell. How stupid.' He tucked the envelope back in place. 'There's a florist's sticker on the back of it, you'd better give them a buzz and tell them they've fucked up.'

'Dan, language,' Keri said automatically.

'Seemed appropriate.' He handed the wreath to her.

She didn't want to take it, her reluctance making her son laugh. 'What? You think it's a bad omen or something? It's a mistake, Ma. It happens.'

Abbie frowned at him. 'Give it to me. I'll put it in the utility room, it'll be cool enough in there. I'll give the card to Dad, he can ring them.'

'No, that's okay.' Keri shook her head and reached for it. 'I was being silly, I'll do it. You two go and enjoy yourselves, we'll see you later.' The wreath hung heavily from her hand as she waved goodbye until the twins had vanished from sight.

Only then did she pull it up to look at it with critical eyes. Even without the stark message on the card, the dark-coloured flowers and foliage made it obviously a funeral wreath. Someone was determined there would be no mistake. No mistake in where it was delivered either.

You'll regret this.

It had to be from Barry. *The bastard.* She tried to focus her anger on him, but it was coming back and smacking her across the face. It was all her fault.

All her damn fault for being so stupid. She lashed herself with the anger, desperately wanting to hold onto it because it was better than the other emotion that was lurking... the one that crept over her, pushed the anger away and seeped in through her pores to leave her trembling... Fear.

Because if Barry had sent the wreath, what might he do next?

10

Keri took the envelope and dropped the wreath to the side of the steps.

Back inside, the TV was blaring and there was a roar of excitement from Nathan. Football. That was him safely out of her way for a while.

To be sure of privacy, she went upstairs to their bedroom to make the call.

'Richter's Florists, how can I help you?'

'Hi.' Keri swallowed, her mouth suddenly dry. 'We had a wreath delivered here today by mistake. Your details were on the card.'

There was a second's silence. 'Goodness, I'm terribly sorry. Could I have your address please, and I'll see if perhaps it was delivered to the wrong place.'

Keri gave their address and waited. When the landline rang, she swore under her breath. It stopped after a couple of rings indicating Nathan had answered. In case the call was for her and he came in search, she stepped into the en suite and shut the door.

'Hi,' the florist's voice came back. 'I'm afraid that's where we were asked to deliver to. The person who ordered it must have given the wrong details.'

'The wreath was left outside. Your people didn't even ring the bell.'

'They were the instructions we were given. I'm reading it now. It says not to disturb the occupant by ringing, that we were to rest it on the front doorstep.'

'Okay.' Keri wiped a hand over her eyes. 'Do you have the details of the person who ordered them? Perhaps you could ask them for the correct address.' The silence on the other end was protracted and she wondered had she been cut off. 'Hello?'

'Hello. Sorry, I was checking our computer. I'm afraid we don't. It was a cash purchase in the shop. They didn't leave a phone number so we've no way of contacting them.'

'Fine.' It was anything but. It was a long bloody way from fine. 'Send someone to pick it up, please, I don't want it here. It's by the front steps. As soon as possible, please.' She hung up without waiting for a reply.

Keri half expected a message from Barry to gloat over the wreath but despite checking frequently over the afternoon and evening there was nothing. Nathan was glued to the football so she didn't have to explain about the wreath lying sadly on their doorstep and next time she checked, it was gone.

She tried ringing Barry's number but it rang off. Did he want her to beg, was that it? She would have done. She'd have done anything to protect her family. Her newly awakened conscience nudged her painfully. *Pity you didn't think about that before.*

It was time for damage limitation, something she was good at after years dealing with such a large cross-section of people in interlinking industries. Her philosophy had always been to get things out in the open so everyone knew where each other stood. She ignored the snide chuckle her conscience gave and concentrated on what she was going to do.

Tomorrow. She'd call into Barry's office and speak to him. Apologise again. Beg if needs be.

On Monday morning it was only Keri and Nathan for breakfast. Abbie and Daniel had left after dinner the previous evening to stay overnight with friends who lived nearer to the university. Since each had 9am lectures on a Monday, it was a frequent occurrence.

Keri poured cereal into two bowls and made mugs of instant coffee. 'Have you a busy day?'

'Not too bad,' Nathan said, pulling a bowl forward and reaching for a spoon. 'What about you?'

'Nothing too exciting.' *Nothing more than confronting the man she'd been having an affair with and begging him to leave her alone.*

11

Monday mornings in the office were always busy. Theirs wasn't a Monday to Friday business and there were issues that had arisen over the weekend that required Keri's input. None were difficult, but all took time.

Mid-morning, Roy rapped on her door and came in with a takeaway coffee from her favourite café.

'Angel,' she said, taking it, flipping the plastic lid into the bin and sniffing the aroma. 'This was what I needed.'

'I thought it might be.'

Roy had been with them for almost eighteen years. The word *godsend* was frequently used in conjunction with his name. Officially the receptionist, his role was much more than that and she and Nathan depended on him. She had considered changing his title to 'front of house manager' or 'administrator' but he'd howled with laughter at the thought, so receptionist he remained.

She nodded toward her laptop. 'I've most of the issues sorted. I need to go out for a bit, the rest can wait till I'm back.'

Roy tugged that day's elaborately floral waistcoat down,

murmured, 'Okey-dokey,' and left her to drink the coffee in peace.

She watched as he walked across to the big semicircular desk that was his domain. *Roy's Kingdom*, Nathan called it, only half-joking.

Roy hadn't queried where she was going but she knew he'd be wondering. She sighed, picked up the coffee and took a mouthful. It was the best thing to do, wasn't it? Face up to the danger, brazen it out, chase it away. She rested her forehead in her hand for a moment. It was times like this that she really regretted the damn glass walls.

No hiding away from what she'd done.

The second hand ticked around the face of the clock that sat on the corner of her desk. It was 11.15, she'd leave at exactly 11.30. But when both hands pointed directly at twelve, she'd still not finished her coffee.

She sipped the cold drink wishing it were something stronger. Something to give her the courage to go to the building next door and face a man she'd been naked with only days before. Face him and accuse him of trying to damage her marriage, when the truth was the blame was all hers.

What had she been thinking?

Draining the disposable mug, she crunched it in her hand and fired it into the bin. If she was going to do this, there was no point in putting it off any longer.

She took her jacket from the coat stand. It wasn't necessary, the building was only next door and it was a particularly warm September. But the smart military cut of the jacket made her feel more in control. She smoothed a hand over it, buttoning the middle button, then unbuttoning it again, a nervous gesture that irritated her.

Roy looked up from his computer screen as she walked

across the reception. Keri raised a hand in acknowledgement but didn't stop.

Outside the office, she joined in the flow of people on the busy footpath and walked the short distance to the entrance of the large multi-occupancy building. She'd never had a reason to go inside before. According to a directory mounted to one side of the front door, apart from Dixon Solicitors, the businesses were arty types: marketing, advertising, graphic designers, a publishing company.

There was a small reception area. A woman sat behind the desk, blonde hair tied in a high ponytail that swished as she turned to look at Keri. She wore a black T-shirt with an asymmetrical neckline that bared one elegant tanned shoulder. Instantly, Keri regretted her jacket, feeling mumsy. *Old.*

'Can I help?'

Keri bit back the words she always wanted to say when she heard this particular phrase. *You. Can I help you. Not 'can I help', you lazy cow.* 'Is it possible to speak to Barry Morgan.'

The ponytail swished. 'Which company does he work for?'

'Dixon Solicitors.'

'And your name is?'

'Keri Metcalfe. Mrs.' Keri didn't know why she added the Mrs. It was a bit late now to remember she was married.

Miss Bare Shoulder turned away and tapped long dark nails on the keyboard. Without looking up, she asked, 'What does this Barry Morgan do at Dixon Solicitors?'

'He's a solicitor.'

The ponytail swished energetically as she turned back to Keri. 'No, there isn't anyone by that name working there.'

Keri looked at her blankly, then laughed unconvincingly. 'I'm sorry, I must have misunderstood. Maybe he works for a different company?' She saw a sudden flash of sympathy in the younger woman's face.

'I shouldn't really,' she said, with a glance around. 'But I suppose I could have a look on the list of names we keep for emergency services. You know, in case we have a fire or something.'

'Thank you, I'd appreciate that.'

'It's going to take me a couple of minutes, the list is organised by company rather than alphabetically.' She waved a hand towards a seating area near the wall behind. 'Why don't you sit and I'll give you a shout when I'm done.'

The seats were those too-low chairs that were impossible to sit on gracefully or to get out of without shuffling awkwardly. Restless, Keri stayed on her feet, wondering how she could have made such a mistake. She remembered the day she and Barry had met, right outside. He'd said he worked there, that he was a solicitor. Her worried expression cleared. She was being silly. She'd assumed he worked for Dixon Solicitors since they were the only law firm mentioned on the directory, but he hadn't mentioned them by name. Maybe he was a legal consultant for one of the other companies.

She'd almost convinced herself she was right when she saw the receptionist wave to catch her attention.

'I'm really sorry,' Miss Bare Shoulder said before Keri could open her mouth. 'I double-checked. There's nobody by that name employed by any of the companies working here.' A long fingernail pointed to the computer. 'I checked last month, in case he might have left or something but–' She shook her head sending her ponytail swishing again. '–no luck, I'm afraid.'

Keri scraped some dignity together and managed a wobbly smile. 'Oh dear, I must have misunderstood, or taken the details down incorrectly, not to worry, no doubt he'll be in touch and we'll get it sorted.' She was babbling and she could tell by the receptionist's increasingly sympathetic expression that she wasn't fooled.

'Thanks for your help.' Keri turned with her back rigid and her chin in the air. The reception seemed colossal, every step across it a forced action she had to concentrate on. She kept her eyes focused on the exit and left the building.

12

Outside, Keri took a deep breath and looked around. It had been about here where she'd met Barry. She'd bumped into him. It had been an accident. Hadn't it? She squeezed her eyes shut as she tried to remember every second but it was impossible. She had been walking on autopilot, her head probably full of the day's business. She remembered feeling a little low because Nathan was away and she wasn't sure if Abbie and Daniel were coming home that night. An empty house didn't hold the allure it once had, when there was always someone wanting to speak to her – one of her children, one of the staff, or Nathan. Days when she'd have killed for a little peace and quiet.

She opened her eyes, ignoring the passers-by who divided like a shoal of fish to get around her immobile figure. Maybe that had been it. She'd looked sad and vulnerable and had stupidly been taken in by a friendly face and an appreciative smile.

Barry Morgan. He didn't work where he said he did, maybe that wasn't even his name. She couldn't believe anything he'd told her. Desperate for a bit of excitement, she'd made him out to be what she needed and ignored the warning signs. Now they were blowing bugles and flashing lights. He was the one who had avowed love, who'd spoken about her leaving Nathan. It was Barry who had clung to her hand possessively with tears in his eyes when she'd had to leave. She'd told herself it was sweet, now she realised it had been seriously odd.

She turned and started the short walk to her office, unbuttoning her jacket and slipping it off as she covered the distance with shaky steps.

There were people in reception so she was able to slip by without Roy seeing her. Always pale, she tended to turn almost grey when she was unwell, or shocked as she was in this case.

The glass walls of her office wouldn't offer her any privacy. She continued along the corridor to the staff toilets, relieved to find them empty. The mirror over the wash-hand basin told her she'd been right, her face had taken on an unhealthy sheen. She turned on the cold tap and held her wrists under the flow of water. Several minutes later, cooled down, she was looking a little better. Good enough not to draw comment from Roy or Nathan.

Back in her office, she sat, picked up her phone and dialled a number from memory. She had to speak to Barry, if he didn't answer this time, she'd leave a message.

'The number you have dialled has not been recognised, please check and try again.'

Grunting with frustration, she dialled again.

'The number you have dialled has not been recognised, please check and try again.'

Keri looked at her phone in disbelief before trying the number once more, pressing each digit carefully, knowing it was a waste of time. She hadn't input his number, afraid Nathan might somehow see it, but she'd a good head for figures, she wouldn't have got it wrong. Barry had obviously changed his number so she couldn't contact him to hold him to account for that blasted wreath.

Perhaps too, he'd have guessed she might have gone to confront him for it so would have discovered his deception. This way, he didn't have to explain. This way, she'd never find out the truth.

She switched on her computer. If anyone looked through the glass walls, they'd assume her frown was from whatever report she was reading or writing.

Perhaps the wreath had been an accident and she was foolishly reading too much into it. Guilt, she was discovering to her cost, had a very loud voice.

The upward swing of optimism didn't last long and when she tumbled she fell further into the trough of guilt and fear. But what if it wasn't an accident? If Barry had sent the wreath and the RIP note as a sick commentary on their relationship... or worse, as a critique of her marriage... would that be enough for him or would he go further to make her regret ending their affair?

She remembered Barry's voice on the phone. How ferociously angry he'd been. Guilt and fear took turns in wielding the lash.

What if he went further?

13

Keri tried unsuccessfully to push the wreath and her guilt over the affair to the back of her mind. But thoughts of both continued to torment her, making her irritable, disturbing her sleep, ruining her appetite.

If Nathan noticed, he made no comment, but she noticed he held her hand as they walked to work in the morning which he hadn't done in a while. She felt the warmth of his hand and relished his unspoken concern even while she acknowledged she didn't deserve it.

They were unusually busy with new contracts which meant she could bury herself in work and by Wednesday afternoon she felt she'd done a full week. A knock on the door dragged bleary eyes from the screen. She looked over to see Roy peer through the glass and waved him in.

'Sorry to bother you but there's a young woman here who is looking for work experience.' He held his hands out. 'I'd have

VALERIE KEOGH

sent her away but she's gone to so much trouble, I didn't have the heart so I thought—'

'That I'd get rid of her for you? You are such a pushover, Roy. Right, go on, show her in, it'll give my eyes a break from staring at numbers.'

Keri saved what she was working on, then looked back in time to see a neatly dressed young woman walk across the reception towards her door. Immediately she was reminded of Abbie who had the same blonde-streaked hair and heavily kohled eyes. But whereas her daughter carried herself with supreme self-confidence, this young woman had the slumped shoulders and rather defeated expression which said she'd been disappointed too many times. Keri, who had intended to say no, gently but emphatically, found herself thinking *why not.*

'Thank you for seeing me.' The woman handed a folder across the desk. 'I've put together my reference and details of jobs I've done so you can see I'm willing.'

'Sit, please.' Keri opened the folder and read through the details of summer and weekend jobs, some voluntary, a few not. Tracy Wirick was eighteen. Keri flicked a look over the young woman sitting nervously on the edge of the chair. She looked older. 'You finished school this year?'

'Yes. I got A levels in English and History.'

There was a reference from the school with the usual overused words. *Diligent, conscientious, pleasant, reliable.* In Keri's experience, they meant little. She shut the folder. 'You want to work in an office environment?'

'Sort of.' Tracy pointed behind her. 'I'd like to work in reception. I'm good with people. Eventually, I'd like to work in a hotel.'

'Have you applied for jobs?'

'About twenty.' She smoothed a hand over her jacket. 'I bought this suit especially,' she said naively. 'I thought if I looked

46

professional I'd have a better chance, but there are so many people looking for the same type of jobs, and so many with experience.' Her sigh said she was getting used to rejection. 'That's when I thought if I had work experience with a good company, I'd be able to use that in my favour.'

And no doubt a reference from Keri and Roy to add to her meagre folder. It was a clever strategy and it might work. 'How long were you thinking?'

Tracy's eyes brightened. 'I was hoping for a month but honestly whatever you allow would be great. I'm a quick learner. I won't get in the way.'

Keri tapped her finger on the desk. Maybe it would show Roy the advantages of having a subordinate in reception. 'Okay. A month. And if you prove yourself useful, we might offer a small payment.' She raised a hand. 'If,' she stressed. 'And it will be Roy who makes that decision, so it's him you'll need to impress.' She tapped the folder. 'I'll have to check your reference, of course, but assuming it's okay, when would you like to start?'

'Tomorrow?'

Keri laughed. 'Why not. Okay, you go and tell Roy the good news and he'll tell you the hours etc.'

Roy would be taken aback, but he was a pushover, he'd go out of his way to make Tracy feel right at home. He would also, Keri knew, be more than happy to impart all his knowledge.

She wasn't surprised when he appeared at her door minutes later.

'A month!'

'You'll love it, someone hanging on your every word. I bet at the end you'll be begging me to keep her on as your assistant.'

He shook his head. 'She seems a nice enough lassie but however nice she may be that won't be happening.'

'We'll see.' Keri waved him away and went back to finishing the last of the contract she'd been reading.

～

At four thirty, she was done. She stretched her hands to the ceiling, feeling muscles groan. Too many hours curved over the computer. Making a snap decision, she picked up her desk phone and rang Nathan's extension. 'If you're not busy how do you fancy slipping away. We could stop for a drink on the way home.' She heard the faint sound of his fingers drumming on the desk before he answered.

'That sounds like a good plan. Give me five minutes.'

There was one advantage to glass walls. When she saw him get to his feet, she grabbed her jacket and bag and left her office at the same time.

Roy smiled when he saw them. 'You two escaping?'

'Before anything else happens,' Keri said. 'Oh, and by the way, I checked that young woman's reference, she sounds a saint.'

'Just what I need.' He raised an eyebrow and winked when Keri laughed.

Nathan wanted to stop in the nearest pub, but since the Hare and Hounds was one Keri had recently visited with Barry, she persuaded him to continue to one nearer the train station. 'It'll be more relaxing,' she said vaguely.

'Sure, I don't mind. The Parson's Nose is nice.'

She'd no recollection of having been there before but jumped at the change of venue. 'Oh yes, let's go there.'

It was only a short distance from the pub to Walthamstow Central station so it was convenient, but it also made it busy and there wasn't a seat to be had. They were forced to have a drink standing at the bar which wasn't what Keri had wanted.

Which was what?

What had she bloody well wanted? She took a large mouthful of the wine the bartender had placed before her.

'Hey, steady on.' Nathan picked up his beer. 'I thought we should make a toast.' He tipped his glass against hers. 'To our continued success.'

The business's continued success. Because that was what was important. If only he'd toasted her or their relationship or hadn't bothered with his stupid toast and simply said *this was nice.* To be together.

Two women with long blonde hair and off-the-shoulder thigh-length dresses passed in a haze of overpoweringly sweet perfume. Keri watched Nathan's eyes automatically sweep over them and follow as they took up a position at the end of the bar.

What was it Barry had said? *That women like Keri, trying desperately to hang onto the idea that they were beautiful and desirable, were two a penny.*

This had been a bad idea. She looked at Nathan's beer. He'd barely touched it. She picked up her glass, drained it in two gulps and waved it at the bartender who lifted a hand in acknowledgment.

Nathan picked up his drink and eyed her warily. 'What's the matter with you tonight?'

'Nothing.' She wanted to try a smile but she knew it would wobble, knew the attempt would end in tears. 'It's been a busy day, that's all. Another glass of wine will hit the spot.'

'You've been a bit odd recently. Why don't you tell me what's troubling you.'

She waited until her wine arrived in a fresh glass. 'Do you still love me?'

He stared, then laughed as if it were a trick question, the laugh fading when she stayed quiet. 'Of course I still love you.'

'We've been together so many years.' She turned to look

down the bar to where the two glamorous women sat. 'We were so young when we met. Do you ever think that we missed out?'

'Missed out?' Nathan moved closer and put a hand on the small of her back. 'Is that because I looked at those women? I'm sorry, it didn't mean anything.'

She knew she was being stupid. He'd only looked... she'd cheated on him. It was her guilt that was making her be so unreasonable. 'Not only because you look at other women when you are out with me, but maybe because you think it's acceptable. That it wouldn't bother me.'

Nathan looked as if she'd hit him. 'I'm really sorry. I didn't think.'

'A bit like your toast.'

Now he looked completely puzzled. 'My toast?'

'To the business.'

'Yes.' One word drawled out as if he were frantically trying to make sense of the conversation. 'We've done really well this week. I know it's been a bit frantic but we've tied up two valuable contracts.'

'What about us?'

'What do you mean *what about us*?' Irritation flashed across his face. He reached for his pint and swallowed quarter before putting it down. 'I don't know what's got into you recently. Abbie says it's the menopause–'

'Abbie says! You've been discussing me with our daughter?'

Nathan looked suddenly sheepish. 'I asked her if she knew what was bothering you, that's all. When she suggested it might be the menopause I did some research and guessed she might be right.'

Keri glared at him. This wasn't the kind of conversation about their relationship she wanted.

'Maybe you should see our GP and talk about your options.'

'My options?'

Nathan, looking mildly embarrassed, leaned slightly closer to whisper. 'HRT.'

Her wine glass was already half empty. She lifted it to her lips, drained it and slammed it down on the bar. A conversation about her aging body was the last thing she needed. He hadn't finished his pint, but she'd had enough. 'Let's go home.' She didn't wait for his answer. 'I'll be outside.'

The footpath was heaving with people making their way to the station. She moved to a postbox and leaned against it as she waited for Nathan to finish his drink and join her. When he came out, moments later, she thought how sad he looked.

Guilt wrapped around her and squeezed. What was she doing? Punishing him for her stupidity. She sighed and slipped a hand into his as he reached her. 'I'm sorry. I'm being a cow. Put it down to the stressful week, okay.'

He pulled her hand up to his chest and held it there as he looked into her eyes. 'I love you, I'm sorry if I don't always show it.'

She pressed a kiss to his cheek. 'You put up with my moods, I think that's a pretty good way of showing it.'

It was a fifteen-minute walk from Highbury and Islington station to their house in Northampton Park. They walked hand in hand, each of them making a conscious effort to keep the conversation away from the business and were laughing about something Daniel had said over the weekend when they turned into their driveway.

The stone steps leading up to the front door should have been bare. They certainly shouldn't have had something dark and ominous on the middle step.

Keri was searching in her satchel bag for her keys so it was Nathan who noticed first.

'What the hell?' he said, holding a hand out to stop Keri moving forward. 'Stop, there's something odd on the steps.'

She looked up in alarm, half expecting to see another wreath, her eyes widening when she saw the dark mess. 'What is it?'

Nathan had approached the steps and leaned over it. 'It looks like a mangled dead rat. Pretty disgusting.' He turned to her with a look of distaste and held out a hand. 'Come on, don't look, get by it and go inside. I'll get something to get rid of it.'

Keri didn't want to look but she had to. Maybe it was simply a coincidence that the bloody mess was on the same step as the wreath had been.

A rat. Was this Barry's way of hinting that he was going to rat on her? She had no way of knowing, no way of finding out. She might have been able to brush away the wreath as someone's silly mistake – but not now.

The card on the wreath had said RIP.

The dead rat didn't need an explanation.

14

Keri put a couple of ready meals in the microwave and sat to wait for Nathan to finish disposing of the creature that had been left on their doorstep.

They'd been in business a long time and had dealt with their fair share of churlish, ungrateful and downright menacing characters over the years. In the beginning, it was the ones who wanted to put them out of business, in the later years, the ones who wanted a piece of it. But this was different. Would Nathan guess it was personal?

'I'll have to put down poison again.' He washed his hands and stood drying them as he stared through the kitchen window, his eyes scanning the length of the garden as he wondered if there were more rodents living there. 'It's a few years since we last saw a rat, isn't it?' He tossed the towel back onto the rail. 'It must have been caught by a dog to be that mangled.'

'Yes,' Keri agreed, relieved when the ping of the microwave distracted them. She took out plates and cutlery, emptied the contents of the packets onto two plates and pushed one across the counter towards Nathan.

He picked up his fork and shoved it into the moussaka. A

spout of steam made him reconsider eating immediately. 'I'll take care of it at the weekend,' he said as he pushed the food around the plate to cool off.

Keri almost smiled. Her action man. He'd put down the poison and never think of it again. He certainly wouldn't dwell on it, wouldn't wonder why a rat had been left spread across their doorstep, would never consider it was a message. 'I think I'll have a glass of red with this, you want one?'

'No, I'll stick to beer.'

Keri stood and crossed the room to the wine rack. She was trying to find the bottle she wanted when she was distracted by the buzz of a mobile and looked over to see Nathan taking his phone from his shirt pocket. Not for her. She could concentrate on her search. Finally, right at the bottom she found the bottle of Merlot she'd known was there.

She replaced the screw-top lid when she'd poured a glassful and returned to her seat. Nathan, she noticed, was staring into his food. 'Something wrong?'

'What?' He looked at her with a frown.

'I heard your phone buzz with a message. Is there a problem?'

'No, it was nothing important.' He picked up his fork again and concentrated on his meal.

She sipped on her wine. Nathan had always been a terrible liar. He became instantly shifty, his eyes slinking away as they were doing now. He had a reputation for being completely honest which amused Keri – he had no choice, the alternative wasn't an option for him. As a result, he'd never been the one who promised a job would be done by a certain date knowing there wasn't a chance in hell. That had been down to her. Down to her too, had been the tough business decisions, the hiring and firing of staff. Nathan's honesty may have contributed to the good reputation they enjoyed, but it was her steely determination, her ability to see problems and instantly search for a solution and fix things that had made Metcalfe Conservation the success it was.

Her fingers tightened on the stem of the glass. He was lying about the message being unimportant, wasn't he? Or was it the guilt that was twisting her brain and affecting her ability to think straight. Guilt that made her see lies everywhere, making her paranoid? She put the glass down. More alcohol was not the answer.

After dinner, they tidied up together. They were past the need to make conversation but usually the silence between them was comfortable. That night, as they tiptoed around one another, it was tense and fraught with the possibility that one or the other of them was going to boil over and say something they would regret.

'I'm going to watch TV and relax. You coming?' Keri was almost relieved to see him shake his head.

'No, I'm expecting a confirmation email from that new company we're going to be working with, and I wanted to read through it. Plus, there's a couple of other things I want to check.'

Working at home was something they tried to avoid but at times it was necessary. It wasn't now, and Nathan's shifty expression made it clear he was lying. As he had been earlier. She was sure of it.

She picked up the remote to switch on the TV, then walked to the French doors to stare into the garden. When Abbie and Daniel had grown too old to want to play in it, she'd had it redesigned by a well-known gardener. Now it was filled with a variety of planting, with something in bloom almost every month of the year. It was looking good now but she couldn't remember the last time she'd sat out in it.

Restless, she dropped the remote on the sofa and went upstairs to change from her work clothes. She pulled a silk robe on, enjoying the feel of the fabric against her skin until a memory slipped into her head. A bedroom, silk sheets, her naked body entwined with Barry's. The thought made her shiver in self-loathing.

Forcing thoughts of their writhing bodies out of her head, she concentrated on the mystery that was Barry. She'd never brought him home, of course, he knew she was married. But why had they never gone back to his apartment? Hatch Lane, where he'd said he lived was only a thirty-minute journey away. It would have been convenient. She'd never questioned it, happy to meet in the discreet boutique hotel in Walthamstow where she'd ignored the knowing look of the reception staff in her belief that what they were doing was something romantic. *Not a tawdry adulterous affair that meant nothing and could cost so much.*

Keri jerked the belt on her robe and fastened it in a tight knot. Maybe they didn't go to Hatch Lane because everything Barry had told her had been a lie.

Desperate to get him out of her head, she went downstairs and picked up the wine she'd abandoned earlier. Grabbing the remote, she sank onto the sofa and tucked her feet under her. There was a crime series on the TV. It was gripping, and normally she would have lost herself in the story, but fear over what Barry might do, guilt over her infidelity, and worry over Nathan's lies all chased round her head as they vied for first place.

Unable to concentrate on the crime series, she switched to reruns of a property show she liked and reached for her wine. One sip, and she put the glass down again. Maybe a cup of camomile tea would soothe her anxieties. It couldn't hurt.

~

It didn't help either, but she sat sipping it as she flicked from channel to channel in search of distraction. The tea was drunk and the 10pm news had started by the time Nathan joined her. He looked preoccupied and sat on the other end of the sofa, eyes fixed on the screen.

'Did it come?' she asked him.

'What?' He didn't turn to look at her as if the report about yet another government fiasco made riveting news.

She didn't know why she persevered, he obviously wasn't going to talk about whatever was worrying him. About whatever was making him lie. 'The email you were expecting.'

'Oh, yes, yes it did. That's what kept me. I had to reply and send a few other emails.' He glanced at her then. 'Before I forget, I won't be going in with you tomorrow morning. I've an early appointment in the city.'

'Really?' Keri frowned. She hadn't remembered seeing anything in the diary.

'Yes, Simon Nicholl rang before I left the office. He apologised for the short notice but he had a free hour and wanted to meet up.'

'Oh, him.' Keri didn't like the president of the Stone Federation but he was an important man to keep on their side and had to be placated. 'Good luck with that. You don't need me to come, do you? I can if you like, I've nothing particularly important on tomorrow. Nothing that can't wait anyway.'

'No.'

She blinked, surprised at the sharp tone.

'I mean, you hate the guy,' Nathan said with a smile. 'You struggle to hide it and I'm not sure he hasn't cottoned on. There's no point in your coming. It's only a routine catch-up.'

Since when did the self-important Simon Nicholl meet anyone as a matter of routine?

Nathan reached for the remote and increased the volume as

the sports results came on. She would have reached over, grabbed the remote and asked what was going on, if their short conversation hadn't worried her.

Nathan was lying about the meeting in the morning. He'd lied too about the phone call earlier and the important email. It didn't take a vivid imagination to link the lies together.

Something was wrong.

She relaxed back and stared at Nathan. He was still focused on the screen as if he were really listening to the sports results but his rigid posture and set expression told her differently. They'd always been able to talk about problems but usually they related to the business. This time, whatever was worrying him was personal.

In that moment, she remembered how much she loved him. Whatever was wrong, whatever was making Nathan need to lie, she'd find out what it was, and she'd do what she did best.

She'd fix it.

15

The following morning, Keri watched Nathan as he ate his breakfast. He had tossed restlessly all night and was obviously preoccupied. She knew there was no point in asking what was worrying him. If it had been something he'd wanted to discuss, he'd have done so by now. There had never been secrets between them before. No room for them in the early days when they'd done everything together, when they'd spent so many hours making a success of the business.

And now?

She had hers, did he have his?

It had to be something personal. Another woman? Nathan was such a terrible liar she'd always thought he'd be incapable of having an affair.

Maybe she'd been fooling herself. After all, on his frequent overnight stays he had plenty of opportunity.

The thought of him with another woman made her squirm.

Was that where he was going that morning?

When she received a series of monosyllabic answers to mundane questions, she put her spoon down. Maybe she needed to give him an opening to talk to her. 'Is everything okay?' She waited with her fingers crossed under the breakfast bar, hoping that he would mention something work-related, something she could laugh off, or help him solve.

But he merely looked up from his half-eaten cereal. 'Everything's hunky-dory.'

She wanted to push it, to say he looked a million miles away from hunky-dory. Instead, she got to her feet and put her bowl in the dishwasher. 'Right. Are you coming to the station with me?' The Stone Federation's head office was in the city, if that's where Nathan was going he could get the Victoria line from the same station.

'Sure.'

They parted in the station: she heading for platform 3, he for platform 5. Rush-hour busy with commuters, it was easy to get lost in the crush. Easy for Keri to double back and follow Nathan, pushing through the crowd to keep him in view. When he turned for platform 4, she knew she was right. The Northern line wouldn't take him to the city.

Half-tempted to continue her amateur detecting and follow him, she shook her head at a sudden descent into farcical Inspector Clouseau territory when she was pushed past the entrance to platform 4 by a sudden swell of impatient commuters. Extricating herself, she retraced her steps to platform 3 and caught the underground to Walthamstow Central.

Roy was standing behind the reception desk when she arrived at the office a little after nine, Tracy Wirick at his shoulder listening intently. Keri said a distracted hello and went into her office where she sat behind her desk, rocking her chair gently as she tried to think of her next step.

Nathan's office would be locked but Roy kept an emergency set of keys. If Nathan were away it wasn't too unusual for her to want access to his office to look for something she'd mislaid or to search for contact details for someone. But this was different, this was snooping.

Guilt made her shoulders tense and her smile become rigidly fixed when she crossed to the reception desk to ask for the keys. 'Nathan's in later, but I don't want to have to wait till then and need to check something in his diary.'

Roy didn't seem to think anything of her request. He opened the bottom drawer of the cabinet behind him, took the keys out and handed them to her without comment.

In fact, he was unusually quiet and looked distracted. Maybe Tracy was being harder work than he'd anticipated.

The thought made Keri smile briefly as she searched through the bunch of keys for the correct one to open Nathan's office door.

Their offices were a similar size, fitted with the same furniture and decorated in the same shades of grey that were in their Metcalfe Conservation logo of a hammer and intertwined M and C. The stylist had insisted it would look professional and luxurious. Nathan had been pleased with the result but Keri had thought it was cold. She'd counteracted the feeling by hanging large colourful paintings on the back wall of her office but Nathan had left his as it had been finished.

She sat behind his desk and picked up a sheaf of reports from his tray. If Roy looked her way, he'd think she was looking for something. Which she was, of course, but she wasn't going to find it in the mass of letters from suppliers.

His desk diary was where it always was. They both used one as well as their iPhones to keep track of various meetings and contract deadlines. She flicked the diary open, not really surprised to see no mention of a meeting that morning. She wasn't sure what she was looking for. What had she expected? To see a note in his diary saying secret assignation?

Feeling stupid, she left and went back to the reception desk to give the keys to Roy. There was no sign of Tracy.

'You haven't frightened her away already?'

'No. I sent her for coffee, thought she might as well make herself useful.'

'How's she doing?'

His sigh said it all. 'I've never met anyone who asked so many questions. Why this, why that. Where does this go, why does it go there; who's he, what does he do, and on and on.' He shrugged. 'I'm trying to keep an open mind.'

'It's only her first day. She's probably trying to impress you.' Keri didn't think it was the time to tell him that she'd promised Tracy remuneration if she succeeded in making a good impression. Maybe that hadn't been one of Keri's better ideas.

Handing back the keys, she returned to her office no wiser. It was possible that Simon Nicholl had arranged a meeting with Nathan at the last minute. And, although unusual, he may have asked to meet somewhere else apart from the Stone Federation's city headquarters. There was only one way to find out.

She found the number for the Federation and dialled. 'It's Keri Metcalfe,' she said when the phone was answered. 'I was hoping to have a brief word with Simon Nicholl, is that possible?'

'Hold for one moment, please.'

Keri's hand tightened on the phone, her brain spinning.

The voice that came on was distracted, the implication in the tone as clear as if he'd said it aloud, *I'm a terribly busy man, why are you disturbing me.* 'Keri, hi, what can I do for you?'

It was tempting to hang up, pretend she'd been cut off, but then she'd have to ring back and explain. Better to come up with something, no matter how banal. 'So sorry to bother you,

Simon. Roy mentioned that he heard from one of our suppliers about a conference the Federation was holding and we've heard nothing about it, so...'

'A conference? No, sounds like someone's got the wrong end of the stick there.'

Keri wanted to apologise and ring off, but Simon liked nothing better than a captive audience. Suddenly, he didn't sound in a hurry. 'We had considered holding a conference on the new technological advances that we've seen in the last year.'

It was a hobby horse of his, Keri raised her eyes to the ceiling and listened, adding a yes or no when appropriate as he droned on. 'Fascinating.'

'What?'

Shit, obviously not the correct word. 'Your knowledge on the subject, I meant.' She cringed and hoped he'd swallow the line, relieved when his ego allowed him to accept the compliment. Despite what Nathan had said, Simon obviously wasn't aware she couldn't stand him. She must be a better actor than she'd thought.

Keri rested her forehead in her hand as he continued his monologue.

'I'll send you an email when we've made a decision on dates etc,' he said finally.

Dates? Had she missed something?

'I think it behoves us all to keep up with technological advances so I'm sure it will be well attended.'

'Oh, I have no doubt,' Keri replied, realising what he was talking about, and pledging to be busy when said conference was announced. 'We'll look forward to hearing from you.'

She put the phone down and sat back. A time-consuming, boring way to prove a point but she'd done it. Wherever Nathan was, he wasn't with Simon Nicholl.

16

Keri checked the time and swore softly. She had a meeting with one of their surveyors in five minutes. Chris Dolan was a good employee when he wasn't complaining about something or other. Worse, he insisted on bringing every gripe to either her or Nathan.

'He simply likes letting off steam,' she'd said when Nathan had complained. 'I'd prefer him coming to us, than moaning to customers or suppliers.'

Keri considered herself to be a good employer, and if that meant taking on the role of counsellor at times, so be it. But she could have done without it that day.

On the dot of eleven, Chris arrived carrying a takeaway tray of two coffees. He put one on the desk in front of her, tossed the tray in the bin and sat on the chair opposite with the air of a man settling in for the long haul.

The coffee was finished and the minute hand had swept around the clock one and a half times before the rather pinched expression on his face softened. 'Thanks for listening, Keri. I feel much better about it all now.'

Weary from listening to him, and from propping up his

incredibly fragile ego, she pushed the corners of her mouth up into a smile she hoped didn't look as false as it felt. 'That's what I'm here for.'

The morning was gone. Sorry she hadn't cancelled a lunchtime meeting with one of their suppliers, she got to her feet. It was almost one, she'd make it with minutes to spare.

She looked over to Nathan's office as she crossed to the reception desk. He'd not yet returned from wherever he'd gone. 'I'll be back in an hour or so,' she told Roy. She waved to the empty office. 'I thought Nate would be back by now, he hasn't rung, has he?'

Roy looked up from his computer screen. 'No, I didn't know he had a meeting this morning. It's not in the diary.'

'Oh, it was a last-minute thing. He hoped to be back late morning but you know the way these meetings can go.' She looked back to her own office. 'I'd hoped to get through some of those emails but...' She shrugged. 'I'll try to get away early.'

'The last time you met Alf Steadman, you didn't return till past four!'

'Well, that won't be happening today. I have too much to do. I know what Alf wants anyway, it's what he always wants, a more favourable contract.' She raised an eyebrow. 'As usual, he'll want too much, I'll offer him a lot less, he'll bridle, say he'll settle for a little less than he demanded, I'll offer him slightly more than I offered and finally, probably over the second bottle of wine, most of which he'll have drunk, he'll extend his big calloused hand and demand we shake on it.'

'Every year, it's the same. I bet you won't get away from him before four.'

'If I were a betting woman, I'd put a fiver on that.' She turned with a smile for Tracy who was standing beside the printer holding a packet of A4 paper. 'How're you doing? Sorry I haven't had a chance to chat to you, it's been one of those days.'

'That's okay. Roy's been great.'

'Good, good.' Keri tried to avoid looking at Roy who was standing behind Tracy staring at the ceiling. 'Okay.' She checked her watch. 'I'd better run, you can ring me if anything urgent crops up.'

~

The meeting went exactly as Keri had predicted. It also, unfortunately, went as late as Roy had bet. Normally, she wouldn't have minded. Alf was one of the nicer people she had to deal with. Happily married for almost thirty years to his childhood sweetheart, he had two children of a similar age to Keri's and much of their conversation that wasn't about supplies centred on them.

She was back in the office shortly after four. Roy looked up when she entered but the quick quip or funny remark she expected didn't come. He was looking unusually serious. Whatever it was, Keri didn't want to hear. She'd had enough for one day and not even the sight of Nathan back in his office lessened the tension that had returned as soon as she'd left Alf's genial company. All she wanted to do now was to get the more pressing of the emails out of the way and head home.

She said 'hello' to Roy and kept walking, but she wasn't going to escape that easily.

'Have you a minute to discuss something?'

'Oh, not now, Roy. Please,' she pleaded. 'First thing in the morning, I promise I'll be all yours. I have to get some of those emails answered today.' She could tell by the downturned mouth that he wasn't happy. More guilt to add to her swiftly growing collection. 'Tomorrow, I promise, okay?' She leaned over and gave him a kiss on the cheek.

Roy wasn't a man to hold a grudge. 'Tomorrow. Right.'

Relieved, Keri went into her office and sat behind her desk. Some of the emails waiting for her attention needed to be sorted that day. She switched on her computer and dived in, keeping her head down and fingers flying across the keyboard. A rap on the door dragged her attention from the screen. 'Come in,' she called out when she saw Roy hovering outside.

'It's five. You nearly done?'

'Almost.' She stretched her arms over her head. 'Another couple to go.' She gave him a weary smile. 'It's been one of those days, but I'm sorry I didn't have time to talk earlier.'

'That's okay. Tomorrow will do fine.' He pointed to her laptop. 'Don't be too late, you'll be exhausted.' And with that final advice, he gave a wave and left.

She was vaguely aware of other staff leaving, shadowy figures in the periphery of her vision as they passed through reception. Finally, she had done as much as she was going to that day. A message from Abbie and Daniel to say they wouldn't be home yet again that night made her half annoyed, half relieved. She didn't know why they simply didn't move out completely for all the time they spent at home.

Through the glass, she could see Nathan still at his desk. It was unusual for them both to need to stay so late, and she wondered what he was doing. Memories of weeks when they left much later than this brought a smile that quickly faded. Those were different times, filled with determination to succeed, hope for their future. They'd shared a desk, elbows bumping, frequent smiles, barks of laughter from him, chuckles from her. It had been a struggle and often they'd despaired. But she never thought of the past without a smile that held a hint of regret for the people they were then.

Was that why she'd agreed to allow Tracy to do work experience? Because the enthusiastic young woman in her M&S suit and cheap shoes reminded Keri of her younger self? She stood abruptly. Looking at the past through tinted glass was rarely a good idea.

She took her jacket from the coat stand and pulled it on. Nathan hadn't moved. Was he so totally engrossed in whatever he was doing, or was it all for show?

They were the last two left in the building and her heels clicked loudly on the tiled floor as she crossed to his office. He didn't look up as she opened the door. 'You coming home?'

It seemed to take an inordinate amount of effort for him to take his eyes from the computer screen and look at her. She wondered again if there was another woman. It would explain his odd behaviour. In the same way as he couldn't lie in business, he'd never be able to hide the lie of an affair. *He wasn't like her.*

She crossed the office to his side and rested a hand on his shoulder. 'You look tired. Let's go home.'

His fingers were on the keyboard but as she'd half-expected, the screen was blank. He hadn't even had the sense to turn the damn thing on.

The journey home seemed to take longer than usual. Nathan barely said a word as they walked to the station and sat silently looking at the floor as the train chugged towards Highbury and Islington. There, they agreed they were too tired to walk and they joined the thankfully short queue for a taxi. When they were sitting in the back of one, minutes later, Keri reached for his hand, half-afraid he would pull away.

Instead, he gripped hers painfully and kept hold of it for the remainder of the journey.

17

Keri wasn't a woman to sit back and wait for things to happen or for problems to magically sort themselves out, but that evening as they sat over the takeaway meal she'd ordered, intuition kept her quiet. Whatever was worrying Nathan, maybe he needed to work through it himself.

It was a small consolation that worrying over him was putting Barry Morgan from her mind.

Her comfort was short-lived because a horrifying thought hit her. Perhaps it wasn't that Nathan was having an affair, but that he had found out about hers.

Was that why he had difficulty meeting her eyes?

Had that been Barry's next step? The wreath, the rat, then ratting?

She looked at Nathan's preoccupied face and wanted to ask him if he knew she'd been having an affair. Cheating on him. Spending hours wrapped in someone else's arms in what she could now admit was a seedy backstreet hotel with black nylon sheets she'd convinced herself were silk.

Nausea brought her to her feet and had her rush from the

room. She barely made it to the downstairs cloakroom in time, heaving the little she had eaten into the toilet.

'Are you okay?' Nathan asked when she returned.

'Something didn't agree with me.' She picked up her plate and scraped the rest of the food into the bin.

He pushed the remainder of his meal away. 'I thought it tasted a bit odd myself.'

'Will I make something else?' She opened the fridge. 'There's some pâté, I could make some toast.'

He shook his head. 'I've had enough. I'll have a beer though.'

Keri took a bottle out and opened it. She slid it across the counter to him and took away his plate, unsurprised to see he'd barely touched it.

Nor was she surprised when he took his beer and made a feeble excuse about having to send an email to someone, a name she didn't recognise, one she guessed he'd made up on the spur of the moment.

Secrets and lies, they were in more trouble than they'd ever been in all their years together.

It was late before Nathan came to bed. Keri stayed curled on her side, pretending to be asleep, afraid to speak in case the wrong words came out, words she could never take back, words that might destroy them if her actions hadn't already done that.

She lay awake for a long time, feeling the bed shudder as Nathan tossed and turned before finally falling asleep. Only then did she drift off, waking a while later to reach for him suddenly desperate for reassurance, only to find the bed empty, her hand sliding across the cold sheet where his warm body should be lying.

Regret brought bitter tears. To have risked so much for so little. How stupid she'd been.

There was no possibility of sleep until she found Nathan. Downstairs, she followed the murmur of the TV to the lounge they rarely used. She opened the door quietly and saw him, stretched out on the sofa, his eyes shut, the TV tuned to a music station.

It was impossible to tell if he was asleep or pretending to be. She retreated upstairs, took a duvet from the spare room, and went back with it bundled in her arms to drape it over him.

It was all she could do.

She returned to bed, tossed and turned for another hour before drifting into a sleep where her sins chased her relentlessly.

18

The following morning breakfast was consumed in an awkward silence only broken by the tinkle of spoon against china as they pretended to be eating cereal. Once again, most of it ended in the bin.

Unable to face the walk to the station, Keri phoned for an Uber.

Nathan looked at her with concern when she told him. 'You feeling okay? You're not still sick from that takeaway, are you?'

She rested a hand on his arm, ridiculously grateful for the worry in his voice. 'No, I'm fine, a little bit tired, maybe. I had a restless night.' She didn't mention his sleeping on the sofa.

'Yes, me too. Must have been that dodgy food.' He made no comment on the duvet she'd draped over him.

There was little conversation in the taxi or on the train to Walthamstow Central where Keri glared at their photograph on the billboard. There were still weeks before it and the poster on the bus shelter would be taken down and replaced by something unremarkable. Until then, every time she saw it she was reminded of how much she'd almost lost.

~

A little after nine, they reached their office building. It was Roy who opened every morning. His day didn't officially begin till eight forty-five, but any time Keri had needed to go in early he was there standing behind his desk. Solid as the building's foundation.

'I like to get ahead of the day,' he commented with a wink when asked why he arrived so early.

The other employees – the accountancy team, surveyors, IT, and marketing gurus – all wandered in from nine thirty. Sometimes, Keri wondered if she and Nathan were too lax, but when she'd broached the subject with him, he'd laughed and told her to lighten up.

'We have good staff. More importantly, reliable ones who stay. You can't put a price on that.'

Keri had a fair idea that they could indeed put a price on the hours that were wasted, but she let it drop and thanked their lucky stars they had the super-reliable Roy.

That morning, as usual, he was behind his desk, his eyes focused on the computer in front of him. Unusually, he didn't look up from the screen to give the big welcoming smile he reserved especially for Keri.

He didn't stir as she and Nathan crossed the reception to his desk.

He didn't look up when Keri screamed.

Nor when Nathan, eyes wide with shock, staggered back to collide with the designer chairs and trendy coffee table that designated the waiting area. The table collapsed under his weight and he crashed to the floor, arms and legs akimbo sending the chairs flying.

Keri only screamed once but the sound echoed around the airy reception and bounced off the glass walls. She was conscious of the noise behind, aware that Nathan had fallen but she couldn't move. Finally, silence floated over the macabre scene.

It was impossible to move or look away from the ghoulish, ghastly vision of Roy, their godsend. There was nothing godlike about the man now. He was sitting on his favourite chair, his hands resting on the desk in front of him, his chin resting on his blood-soaked chest.

So much blood.

Keri was panting – she stopped when the metallic smell hit her and clamped her lips shut against the noxious, levelling, classless smell of death. Because there was no doubt in her mind. Roy was dead. Nobody could survive such catastrophic blood loss.

Her mobile was in her jacket pocket. She pulled it out with a damp shaking hand, flipped open the cover and stared at it. What was her PIN number? It was seconds before she remembered she didn't need it in this situation.

'Emergency, which service do you require?'

There was no need for an ambulance. Roy was dead. *Dead.* She hadn't realised she'd said the last word aloud until she heard the voice asking her who was dead.

'Roy. Our receptionist. He was dead when we... my husband and I... arrived.' She swallowed and answered the questions she was asked as best as she could, the calmness of the voice on the other end helping her to respond.

'The police are on their way,' the operator said. 'You sure you're both safe?'

'I think so.' Keri looked around reception. There was nowhere for anyone to hide. Nor was there anywhere to conceal a person in either her or Nathan's office. The short corridor that lay between the two was empty and the back-office doors were kept locked after hours. 'There doesn't appear to be anyone here.'

'Okay, stay where you are, don't touch anything, they'll be with you in a few minutes.'

Keri stood staring at Roy a moment longer. He was wearing a waistcoat she and Nathan had bought him. She remembered he'd put it on straight away, professing it to be his favourite.

He wouldn't be happy that it was ruined.

With a sob, she turned away.

19

K eri kept the phone in her hand and went to help Nathan. He was lying among the debris of the smashed table, tears running down his face, a look of terror in his eyes. She pushed broken pieces of the wood and glass out of her way and reached a hand down to help him to his feet. He pulled her into his arms and they held each other tightly in the eerie silence.

They didn't move, even when the scream of sirens got louder and armed police burst through the door, ignoring them, ignoring the body, moving quickly through the offices, kicking open the locked doors at the rear of the building. The noise, the chaos. Roy's bloody body. All of it was so unreal.

When the commotion died down, Keri and Nathan separated slightly. They stood together with his arm across her shoulder giving the impression he was comforting her. She could feel the tremble in it, and the pain as his hand gripped and released her arm.

A slim, unremarkable man with thin brown hair stepped away from the armed police and walked towards them. He was wearing a tan suit, white shirt and the most luridly coloured tie

Keri had ever seen. It was a bizarre addition to a surreal morning.

'I'm Detective Inspector Sam Elliot.' He held his identification forward as if they might doubt he was telling the truth.

Keri didn't look at it, she was searching his face, looking for answers he couldn't possibly have. It was pleasant and unremarkably bland. If he knew anything, he wasn't giving it away.

'Who would have done such a thing?' Nathan's voice held the same tremble Keri felt in his arm.

Rather than answering, DI Elliot pointed to the offices behind. 'This area will be sealed off soon. Perhaps we could go into one of those?'

Keri's keys were in her pocket, she took them out. 'We can go into mine.' She stepped away from Nathan's arm and navigated the edge of the room to her office. Thanks to the glass walls giving a clear view of the interior, the police hadn't needed to break the door down. She unlocked it and went inside, Nathan and the detective following behind.

It was automatic for Keri to take her seat behind the desk but she got to her feet immediately and walked to a chair on the other side, facing away from the traumatic sight of Roy's body. She was relieved when the detective seemed to understand, taking the chair himself, leaving the other spare chair beside her for Nathan.

'Not sure I'd like an office with glass walls myself,' Elliot said.

'It was the interior designer's idea. It was supposed to reflect our ethos of transparency.' Keri shrugged. Never did it sound more pretentious than at that moment.

'I suppose she wasn't expecting this particular situation.' The detective's eyes drifted over her shoulder to the scene behind, then back to her face. 'Tell me about Roy Sheppard.'

Keri darted a look at Nathan. He hadn't spoken a word since they'd seen poor Roy's body. His expression was fixed into a cartoonish depiction of shock: wide eyes, mouth slightly agape, body held rigid. She slipped her hand into his and looked back across the desk.

'Roy has been with us for about eighteen years. He's... he was the nicest guy you could meet. Reliable, professional, kind, generous...' Her voice faltered as the enormity of their loss hit her. She lifted her free hand to her trembling lips. 'I don't think you'll find anyone with a bad word to say about him. The other staff, suppliers, customers, everyone liked him.'

'What about his personal life?'

'He was living in the US for a few years before he came to work with us. I'm not sure what he was doing there. He never really spoke about it. We speculated that it might have been a failed romance but–' She shrugged sadly. '–we don't know for sure. He lives alone but he has lots of friends and is always busy doing something. He liked taking up new hobbies. Mixology was his latest. Making cocktails,' she said in answer to the puzzled look on the detective's face.

'Mixology, right.' He shook his head as if rejecting this as a reason to be killed. 'He lives here in Walthamstow?'

'Yes, he has an apartment.' She gave him the address.

'Thank you, I know where that is.'

'He has an allotment too. He's a keen gardener.' Memories brought a quivering smile. 'He'd often arrive with bunches of carrots or big misshapen marrows and give them to anyone who wanted them.' She spoke of other memories, other good times they'd spent together.

DI Elliot listened intently and when she'd finished, said, 'Thank you, you've painted a good picture of Mr Sheppard.' He glanced at Nathan, then kept his focus on Keri. 'The front door was unlocked when you arrived?'

'Yes, Roy always opened up. Nathan and I were usually in by nine, and the rest of the staff around nine thirty.'

'And this morning?'

She looked at him blankly.

'You said you were usually in by nine, what time did you arrive this morning?'

'Oh.' She looked to Nathan who shrugged helplessly. A dart of angry resentment that he was leaving it all to her made her pull her hand from his. 'I think it was a few minutes after nine.'

'And Mr Sheppard arrived at what time?'

'Officially he didn't have to be here till eight forty-five but he was always in way before that.' Her expression brightened when she remembered. 'The alarm. He'd have turned it off when he arrived. It'll tell you what time it was deactivated.'

'Good, thank you, I'll have it checked.' He frowned. 'If you and your husband usually arrived at nine, and he was in at eight forty-five at the latest, it only gave someone a small window of opportunity to kill him.'

Keri wouldn't ever forget her first sight of Roy's blood-soaked body. 'He was sitting where he always did. It looked as if he was engrossed in his computer. Until we were quite close, we didn't realise there was a problem. Then we saw the blood.' Her face creased with the dual attempt of handling her sorrow and processing what she'd seen. 'It looked as if he hadn't known what was coming.' She looked at the detective, trying to read his expression. 'He knew who killed him, didn't he?'

Another thought hit her. 'Oh God.' She pressed her hands over her face.

'What is it?'

There were tears in her eyes when she took her hands away. 'Yesterday, late in the afternoon, Roy said he'd wanted to talk to me about something but I'd had a difficult day and brushed him off. I told him we'd talk this morning.'

Elliot's frown returned. 'He gave you no indication what it was about?'

'No. But I wondered if it was about Tracy.' Keri held a hand up to stop the questions she knew would follow. She took a deep breath before she could continue. 'Tracy Wirick. She's doing work experience for a month. Yesterday was her first day. I noticed she wasn't here when I got back from my meeting yesterday and wondered where she was. That may have been what he wanted to talk about but I've no idea. It could have been about one of the suppliers, anything really.'

Elliot reached into his jacket pocket for a notebook and pen. 'We'll have a word with the young woman and see if she can tell us... Tracy?'

'Wirick.' Keri spelled out the surname.

He scribbled the name down, shut the notebook and put it away. 'Is it usual? Taking on people for work experience?'

'Not really.' She wasn't surprised when the detective's eyebrow rose in question and heaved a sigh. 'We get schools ringing us wanting us to take students who are either interested in the stonemasonry side of the business or the surveyor side. It's unusual for someone to want to do work experience in reception, and very unusual for someone to walk in off the street like Tracy did.'

'But you checked references, I assume?'

Keri gave him a sharp look. 'Of course. In fact–' She pointed towards the corner of the desk. '–if you open that top drawer, her CV's there somewhere as I'd not got around to giving it to Roy to file.'

And she never would now. How were they going to cope without him? Over the last few years, they'd spoken about getting a junior office administrator to relieve Roy of some of the heavy workload, and to cover for him when he was off on holidays. But he'd resisted, saying each time that he preferred working on his own. He took holidays when the office closed for the first two weeks in August every year and the week over Christmas, plus he took the occasional day now and then. He'd never, that she could recall, taken a day off sick.

The detective was rifling through the drawer. 'Here it is,' he said, pulling stapled pages out. He put them on the desk, took out his notebook again and jotted down the details before returning them.

'There have been no issues with suppliers or customers. Nobody who would have had a gripe with the company, Mr Sheppard, or either of you?'

'I can't think of anyone.' She looked at Nathan. 'Can you?' When he looked at her blankly, she turned back to the detective. 'We've a particularly good relationship with all our suppliers and customers. I can't think of anyone.'

Elliot reached into his jacket pocket and withdrew a business card. 'You've had quite a shock. Later, you might think of something. If you do, you'll get me here.' He slid the card across the desk. 'Final question, what about next of kin?'

'He said there was nobody.' He'd left it blank on his application form. She remembered querying it with him at the time and had felt sorry for him when he'd admitted to having no relatives. 'I suppose we're the closest to family he has. We'll take care of the funeral, of course.'

'Okay.' The detective got to his feet. 'That's it for now. If you want to leave, I can have one of the officers lock up when the team are done and drop the keys to your home address.'

Keri, who had pictured having to hang around for hours trying to avoid looking at the body of a man she'd been so fond of, slumped in relief. 'Oh, thank you. I think it would be better if we could get out of here.'

'I might be able to get a car to take you home.'

'Thank you, but no, that's fine.' She took her mobile from her pocket. 'I'll order a taxi to meet us outside.'

DI Elliot escorted them from the office, past the area that had been cordoned off. Keri knew he was trying to protect them from the hideous sight of Roy's bloody body. She appreciated the kindness but she needed to say goodbye, and letting Nathan walk on with the detective she stood and stared across to where Roy still sat.

At his post to the end. He'd have liked that idea.

20

At home, Keri rang Abbie and Daniel. They were at a students' union meeting in Edinburgh but they needed to hear about Roy from her before they heard it on the news or read it in the papers.

Both were shocked: Daniel stunned, Abbie distraught. Roy had been part of their lives for so long. He'd been at every birthday party, every Christmas and New Year celebration.

'Who would have killed Roy?' Abbie asked, her voice thick with tears. 'He was the most unassuming man you could possibly meet.'

The same thought had been in Keri's mind. 'I don't know. It'll probably turn out to be a case of mistaken identity.'

Daniel agreed. 'There's no other explanation. It wasn't as if you kept money or valuables in the office either. No reason for anyone to kill him.'

No reason at all.

Keri was wracked with grief and guilt. If she'd simply given Roy five minutes the previous day. Maybe she'd know why he died. Maybe... and this was the worst thought of all... she could have prevented it.

It would have helped to have been able to talk to Nathan but he'd closed in on himself as if the pain of loss were his alone.

Abbie and Daniel had wanted to come home immediately but she persuaded them not to, unable to handle their grief on top of hers. There was no guilt in keeping them away, they'd be with their friends, away from the tense, painful atmosphere that had settled around Keri and Nathan like a winter duvet. 'Your dad and I will be okay,' she told them when they asked was she sure. 'We'll see you tomorrow.'

The news of Roy's murder had leaked and the phone rang all afternoon, one shocked voice after the other offering sympathy, expressing horror and dismay, asking unanswerable questions. Finally, Keri took the house phone off the hook and turned off her mobile.

She changed into thick winter pyjamas, wanting the comfort of their softness and their warmth to melt the chill that had settled in her core when she'd seen that blood-soaked body. She made a mug of hot chocolate and stretched out on the sofa in the living room with it cupped in her hands.

Every now and then, she heard the faint sound of Nathan's mobile ringing and wondered why he hadn't done as she had and switched it off. The vague notion that maybe he was waiting for a call from an unknown person... a female unknown person... flitted in and out of her mind. Perhaps tomorrow she'd bring herself to care.

She still hadn't spoken to Nathan by the time she trudged upstairs to bed and lay awake waiting for him to join her. He didn't and she wasn't sure where or if he slept. She lay in their bed, tears rolling down her cheek to soak into the cotton pillowcase, wishing she could turn the clock back to that moment where she'd said no to Roy's request, to have the opportunity to say what she should have done, that she always had time for him, for a man she'd held dear for so many years.

It was too late.

Guilt didn't make a good bedfellow. Neither did grief. Sometime in the early hours, she pulled a robe over her pyjamas and went downstairs. She made coffee, opened the French doors, and headed out into the garden. Early morning dew wet her feet as she crossed to the furthest of the seating areas tucked away behind tall grasses that shushed in the slight breeze.

In the murky half-light, she sipped her coffee and let her thoughts wander. She'd tried to explain to Nathan once that this was her way of coming up with solutions to problems... letting her imagination run riot, bouncing from one vague idea to another until the pieces finally clicked into place.

But nothing made sense and she couldn't come up with any explanation for why someone would want to kill Roy. It was easy to think of it as a case of mistaken identity but the more she considered that the less likely it became. Roy was... had been... an astute, clever man. He wouldn't have let an unknown person into the building that early, certainly wouldn't have turned his back on them.

It had to have been someone he knew and it followed, since they'd known each other so long, socialised together at times, it was also likely to be someone she knew.

That horrifying thought drowned out her worry about Nathan. Roy would have laughed at the thought that his death had given her something more important to think about. She could hear that strange raspy laugh of his now, it brought a smile and tears. She'd miss him so much.

Someone she knew.

Barry Morgan. She tried to laugh the thought away but it curled tendrils around her brain and no matter how hard she tried to shake it away, the idea stayed. *Barry Morgan.* Was it possible?

Keri put her empty mug down on the seat beside her. The

VALERIE KEOGH

breeze had picked up. She pulled her feet up and wrapped her arms around her knees for warmth as a shiver ran through her.

Guilt over her affair was making her paranoid, turning Barry into a monster. He couldn't have had anything to do with it. *Could he?* He'd been so angry. And the wreath and the mangled rat were pretty gruesome... but murder... would he go that far to make her regret ending their affair? She'd like to be able to say he wasn't that kind of man, but the sad truth was that she'd no idea what kind of man he was.

But Barry was a stranger to Roy. He wouldn't have let a stranger into reception that early, would he? Or, like Keri, had he been fooled by a sharp suit?

If only she knew what Roy had wanted to speak to her about.

Was it about Tracy? She hadn't been in the office so it was logical to think it was something to do with her, but what could it be? And whatever it was, was it linked to his death? Keri shook her head at the far-fetched notion that the rather browbeaten young woman was somehow involved in Roy's murder.

That detective, Elliot, his tie had been ludicrous, but his eyes were sharp. If there was something connecting Tracy to Roy's death, he'd find out.

And if Barry Morgan were involved, he'd find that out too.

And Keri's sordid secret would be revealed.

21

The sun had come up but there was little warmth in it, and none in the shady spot where Keri had chosen to sit. She was shivering by the time she went inside.

There was no sign of Nathan. She stood in the kitchen and debated whether to make more coffee or have a hot shower to warm up. The shower won, and it worked.

Thirty minutes later, warm and cosy, she went back to the kitchen for breakfast.

She'd heard Nathan moving around in their home office. When the kettle boiled, she went up and stood at the door. In a different time, she'd simply have pushed it open but now, uncomfortably aware she was nervous of what she might find, she rapped her knuckles against it and waited a second before turning the knob slowly.

She peered around the edge of the door. 'Hi. You coming down for breakfast?'

When he turned from the computer to look at her, she was shocked at his pallor and the dark circles under his red-rimmed eyes.

Quick sympathy rushed through her. 'Did you get any sleep?'

'A bit.'

Less than she had, she guessed. She crossed to him, put an arm around his shoulder and kissed his cheek. 'Come and have something to eat.' She took his hand and tugged. 'Come on. Coffee will start your engine.'

'Not sure anything can start it this morning,' he said with an attempt at humour. But he got to his feet and allowed her to lead him downstairs.

'Abbie and Daniel will be home in a while,' she said, putting a bowl of cereal in front of him. 'They're devastated over Roy. It will be good to be together.'

'Hard to think of Metcalfe Conservation without him. He's not going to be easy to replace.'

Keri wanted to snap that they weren't going to *replace* him but she swallowed the words. It wasn't the time to be pedantic. 'He did so much without complaint but he loved it. I mean how many times over recent years have we suggested he get a junior admin person.'

That raised a smile on Nathan's face. 'Probably about once a month.'

'Do you remember the time in our previous office when he thought he'd mislaid a contract and spent all day searching for it until I confessed that I'd taken it home and forgotten to bring it back.' She laughed at the memory. 'He was so sweet about it, never complained about the hours he wasted.' One anecdote led to another and soon they were laughing together about the funny things Roy had said or done.

Keri was relieved to see tension leave Nathan's face. Pleased, too, to see him eating a little. She made a pot of coffee and was about to fill their cups when the doorbell rang. 'You weren't expecting anyone, were you?' When Nathan shook his head, she frowned. She'd spoken to everyone yesterday, there was no reason for anyone to call.

When the doorbell chimed again and Nathan made no attempt to stand, Keri slid from her stool and went to answer it.

It was the detective from the previous day, a short, stocky, grim-faced woman on the step behind. 'DI Elliot and–' He waved a thumb behind him. '–Detective Sergeant Burke. I hope this isn't an inconvenient time.'

Yes, Keri wanted to say, it was a bloody inconvenient time. 'No, of course, come in.'

She brought them through to the kitchen, Nathan looking up in alarm as they entered, his eyes flicking between all three. 'What?'

Elliot raised a hand. 'A few queries, that's all. We're hoping you'll be able to answer them for us.'

'Sit, please.' Keri waved to two free stools. 'I've made coffee, would you like some?'

'That would be good, thanks,' Elliot said.

Burke, who was looking around the room with assessing eyes, gave a shake of her head and muttered, 'No, ta.'

Keri put a mug on the counter in front of the detective, filled it with coffee, and pushed the milk jug and sugar bowl towards him.

Burke was prowling around the living room, stopping to look at photographs on the bookshelves. Keri wanted to tell her to sit or at least stand still, but she couldn't think of anything to say that didn't sound rude and didn't want to antagonise the unfriendly-looking woman.

Instead, Keri sat, picked up her coffee and looked at Elliot, her eyes drawn to a different but equally dreadful tie.

He must have noticed because he grinned and ran a hand down it. 'My daughter buys them for me. When she bought the first one, I lied and told her how much I loved it, now she

VALERIE KEOGH

buys one for every birthday and Christmas. All are equally garish.'

It was so unexpected, Keri had to smile. 'The things we do for the people we love.'

'Indeed.'

He picked up his coffee, took a mouthful, then put the mug down. Reaching into his pocket, he took out a bunch of keys and slid them across the counter. 'My apologies, I meant to have them returned to you yesterday.'

'Not a problem.' Keri looked at the keys hanging from a big ornate R, Roy's distinctive key ring. 'We all have our own set of keys anyway. With this being a bank holiday weekend, we're planning to reopen on Tuesday.' A thought crossed her mind. 'That's okay, isn't it?'

'Yes, of course, the team have completed their work there anyway.' He hesitated. 'You should organise for a specialist trauma-scene clean-up team to go in first.'

Keri remembered all the blood and gulped. 'Yes, of course, I didn't think of that.'

'There are a few companies.' He pulled a card from his pocket and scribbled across the back. 'Any of these three would do a good job.'

'Thank you.' She took the card and looked at it. Names and phone numbers. 'You have a good memory.'

'It's helpful in this job.'

Keri looked at Nathan whose face was wearing the same shocked expression as the day before. 'What did you need to ask us?' The sooner the detective was gone the better. His hesitation worried her. She'd assumed any questions were merely routine dot the i, cross the t kind of questions. It was becoming obvious there was more.

Elliot reached into his inside jacket pocket and pulled out a sheet of paper. 'Tracy Wirick's personnel form,' he explained.

'We found it in a file in reception.' He opened the sheet out, turned it around and pushed it across so Keri and Nathan could read it. 'It's pretty basic–'

'She was only doing work experience,' Keri interrupted him quickly. 'There was no need for anything more complicated. We have more detailed forms for our regular employees.'

'It wasn't a criticism, actually, I was simply stating a fact,' he said evenly. He tapped the sheet with a finger. 'The address she gave, unfortunately, doesn't exist.'

'What?' Keri blinked, pulled the sheet closer and stared at the address. 'She filled it in herself.'

'Yes. She lied.'

Keri sat back, stunned. 'What about her reference?'

'They've never heard of her, I'm afraid.'

'But I rang, I spoke to the school administrator. She confirmed the reference was accurate.'

'You rang the phone number on the paperwork Tracy gave you?'

'Of course.' Keri shut her eyes. A classic con and she'd fallen for it. 'This was all a set-up?'

'Looks very much like it, I'm afraid.' Elliot pulled the sheet of paper back, folded it and tucked it into his pocket.

'Let me get this straight,' Nathan said. 'You think this woman inveigled her way into our company to kill Roy?'

'I'm not thinking anything yet, Mr Metcalfe. Just finding answers to all the questions that have arisen.'

'It's too much of a coincidence though, isn't it? She worms her way in and the next day he's killed. Sounds like two and two equalling four to me.'

Burke, who had sat on the spare stool, sneered unpleasantly. 'Detective work unfortunately isn't as simple as basic maths.'

Keri saw a flash of anger on Nathan's face and reached a

hand over to grasp his arm. 'It's all difficult for us to take in, you understand.'

'This is the early stages of the investigation. We don't rule anything in or out yet. Instead, we collect all the information and see what fits where. For the moment, this Tracy Wirick, is a piece that doesn't fit anywhere.' Elliot took out his notebook. 'It would help if you gave us a description of her.'

'Yes, of course.' She thought back to her first sight of the woman crossing reception to her door. 'My first impression of Tracy was that she looked downtrodden and defeated. I wonder how much of that was an act.' She lifted her coffee and took a sip. 'A description... about five six, slim build, dark hair streaked with blonde. She wore heavy eye make-up.' Keri shrugged. 'That's it really, I'm afraid. She was pleasant-looking but nothing out of the ordinary, nothing that stood out.'

When the detective pocketed his notebook, Keri squeezed Nathan's arm gently before taking her hand away. 'Is that it?'

'I'm afraid not,' Elliot said slowly. 'And that, unfortunately, was the easier of the two things I had to ask you about.' He reached into his jacket pocket again, took out a photograph and slid it across. 'You recognise this person?'

'Yes, of course.' Keri gave a brief smile. 'It's an old one but he hasn't changed that much. It's Roy Sheppard.' She felt her insides lurch when Elliot shook his head.

'No, I'm afraid, it isn't.'

22

Keri looked from the detective back to the photograph. She picked it up, held it closer to her face. It was Roy, she was sure of it. Handing it to Nathan, she said, 'What do you think?'

As she had done, he held it closer to his eyes before putting it down. 'Looks like Roy to me too.'

'Sorry,' Elliot said, 'I should have made myself clear. It is the man you knew as Roy Sheppard, but that's not his real name.'

'What?' Keri waited for the punchline. This had to be a joke. 'Roy has worked for us for eighteen years.'

'Yes. A year after he was released from prison in Dundee. He was supposed to report to his parole officer every week which he did for nearly a year. Then he vanished off the grid.' The detective played with the handle of his mug as he waited for them to take this news in.

'Shit!' Keri ran a hand over her head. 'Eighteen years ago, we were beginning to make a success of the business and still working with minimum staff. Roy walked in off the street one day and stood watching me with a smile on his face while I tried to juggle dealing with two phone calls and a customer.

'He said he'd been in America, had got back recently and was looking for work but didn't have any references.' Keri remembered feeling so exhausted that she almost threw her arms around his neck, but she'd already learned the hard way that if something looked too good to be true it generally was. It seemed that all these years later, she'd been proven right. 'Desperate as we were, I told him to take a hike, that we weren't that green that we'd take someone on without a reference. But he simply said he'd work for nothing for a week, and if we didn't think he could do the job, he'd leave and nobody had lost anything.'

'I remember,' Nathan joined in. 'We were worn out trying to do everything. He was like an answer to a prayer, especially when in only a couple of days he had everything sorted and running more efficiently.'

'At the end of the week, we begged him to stay.' Keri frowned. 'There was no issues with the revenue. He had all the correct paperwork.'

'Prison is a good place to make friends with certain skills,' DS Burke said.

Keri looked at the sergeant, at her bad teeth and mean begrudging eyes. 'He's worked hard for us since, never let us down, never gave us a moment's pause where we regretted our decision to give him a job. Whatever he did all those years ago, he's been straight since.'

'How do you know?' Burke screwed up her face. 'Do you know what he did in the evenings, at the weekends, at night?'

Keri glared at her.

'What was he in prison for?' Nathan asked, breaking the tension.

Elliot ran a hand down his tie. 'He served time for sexual assault.'

'Of a twelve-year-old girl,' Burke added bluntly.

Keri and Nathan exchanged horrified glances. It was left to Keri to put it into words. 'Roy was a paedophile?' Her hand crept over her mouth. All the nights he'd babysat for Abbie and Daniel. Surely not. Wouldn't she have known? *Oh God, wouldn't she have known?*

She felt the cereal and coffee churn in her belly and with her hand clamped over her mouth ran from the room.

'I'm sorry,' she said when she returned.

'There's nothing to apologise for,' DI Elliot said. 'You've had a shock.'

Burke pointed to the framed photographs of Abbie and Daniel on the shelves behind her. 'If Sheppard has been alone with them over the years, it might be a good idea to ask if he'd ever been inappropriate.'

Elliot shot her a quelling look before turning back to Keri. 'Roy has kept off the radar all these years so it's likely he was a one-time offender but for your peace of mind certainly have a word with your children.'

'Yes, I will.' Abbie had adored Roy. There'd been nothing more to it than that. She was almost sure of it. She blinked away tears. 'Okay, so is that why he was killed? Someone getting revenge after all these years.'

Instead of answering her, Elliot asked a question of his own. 'This woman, Tracy Wirick, it says on her form she was eighteen. Could she have been older?'

Quick thinking was Keri's forte so she saw immediately where he was going. 'Could she be the girl he assaulted twenty years ago, you mean?' She shook her head slowly. 'I did think Tracy looked older than the eighteen she claimed, but only by a few years, not more than ten, no.'

'It was worth considering.'

'But there must be a connection, mustn't there? She turns up one day, lies about who she is and where she lives, and the next day she's gone and Roy is dead.'

'It could simply be a coincidence, couldn't it?' Nathan said.

Elliot looked at him in surprise. 'They do happen, more often than people believe. However, I do think it's a little beyond the realms of possibility in this case.' He pushed the stool back and got to his feet. 'It's early days yet, if there's a connection, we'll find it.'

'You'll let us know, won't you?'

'As much as I'm able,' he said.

Keri saw Burke raise her eyes to the ceiling, her mean mouth downturned. Perhaps she was being more honest than the pleasant DI Elliot.

Nathan seemed once again to be off in a world of his own, so Keri got to her feet and showed the detectives to the door. 'We'll be opening the office on Tuesday,' she reminded them, as she stood back to let them pass. 'You can get us there if you've any more questions.' She shut the door after them and rested her forehead against it for a moment. It was impossible to think of Roy as a paedophile. A one-time offender Elliot had suggested, as if somehow that made it less dreadful, less disgusting, less downright unbelievable.

If she discovered he'd ever touched Abbie or Daniel, she'd wish Roy were still alive so she could kill him herself.

23

Abbie and Daniel arrived home together a little after 4pm by which time Keri and Nathan had gone over every memory they had of Roy. There was little joy in the recollections this time, each of them dissected for possible evidence of his skin-crawling tendency.

It was Keri who did all the talking, mentioning with horror all the nights Roy had babysat for Abbie and Daniel. It was she, too, who shook her head, still unable to believe a man she thought she'd known had been involved in anything so vile.

Nathan mostly sat in continued silence. He added a yes or no when she asked him directly for a comment but otherwise he seemed lost in his own thoughts.

Their children's arrival brought relief and more sadness. They arrived late afternoon, bursting through the kitchen door together to envelop Keri in hugs and tears. 'I can't believe it,' both said at the same time.

Abbie was the first to pull away. She tore a sheet from a roll of kitchen paper and blew her nose, using a second sheet to dab her eyes. 'How awful for you to have found him.'

'Do the police know who did it?' Daniel asked, giving Keri a final hug before letting go.

'No, the investigation is ongoing.' Keri looked to where Nathan sat on the sofa, saying nothing. It was going to be left to her to tell them the awful news. 'The police were here earlier asking questions, I'll tell you all about it in a bit.' Her deliberately casual air did the trick and neither commented beyond a muttered *okay*.

Abbie went back to where she'd dropped her bag and pulled out a bottle of wine. 'Merlot, Roy's favourite, I thought we could drink to his memory.' Nathan's harsh laugh startled her into a step backwards, bumping into Daniel who put an arm out to stop her stumbling further.

'Careful, you clumsy clot. Have you been drinking?'

'No.' She put the wine down on the counter and stared across at her father. 'But I think Dad must have been.' She turned to Keri. 'What's wrong with him?'

Keri didn't answer, instead she reached to rub the pad of her thumb under Abbie's eye. 'Take your stuff upstairs, Panda-eyes, then we'll have a glass of wine and talk.'

When they came back, minutes later, Abbie had repaired her make-up and each held armfuls of laundry that they shoved in turn into the washing machine in the utility room. They hadn't bothered sorting it out, Keri noticed. Some of Abbie's clothes wouldn't be machine washable, the colours were bound to run. Normally, Keri would have remonstrated with them, taken it all out and sorted it into piles. Now, she left them to it, it was time they learned.

When they finished, and rejoined Keri and Nathan in the living room, they were laughing and joking. The resilience of youth. Keri envied it.

'I ordered a takeaway,' she told them. 'Chinese. It'll be here at 7pm.'

Daniel groaned. 'I'm famished. Is there anything to nibble on?'

Keri looked at him with affection. Her greyhound son with the rangy body that belied his enormous appetite. She opened the cupboard, took down a large packet of crisps and emptied them into a bowl. From the fridge she took an open jar of olives. She drained it, emptied them into another bowl, and put both on the breakfast bar.

Abbie had taken wine glasses out and was pouring red into each.

'I'll stick to beer.' Nathan waved a hand to get her attention.

Keri hurried over to get it before a comment was made about his drinking. This would be his fourth beer in as many hours. She had suggested he slow down, that they had a difficult evening ahead telling the children the truth about Roy, but Nathan dismissed her with a growling comment that he needed it.

She felt a quiver of resentment that he was drowning his sorrows in alcohol and leaving to her the grim task of telling Abbie and Daniel the truth about a man they'd regarded as an uncle. Worse, it was left to her to pry them gently for the truth.

'Let us all sit down,' she said. 'Come on, Nathan.' She waved the bottle of beer as a lure when he seemed reluctant to move, relieved to see him getting to his feet. He took the beer from her, opened it, and glugged from the bottle.

'I still can't believe Roy's dead,' Abbie said taking a seat opposite. 'I mean, who would want to murder him. He was so sweet. I can't imagine someone hating him enough to do such a thing.'

Sweet. Keri swallowed. Hearing that Roy had been murdered was bad enough, hearing the truth about his past was going to be traumatic. She reached for her wine and took a mouthful. 'There's something I need to tell you...'

When her voice faltered, Abbie reached a hand across the counter and held hers. 'Oh Mum, it's all been so awful for you.'

Keri took comfort and strength from the warmth of her daughter's touch. She cleared her throat. 'As I said, we had a visit from the police this morn–'

'They have a suspect?' Daniel interrupted and banged his fist on the table. 'Good, I hope they lock the bastard up and throw the key away!'

'No, that wasn't it.' Keri looked at Nathan, wishing he would say something but he sat nursing his beer, leaving it to her. 'I'm afraid they had some distressing news for us.' She took another mouthful of wine. She'd have liked to have drained it, asked for a refill, and drank that too, but she didn't. One of them hitting the booze was enough. 'It appears that Roy Sheppard wasn't Roy's real name.'

Abbie laughed in disbelief. 'What? But you've known him forever!'

'That's what I said.' Keri drained her glass then and didn't refuse a refill when Daniel held the bottle towards her.

'So, if he wasn't Roy Sheppard,' he said, 'who was he?'

Keri frowned. 'I don't know his real name, they never said–'

'But you know why he changed it.'

She looked at her handsome son. He was so like Nathan at that age, nothing of her in his face. Such a good man, honest, conscientious. But hadn't she thought the same of Roy? Did you ever really know anyone? With that, she looked over to her husband. Didn't she think she knew him so well, believed there were no secrets between them. Now she didn't know anything.

'Mum?'

'Sorry, Daniel, this is so hard.' She took a sip of her wine to moisten her suddenly dry mouth. 'There's no easy way to say it, but it seems that Roy had been in prison before we knew him.'

She held a hand up when she saw the question poised on her son's lips. 'He served time for the sexual assault of a twelve-year-old.'

Daniel reared back as if she'd struck him. Abbie gasped. She pushed her stool back and got to her feet with her eyes fixed on Keri in horror. 'They're saying Roy was a paedophile? I don't believe it!'

Abbie was so obviously shocked, her words so emphatic that Keri relaxed a little. Surely she wouldn't have been had Roy ever... Keri didn't finish the thought.

'Unfortunately, it's true. The detective inspector who was here said that Roy, or whatever his name was, had vanished months after leaving prison. The detective also suggested that as Roy hadn't been in trouble since, he may have been a one-time offender–'

'Like that makes it any better! A paedophile! All the times I sat on his lap when I was a child, was he getting off on that?' Abbie's face twisted as she tried not to cry. 'It's all so disgusting.'

Daniel got to his feet and went to the fridge for a beer. He grabbed the bottle opener and levered the lid off. 'I understand now why you two are downing the booze.' He put the bottle to his lips and glugged a mouthful. 'Is that why Roy was killed?'

'Seems likely,' Nathan said, speaking for the first time.

Keri told them about Tracy. 'It's possible she was linked to his murder in some way.'

'Possible?' Abbie pressed her lips together as she struggled with tears. 'She appears out of nowhere, gives you a made-up name and fake reference and the next day Roy or whoever that pervert was, is killed and she vanishes. It doesn't take a bloody detective to see there's a link there.'

'If there is, they'll find it.'

'Ha.' Daniel waved his beer bottle to emphasise his point.

VALERIE KEOGH

'Seems like it's easier to disappear in this country than I'd have guessed. If they didn't find Roy after he absconded, what makes you think they'll find her?'

Keri held her hands up. 'I'm not the guilty party here. I'm as shocked by all of this as you are. More.' Despite what she now knew about Roy, it was the last eighteen years of friendship she was remembering, that and seeing his bloody mess of a body. 'I need to know, did he ever...' Her voice faded, the words weren't there for the questions she wanted to ask, for what she needed to know. 'Did he ever... you know...'

Abbie's eyes grew round. 'Yuk, no, never! I'd have told you if he had.' Her expression lightened a little. 'And you'd have killed him.'

Keri turned to Daniel who shook his head. 'No, there was never anything iffy. I always kinda thought of him as being the granddad we never had. He was always sneaking me a few quid, even in the later years when I kept telling him I had a good allowance and didn't need it.' He jerked his head towards his sister. 'I agree with Ab, if he'd touched us that way, you'd have killed him.'

The doorbell ringing into the silence that followed startled them all. Keri smiled shakily and stood. 'It'll be the takeaway.'

It was, and over the next few minutes the mundane actions of setting out plates and cutlery, taking the lids from the various containers and putting out serving spoons – all done in silence – helped to restore the normal family dynamics. Abbie put an arm around Keri's shoulder, Daniel topped up her glass before going to the fridge and taking out another beer for Nathan.

Alcohol wasn't the solution, but it certainly blurred the scratchy edges of reality.

Over dinner, by subconscious decision, conversation consisted of chat about Abbie and Daniel's university courses.

They attended the same university, Abbie reading business and economics, Daniel reading social media studies. Normally they had plenty to say, but that night they struggled, and conversation slowed to the odd comment before fading into silence.

Finally, Abbie put her cutlery carefully down on her plate, lining them up neatly, fiddling with getting the end of each handle level with the edge. 'What about the funeral?'

Keri had told the police they'd pay for everything but that had been before she'd learned about Roy's terrible secret. But eighteen years was a long time. 'Do you remember the Christmas when you were six, Abbie, and you wanted that stupid doll whose name I've forgotten.'

'Matilda. Yes, I remember.'

'Online shopping wasn't so big in those days and it was sold out in the local shops so I was going to get you something else, but when Roy heard how much you wanted it, he said to leave it to him. He went to every toy shop for miles around until he found that damn doll.' Keri played with the stem of her glass. 'We'll have a funeral for the man we knew, the man who wanted to make a six-year-old's Christmas a happy one, and for the times he was good to us, his loyalty and hard work over all these years.'

Daniel frowned. 'If it gets out, and it's sure to, there will be plenty to criticise you for that position.'

'I have no doubt.' She ran a hand over her face, brushing away the tears that always seemed to be waiting in the wings. 'If the police find anything that shows he has crossed the line while he's been with us, then that's a different situation. But if not, my position will remain unchanged. I'm certainly not condoning his behaviour, but Roy, the man I knew, deserves a decent funeral attended by those who loved him.' She looked around, slightly embarrassed by her speech. But in the faces of her children all she saw was loving support. Nathan's face though, remained shadowed with concerns she didn't understand.

She couldn't deal with them now.

24

Abbie and Daniel vanished to their rooms shortly after dinner leaving Keri and Nathan to linger silently over the last of the wine.

It would have been the perfect time to have asked him what was troubling him but there were too many stressful fingers squeezing her brain already. Whatever was bothering him would have to wait. One of the stressful fingers that was poking her was resentment that he was leaving everything to her. Perhaps it was time that changed.

'Nathan.' She waited until he looked up from the bottle of beer he was holding to meet her eyes. 'Tomorrow, will you contact one of those companies DI Elliot told us about? You know, the clean-up specialists.'

He looked at her blankly for a moment, then shrugged. 'Okay.'

'You won't forget. We don't want to go into the office on Tuesday and see...' Her voice faded.

'I said I'll do it, didn't I?'

But there was no conviction in his voice and Keri knew she'd end up making the call herself. She finished the wine in her

VALERIE KEOGH

glass and got to her feet. Barely touched cartons of Chinese food were strewn across the table. Abbie and Daniel hadn't even removed their plates. It wasn't their fault. How many times had they offered to help and she, wearing her superwoman cloak, insisted she could manage. Lately though, it was becoming less a cloak, more chainmail. It was time things changed, but that was a discussion for somewhere in the future, not now.

She cleared the table, debated saving the takeaway food, then shook her head and threw it into the bin. Nathan would normally have helped but that night he seemed glued to his seat, his hand stuck to a bottle she was convinced was empty.

It took only minutes to tidy up. She shut the dishwasher with a bang and looked back to where he sat. 'I'm exhausted, I'm going to have a bath and head to bed.'

'Right. I'll be up in a bit.'

Her heart twisted to see him looking so woebegone, so defeated, and it twisted further when she realised the one person she would have talked to about him was dead. Roy had always been able to see the overall picture in business and personal relationships. He'd have put her worries to rest with well-chosen succinct words. She missed the man she'd known.

Upstairs, she heard the murmur of voices from Abbie's room and the low thump of music from Daniel's. They were strong and resilient, they'd get through this in their own way.

Keri ran a bath and added a generous amount of her favourite oil before switching out the light and easing into the hot water. She rested her head back. A soft glow slid under the door from the hallway to make a dim, warm, womb-like cocoon. At last, she could allow the tears to come. Their release relaxed her a little and gave her space for thinking.

But for a change, everything seemed to be beyond her control. Roy. Nathan. That blasted Barry.

Barry. If Roy was murdered because of his past, didn't it put her ex-lover in the clear? She wanted to believe so, wanted no risk of her own secret escaping.

Usually, she stayed until the water cooled around her, but not that night.

Restless, she climbed out only minutes later, wrapping a bath towel around her foam-flecked body.

She preferred to sleep naked but once again she needed the comfort of pyjamas and pulled a fresh, light cotton pair from a drawer. When she was in bed with her head nestled into the pillow, she could hear murmurs of conversation from Abbie and Daniel's rooms. Comforting sounds. It was good for them to be talking to their friends.

Tears came again then. Friends, the two she'd choose to talk to... one dead, Nathan lost in worry that he seemed unable to share. She couldn't bring Roy back but she could get to the bottom of whatever was ailing Nathan.

Tomorrow.

That one word seemed to work like a magic spell and Keri, who had expected to shuffle restlessly all night, drifted off to sleep.

25

Nathan's side of the bed was empty when Keri woke early the next morning, the unrumpled sheets indicating he'd not come to bed even for a short while. She lay for a moment listening to the sound of voices drifting up from downstairs. Daniel, she guessed. He was always an early riser unlike Abbie who would sleep till mid-morning if she could.

Keri dressed and headed down, pleased to hear laughter.

Daniel and Nathan were sitting around the breakfast bar but they weren't alone. Two of Daniel's friends lifted smiling faces to her when she opened the door.

'Ben and Jason came over to offer their condolences,' Daniel said. 'I invited them to stay for breakfast. That's okay, isn't it?'

'Of course, there's plenty.' Keri greeted the two friends and opened the fridge to take out eggs, bacon, and sausages. She'd lied, there wasn't enough for six but she wasn't feeling hungry anyway, and from the look of Nathan's pale face, she thought he mightn't want too much either.

In fact, Nathan shook his head when she put a plate in front of him. 'I've had something already,' he said. 'I was awake early.'

He tilted his head towards the sofa. 'Fell asleep there and woke up with a crick in my neck.'

Daniel looked from Nathan to Keri and back again. 'You slept on the sofa, all night?'

Nathan laughed. 'Don't sound so surprised, how many times have we found you asleep there in the morning after a few beers.'

'I know but–'

'But what? You think it's the prerogative of the young?' Nathan got to his feet and left the room leaving an uneasy silence behind him.

Ben and Jason shuffled on their stools and looked uncomfortable. 'Maybe we should go,' Jason said.

'Nonsense.' Keri patted him on the arm. 'I'll have breakfast ready in a jiffy.' She turned to Daniel. 'Make a pot of coffee, I could do with a mug.' She kept up a stream of light conversation, asking questions about university, their individual courses, their social lives. By the time she put a dish of bacon, sausages and fried eggs on the counter and told them to help themselves, the tension caused by Nathan's snapped comment had eased completely.

Abbie arrived as the boys were scraping their plates. 'I hope you left me some,' she said, planting a kiss on Keri's cheek.

'I have some in the oven for you. Sit, and I'll get it.'

Abbie greeted her brother and his friends, accepting the mug of coffee Daniel slid her way with a grateful smile. 'I needed this.' She took a mouthful and put it down, twisting in her seat to look at Keri. 'Where's Dad gone?'

Keri jerked her hand, hitting it off the rack as she reached for the plate. 'Blast,' she said, putting the plate down and hurrying to the sink to turn on the cold tap and hold her hand under the stream of water.

'You okay?' Abbie came to stand beside her looking down in concern.

'I'll live.' Keri looked at her. 'Dad's gone out?'

'I saw him going out the door as I came down the stairs. I called him but he mustn't have heard me. Seemed to be in a bit of a hurry.'

Keri turned the tap off and grabbed a towel. 'Oh, he's probably gone for the newspaper.' It was a possibility of course. Nathan might be worried about the reports on Roy's murder. It was a definite possibility. Her eyes flicked to the clock over the kitchen door. Ten thirty. The closest shop was a ten-minute walk. She sat and tried to join in the conversation between her children and their friends as the minutes passed. Thirty minutes ticked by. Thirty-five.

Keri put on a good act. She didn't think anyone present realised she was worried. She should have spoken to Nathan the day before... should have learned from Roy's death that sometimes tomorrow didn't come.

26

'He's probably met someone he knows and gone to the pub for a pint,' Keri said an hour later when Daniel and Abbie looked concerned at their father's continued absence. She waved a dismissive hand as if this were something that happened regularly. Truth was, it had never happened before. Nathan would never go anywhere without telling her.

'Wouldn't he have rung you?' Abbie said.

'He will eventually when he realises the time.' Keri forced a laugh. 'You know what your father's like.'

'I thought I did, now I'm not so sure.'

Keri heard the note of criticism and jumped to Nathan's defence. 'He's taking Roy's death and the news about his past hard. We all cope with things in different ways, this is his.'

'Still–'

'Leave it, Abs, I understand your father.' Keri pulled her daughter into a quick hug. 'Honestly, it'll all be fine.' It would because when Nathan returned she was going to make him sit down and tell her what was going on.

'We were thinking of maybe going out to the pub,' Daniel said. 'Will you come with us?'

'Thank you, that's sweet of you, but I'd rather stay here and catch up with some reading. When your dad gets back I might drag him out for a while.'

'I'll stay and keep you company,' Abbie said, throwing an arm around her mother's shoulder.

'Not necessary, honestly.' Keri pushed her away. 'Please, I'd be happier if you all went out together.'

With only a little more encouragement, Abbie agreed and twenty minutes later each of them, including Ben and Jason, gave her a hug and left. When she heard the front door slam, Keri picked up her mobile and rang Nathan's number. It went directly to voicemail. She hated leaving messages so hung up without doing so. She didn't need to anyway, he'd see the missed call from her and get the message.

She slumped down on the sofa and rested her head back. Nathan would return eventually. She wouldn't put it off any longer and would insist he told her what was going on. The truth couldn't be worse than what they'd heard about Roy. Could it?

If it was another woman?

Another woman who was as meaningless as Barry had been to her, Keri could cope with. But if it was more serious. If Nathan had fallen in love with someone else and wanted to leave. A sob broke from her, a sad, forlorn sound of distress. Life without Nathan was unthinkable.

She brushed the tears away and sat up. There had been tough times in Metcalfe Conservation through the years, but they'd battled through. Giving up wasn't in her DNA. Twenty-five years she and Nathan had been married, that was worth fighting for.

Wanting distraction, she looked for the book she was reading and remembered it was upstairs beside her bed. She thought about going up to get it but worry kept her pressed to the sofa. It wasn't until she heard the hall clock chime the hour that she grunted in frustration and got up. She needed to be doing something. Then she slapped her hand to her brow. The trauma-scene clean-up specialists. She bet Nathan hadn't rung them.

The card the detective had given them with the names was on the coffee table. She picked it up. Three names. Had Nathan rung one of them? She tried his mobile but as before it went to voicemail; this time she left a message and followed it up with a text. *RING ME.* She hoped he'd see the capitals as a deliberate act to emphasise the urgency rather than an accident. When ten minutes passed without reply, in the hopes that he might answer a question, she quickly tapped out, *did you ring the clean-up team* and sat staring at the screen as she waited for a reply.

When one didn't come, Keri gritted her teeth and picked up the card. She'd have to ring all three to check he hadn't already organised someone to call to the office. It was a frustrating few minutes. The first two hadn't been requested to do the job and when the third company also denied being asked she was relieved to be reaching the end of this fiasco. 'Fine, how soon can you do it?'

'We have availability on Wednesday.'

Wednesday! 'No, I'm sorry we need this sorted sooner than that. Thanks, I'll try someone else.'

The first company on the list were equally busy. On the fifth frustrating phone call, she got lucky, the second was able to send a team the following day. She gave her credit card details to secure the contract and promised to have the keys delivered to the office that afternoon. The easiest thing to do was to order a taxi to bring them, and twenty minutes later she handed the set of keys to the driver.

With that out of the way, she sat back on the sofa, picked up her phone again and scrolled through the contacts to find the employment agency they used. 'Hi Marianne,' she said when it was answered. 'We need someone for reception from Tuesday for a couple of weeks, maybe longer.' The thought of interviewing for someone to take Roy's place was too hard to contemplate. Using an agency was expensive but it was worth it to give them some leeway.

'No problem,' Marianne said. 'Is the amazing Roy taking time off?'

'Not exactly.' Keri squeezed her eyes shut on the image of his blood-soaked body. 'He was killed. Friday morning. In the office. So you'd better not send someone squeamish.' The silence lasted so long she thought she'd been cut off. 'Hello?'

'Sorry, I'm stunned. I met Roy a couple of times. A nicer guy you couldn't meet.'

Keri's fingers tightened on the phone. 'Yes. We'll miss him.' She swallowed and kept her focus on the business. 'If you could send someone who has been with us before, that would be so helpful.'

'Roy took so little time off, but you did have someone recently, I'll check who it was and see if he's free. I'll do the best I can and promise you'll definitely have someone on Tuesday morning.'

Keri had to be satisfied with that and thanking the administrator, she hung up.

This is what she was good at. Getting things sorted.

It was too late to help Roy. Whatever he'd wanted to speak to her about had gone with him. It was up to the police now to find his killer.

Barry Morgan... it was preposterous to think he'd anything to do with Roy's death. *Wasn't it?* He'd been angry she'd ended their affair, the wreath and rat a nasty touch of revenge, but it was a huge leap to murder. Hopefully, he'd have moved on. She needed to stop beating herself with a stick made of guilt and put him and that stupid period of madness behind her.

Her priority now was Nathan. She'd find out what the hell was going on with him and she'd fix it.

She would fix it.

27

Unfortunately for Keri's renewed determination, Nathan didn't return. Late afternoon, her phone buzzed with a brief message from him.

I'm ok. Trying to sort a few things out in my head. Don't worry. See you in the office Tuesday.

Tuesday! Keri rang his number but it went straight to voicemail. Frustrated, her thumb flew over the keyboard. *Why can't you come home now?* It was tempting to add *we need to talk* but she knew that would be the last thing he'd want to hear. Instead, she added, *I love you*, and pressed send.

The reply was immediate. *Love you too. Cu Tuesday.*

Where are you staying? She stared at the screen waiting for an answer till her eyes stung. None came. Blinking, she tossed her mobile down and slumped back with a groan. Tuesday, she might kill him before sitting him down to find out what the hell was going on.

By the time Abbie and Daniel returned, thankfully alone,

Keri had resigned herself to waiting. She met their queries about their father with a smile and a ready-made lie waiting to be used. 'He met an old friend, they went to the pub and ended back in the friend's house. He's going to stay over.'

'He's not coming home?' Abbie's face fell.

Keri hoped her laugh didn't sound forced. 'You sound shocked. It's good for him to be with his male friends, talk about man stuff.'

'But now? With all this about Roy... don't you need him here?'

Keri put her arm around Abbie's shoulder and pulled her into a hug. 'Darling daughter, I'm fine. To be honest, it's been so busy recently that we've been getting on each other's nerves a bit and now the added stress of Roy's murder on top of it all. It's good to have a break from one another.'

Abbie kissed her cheek and pulled away. 'I've never understood how the two of you work together every day without driving each other crazy. As long as you're okay.'

Apart from a derogatory comment about his father's drinking habits, Daniel merely raised an eyebrow when he heard but didn't question his absence.

Keri rang Nathan's mobile at intervals the remainder of the evening but each time it went to voicemail. In desperation, she left a voice message in the end. *'I don't know what's wrong, Nate, but whatever it is, we'll get through it. We always do. I love you, remember that.'*

For the moment, it was all she could do.

Keri didn't hear from Nathan again that night although she lied and told Abbie and Daniel that he'd said hello. Annoyance vied with worry leading to a restless night's sleep. Usually, she enjoyed bank holiday weekends but all she wanted was for Monday to be over. That she was lying to the twins was added guilt she didn't need and found hard to bear.

They insisted on taking her out to a pub for brunch rather than her having to cook again. She was easily persuaded, happier to be in the noise and jolly atmosphere of a pub than sitting at home wondering where Nathan was. *How he was. Who he was with*.

Abbie kept Keri amused with choice anecdotes about the men on her course. She recounted a story of one student who considered himself to be a cross between Don Juan and Casanova. 'He was desperately trying to chat up Tanya and–'

'Tanya? The girl I met last year? One of your uni mates?'

'Yep. He was agreeing with everything she said. I swear he nodded so hard he was unable to nod anymore because his head fell off his shoulders and rolled onto the road and got squashed by an Uber driver delivering a kebab.'

Like many of Abbie's anecdotes, it didn't make a lot of sense but it made Keri laugh and that was what she needed. The food was good, she ate better than she had in days and had sparkling water in preference to more alcohol. A clear head was essential to get through the next day.

She guessed Abbie and Daniel had been talking when neither asked when Nathan was coming home and she was relieved not to have to lie again.

It was late afternoon before they returned home. If Keri had half-hoped Nathan would have changed his mind and returned, she was disappointed. 'I think I'll make a pot of tea,' she said, throwing her jacket over the banisters. 'Any takers?'

'Sure,' Abbie said.

Daniel merely nodded and, as Keri put the kettle on to boil, made himself useful taking out mugs and the jug of milk while Abbie sat with her elbows on the counter.

'You sure you're going to be okay?' she said when Keri brought over the pot of tea.

'It's going to be a difficult few days, I won't lie, but yes, we'll be okay.' She emphasised the *we* and smiled.

'We could stay tonight.'

Keri shook her head firmly. She knew they had plans, knew too they'd want to stay over with friends for convenience. There had been enough upset, it was good to return to normality. Truth was, she was looking forward to their departure, to being able to stop pretending. 'No, that's not necessary, honestly. I'm planning an early night. Tomorrow is going to be a tough day.'

She walked them to the door when they were ready to go and waved them off. It wasn't till they'd disappeared from view that she shut the door and locked it. It wasn't the first time she'd spent the night on her own in the house but it was the first time she felt uneasy.

It was understandable. Roy had been murdered by someone he probably knew. Someone she might know. She slipped the security chain in place, then hurried through to check the back door was locked. And the French windows. In the end, she wasn't content till she'd checked every window downstairs. They rarely closed the curtains, but that night she went from room to room and pulled them all.

It didn't take away the sense that something bad was lurking outside. She was being silly. Stupid too, to worry suddenly if there was a connection between all the unsettling happenings... that damn wreath, the mangled dead rat, Barry's lies, Tracy's lies. Even Nathan's. Was Roy's murder the endgame or simply the next step in some twisted plan?

Back in the living room, she picked up the detective's card. Maybe she should tell him about Barry and the choice gifts he'd left for her.

She took the card with her as she plodded up the stairs. Their sophisticated alarm system allowed her to isolate her bedroom and she felt safer when it was done and she was inside the room with the door locked. Sitting on the bed, she flicked the card against her lip. Too many bizarre things had happened in a short space of time. Too many people had lied. She was surprised she hadn't considered a connection before. Because it was suddenly clear to her, there had to be one.

But what the hell could it be?

She flopped back on the bed and stared at the ceiling. The answer unfortunately wasn't written there. She wished Nathan was beside her. They could've talked through it, bounced ideas around. The way they used to.

When she felt tears gather, she sat up. No more damn tears. They weren't going to bring Roy back. Or solve whatever the hell had gone wrong with her life.

She'd have liked to go to sleep. Preferably for weeks. Hibernate until everything was right again. But it was only 7pm, too early to even try. Her book was on the bedside table. It was good, but reading didn't appeal. She reached for the remote and switched on the TV. Channel-hopping to find something to watch, she switched off when nothing took her fancy, threw the remote to one side and got to her feet.

A bath would have been nice. Relaxing too. But the idea of lying naked in the empty house sent chills down her spine. Camomile tea might help but that would mean switching off the alarm and going downstairs. She stood, shuffling from foot to foot, annoyed with her inability to make a simple decision, annoyed even more by unaccustomed fear that fluttered around her like a persistent bluebottle.

She batted it away and switched off the alarm at the upstairs panel but the flash of bravery didn't last past the first few steps downward. It was still bright but the setting sun was throwing shadows and shades. Halfway down, she stopped and waited, head tilted. There was nothing to hear apart from her own stupid thumping heart.

The remaining steps were taken one at a time, her hand sliding along the banisters, eyes flicking from shadow to shade. She pushed open the kitchen door, the room in darkness thanks to the curtains she'd pulled earlier. Her fingers felt along the wall for the switch and flicked it to flood the room with light.

The curtains over the French doors to the garden were heavy and usually looped back on each side, day and night. They didn't lie flat as a result, the material forming deep folds that could easily have sheltered someone. Ridiculous. It would have to be a very skinny someone. But she couldn't take her eyes from the curtains as she filled the kettle and switched it on.

It seemed to take an eternity for the water to boil. Keri knew there was nobody behind the damn curtains. That it was only her fixed unblinking stare that made them look as if they were moving.

But before the kettle had boiled, she crept from the room without taking her eyes from the undulating folds of fabric. At the stairs, she turned and ran, taking the steps three at a time. Only when the alarm was on, and the bedroom door shut and locked, did she slump against the wall feeling ridiculously foolish.

She felt a little safer until, with another flash of stupidity, she remembered *The Shining* and Jack Nicholson's crazed cry, '*Here's Johnny.*'

Stupid! There was nobody outside with an axe waiting to smash through the door. She was still telling herself this as she crawled under the duvet fully dressed and curled up.

It was sometime in the early hours of the night that fear, having exhausted its host, took a step back and allowed her to fall asleep.

28

The morning light chased away some of the demons and Keri gave a half-hearted laugh as she climbed from the bed. Sometime during the restless night she'd kicked off her shoes. One was on the floor, the other tucked under the duvet. She brushed away the scuff marks they'd made on the sheets and gave a brief but quickly dismissed thought about changing them. Instead, she shook the duvet and fluffed the pillows. That would do.

Her plan was to get to the office early to check that the clean-up specialists had lived up to their name. Early enough too, to face the memory of the last time she'd been there. Of course, she'd hoped Nathan would be with her. Mutual support. She tried his number but once again it went to voicemail. She tapped out a message. Resisted the temptation to beg.

I'm planning on being at the office by 8.30am. Meet me there. Please don't be late, it's going to be tough.

Surely he wouldn't let her down.
Keri always liked to portray a professional appearance but

that morning she took extra care. Whatever Roy's past, he'd earned respect from her and Metcalfe Conservation and she'd make sure he got it.

All black seemed appropriate. Her Armani jacket and trousers, black silk Chanel shirt. She tied her hair back in a French knot but rather than allowing strands to curl around her face as she normally did, she pinned every hair back. It was severe. Funereal. A suitable reflection of their loss.

Dark-grey pearl earrings, an overlarge black clutch bag, and she was ready to go.

The Uber she'd called arrived within minutes. She'd decided to take it to the office rather than the station. It might take a little longer but she was even earlier than she'd planned and it saved having to push through the crowds at the station. She refused to admit that she was nervous of being in such an open place where Roy's killer might have easy access.

She checked her phone as the taxi chugged through busy London streets but Nathan hadn't replied. She left a voicemail, trying to keep the hint of desperation from creeping into her words. *I'm almost there, hope you're on your way. Love you.*

There was still no reply by the time the taxi stopped outside their office building. She stared at it for a moment noting that only the emergency lights were on and the alarm was still engaged. Nathan hadn't arrived yet. She swallowed the lump of self-pity that had lodged in her throat and climbed from the taxi. They had an account with Uber that covered the journey but she pulled a ten-pound note from her purse and handed it to the driver. 'Wait until I'm inside please, will you?'

He pocketed the bill. 'Sure.'

With the office keys in her hand, she walked up the broad steps to the glass front door. There was a clear view through to the reception area. Nothing to be seen. Nothing out of the ordinary. Just a huge sense of absence.

She opened the door, the beep of the alarm confirming it was engaged and turned to wave a thanks to the driver before shutting and locking the door behind her.

Once the alarm was switched off, she approached the reception desk, her heels clicking loudly in the silence. She kept her lips pressed together as she edged around to the other side but the clean-up team had done a good job. There was nothing to see. No evidence that this was where Roy had bled to death.

His chair was missing. She'd told them to remove anything that was too heavily contaminated, but everything else that had made this area Roy's kingdom was still there. A piece of stone, from every project the company had worked on since he joined, stood on the freestanding shelves that were angled in a V behind the desk. Roy remembered each and was happy to tell potential customers their story. Often it had swayed those who hadn't quite decided to avail of Metcalfe Conservation's services.

The spinning desk organiser still held Roy's eclectic mix of pens and multicoloured paperclips. Photographs of various events were slotted along the back of the countertop – Roy's smiling face in each surrounded by Keri, Nathan, Abbie and Daniel along with various customers and suppliers over the years. Happy pictures.

A vase stood empty. Every Monday morning, Roy would arrive with a bunch of fresh flowers from his local florist. She was pleased the clean-up team had removed the withered remains. Later, she'd ring a florist and have a suitable arrangement delivered.

The desktop computer was missing. She had a vague memory of DI Elliot telling her they'd be taking it for forensic investigation. Damn, she'd left his card at home. She'd try to get him through the station to ask when it would be returned. Hopefully, they'd have found nothing suspicious on it. Or on Roy's home computer. She wanted to cling to the memories of the man she knew. They would be invariably tarnished if... She couldn't finish that thought.

In her office, she sat and took a deep breath. One dreadful step over. Many more to get through before the end of that day.

There was still no word from Nathan by the time the agency temp arrived on the dot of 8.45. He was someone who'd done a day in reception only a couple of weeks before when Roy had taken a day off for a friend's wedding. Only a day, but it meant Keri was spared having to show the temp around.

'It's Luke, isn't it?' She remembered thinking when she saw him the previous time that the young man bore a resemblance to Tom Cruise. Short dark hair, charismatic smile, a little shorter than average. Now it was the kindness in his eyes she noticed. 'The agency filled you in, I assume?'

'Yes.' He then shook his head. 'I never met Roy but he left me a helpful note when I came a few weeks ago. Seemed to be a nice guy. A sad loss.'

'Yes.' She would no doubt hear that sentiment expressed a million times that day. 'It's going to be a difficult morning for us all.' She looked along the desk and frowned. 'You'll need a computer. You can use Nathan's for the moment.'

She unlocked his office, switched on the laptop, and waited for it to power up before entering his password. When Nathan arrived, he'd have to share her computer. She left the door unlocked. Surely, he'd be in soon. Not leave her struggling alone with this hideous morning.

'Here you go.' She put the laptop on the reception desk and plugged it in. 'I have no doubt the phone will be hopping. Do the best you can. Any business calls you can put straight through to me until Nathan gets here, then share them as appropriate. Okay?'

Luke pulled a chair over, sat, and moved the phone closer.

Making himself at home. *In Roy's kingdom.* Keri took a step away. 'I'll leave you to it, shout if you have any problems.'

She sat behind her desk and pressed her fingers against her eyes. How could Nathan leave her to cope alone? The selfish bastard.

It was by sheer willpower that she managed to set her expression into a professional one before the first of the staff arrived, their shocked faces lingering on the reception desk. And each of them called into Keri with words of sympathy, sorrow, loss.

By mid-morning, she was exhausted. From their sadness, from her own, from the constant stream of phone calls. Some genuinely upset, some simply wanting the gory details. She handled them all with the same standard phrases of loss, how much they'd miss Roy, how much he meant to her, to the company, how shocking it had been. She didn't tell callers it was a nightmare, that she was afraid she might know the killer, that everything seemed to be falling apart. That fear seemed to have taken up residence and she couldn't shake it away.

Luke, thank goodness, seemed to be coping. A quick call to the agency reassured her that he could stay with them for as long as necessary. She'd have to advertise for the position eventually. It wouldn't be an easy job. How could she replace the irreplaceable?

At least with Luke manning the desk, she could put that off for a while.

She was grateful when Chris Dolan knocked on her door at midday and offered to get her something for lunch.

'I'm not hungry, Chris, but I'd kill for a coffee.' The words were out before she considered what she was saying. She lifted a hand in defeat. 'You know what I mean. Yes, please, a large cappuccino would be great.'

When he returned she accepted the disposable mug from him with thanks, grateful when he left her to have it in peace. She took her phone off the hook and sat back. Through the glass walls, she was able to watch Luke. She'd no idea what he was doing about lunch. Roy used to have it at the desk. Occasionally he'd grab one of the accountancy team to cover for him while he nipped out for coffee, always returning with one for her too.

Luke seemed sensible. No doubt he'd cope.

The way she was having to.

She wanted to put her head down and weep. Instead, she drank the coffee and came to a decision. As soon as her world returned to something resembling normal she was going to do a major redecoration. The first thing that was going to go was those damn glass walls.

By early afternoon, worry vied with annoyance at Nathan's continued absence. She'd left voicemails, saying the same in each, *Nathan can you ring me, I'm worried,* and checked compulsively for replies, slamming the mobile down on the desk when there was nothing from him.

It might have been a good idea to ring the police station to enquire about the return of their computer, but she couldn't bring herself to do it. Fear of what they might have found on it combined with worry that she'd reached the limit of what she could deal with alone.

Abbie and Daniel rang to ask how she was. 'Just getting through the day,' she said giving the same answer to each. 'The agency sent someone for reception who was here before so that's been a help.' She didn't mention their father's continued absence knowing they would be worried and distressed that she was on her own.

A day that felt like a year finally ended. At five to five, she went out to reception to speak to Luke. 'Would you be able to lock up and open again in the morning?' She waved to the offices at the back. 'Most of the staff are usually gone by five, there might be a couple who are late but we'll pay you till five thirty to cover that, if that's all right with you?'

'Sounds fine, Mrs Metcalfe.'

'Good, thank you.' She handed over the two keys she'd removed from Roy's key ring. 'Here you go. You'll need to put the alarm on too. The panel is to the right of the door, the code is 0078.'

'That'll be easy to remember.'

'Yes, it was Roy's idea.' She slipped her arms into her jacket. 'Right, I'll see you in the morning.' She moved towards the door, then turned again with a final word for him. 'Thank you, by the way, you managed well today. It is much appreciated.'

The Uber she'd ordered was idling outside. She climbed in and sat back, shutting her eyes, grateful the day was over.

She got through it. She'd get through everything else.

But first she had to find Nathan.

29

The traffic on the journey home was horrendous and Keri regretted her decision to take a taxi rather than the train. But like most things, it was too late for regrets. She kept her eyes shut and longed for a few minutes' sleep envying those people who could catnap. It didn't work for her and she opened her eyes and gazed listlessly out the window.

It was almost an hour later before the taxi pulled up outside her home.

Beyond weary, she trudged up the steps to the front door and unlocked it. In the hallway, working on autopilot, she went to the alarm panel to key in the code. Only then did she realise it wasn't on. She turned from it, the silence unnerving, then looked towards the door wondering if she should run outside. Her mobile was in her pocket, she took it out, flipped the cover open and held her thumb hovering over the emergency key.

It brought her enough reassurance to allow her to move further along the hallway. Maybe one of the children had come home. 'Hello? Abbie? Daniel?' When there was no answer, she tried a less assured, 'Is there someone here?'

With every step forward, she stopped to listen and she was halfway to the kitchen before she heard someone's voice. A low mumble. She tilted her head one way, then the other, trying to hear what was being said, or where it was coming from. Convinced it was from upstairs, she took a step backward, cocking her ear to listen for sound drifting down the stairway, then convinced she was wrong and it was from the kitchen, she retraced her slow steps in that direction.

The kitchen door was shut. Keri rested her hand against it and looked back down the hallway to the front door. She should have left it open for a quick getaway. Perhaps it would be wiser to leave and call the police. Instead, she rested her ear against the door, pressing it tightly when she heard the murmur again. Impossible to make out what was being said but there didn't appear to be anything threatening about it... in fact, it sounded sad.

Her hand moved to the door knob and slowly, quietly, she turned it and pushed the door open an inch, peering through the gap to see who was there. It wasn't until the door was almost fully open that she saw who it was and her breath came out in a noisy gust. 'Nathan! You idiot! You scared the bloody wits out of me!'

He was seated at the breakfast bar, his head resting forward on his arms. The sound, that sad rhythmic murmuring, was coming from him. But with his face buried in his arm, she still couldn't make out what he was saying.

'Nathan? Nate?' When he didn't respond she wondered if he was talking in his sleep. She put a hand on his shoulder and shook it slightly, then harder until finally he lifted his head to look at her.

Her gasp was automatic and came as a bolt of terror shot through her. This man with his blotchy face and defeated reddened eyes was barely recognisable as her handsome husband. 'Nathan, for God's sake, what's wrong?' When he didn't answer, anger replaced the terror. She'd been abandoned that day, left to deal with all the ramifications of Roy's death. 'Where have you been? I needed you today, what the bloody hell happened to you?'

He pulled her to him, wrapping his arms around her waist, burying his face in her chest. She wanted to pull away, demand answers, but this was so unlike her usually rather devil-may-care husband, that the terror returned and ratcheted up a notch. It had to be something beyond serious to affect him in this way.

She couldn't think of anything else to do, held captive as she was, but to murmur words of endearment and stroke his head as if he were a baby.

It was a long time before he pulled away. Snuffling, he wiped his nose and eyes with his arm leaving a snail-trail of snot and tears on his navy shirt.

Keri reached behind for a stool and sat. 'Do you want to tell me about it?' When he stayed silent, she reached for his hand. 'We always used to talk about everything. It'll make things easier. And whatever it is, whatever's wrong, I can help you fix it.'

'Oh yes, the great Ms Fix-it.' Sarcasm laced his voice. 'Not everything is fixable, Keri. You're bloody superwoman, but even you would be beaten by this.'

Hurt by the words, she kept a grip on his hand and a tighter hold on the impatience that was threatening to explode. There didn't seem to be any point in replying that he wouldn't know till he told her.

After a few seconds of uneasy silence, he turned to look at her. 'Do you remember the early days? The time when we took every job that was going, desperate as we were to make a go of the company?'

It wasn't the time for a trip down memory lane but she kept a rein on her exasperation. 'Of course.'

Nathan snuffled again and used his free hand to brush tears from his eyes. 'Every damn job. Even ones we shouldn't have taken.'

Keri remembered it all. Counting the pennies, the long hours, the exhaustion, the faith that they'd make it. And they had. But those days had been tough. She remembered that Nathan had grown progressively more depressed by the type of work they were accepting, the below-minimum-pay jobs on dodgy sites for even dodgier people. 'We stopped as soon as we could, didn't we? We came up with that new philosophy and only took work we believed in. It was a success, too, we never looked back.'

'It was too late though.' He jerked his hand away from hers and dropped his face into his cupped palms.

Too late? 'If you don't tell me, I can't–'

He lifted his head at that. 'Can't? Can't what? Fix it? Not everything is fixable. You're not God, you know. Keri the almighty fixer.'

She reeled at the scathing anger in his voice and felt the sudden wash of tears at the unfairness of his words. He had always been happy to leave things to her... hadn't he? He sounded resentful, had he always begrudged her ability to sort things out?

It was all so unfair on top of the horrendous day she'd had but there was no point in crying. Not yet. She got to her feet and walked across the kitchen to the sink, took a glass from the draining board and filled it with cold water. It gave her time to get back in control. Because like it or not, she knew whatever was wrong, it would fall to her to make right. It always did.

With the cold glass between her hands, she turned back to glare at him across the room. She loved him but would be the

VALERIE KEOGH

first to acknowledge he was a weak man. If there was an easy road, that's the one he'd take.

'You'd better tell me what's going on.'

He lifted his face. 'Nothing you can fix, not this time. You see, years ago, I killed someone.'

30

The glass slipped from Keri's hands and hit the tiled floor with a loud crack, shards of glass flying across the surface, the water making rivers in the grouting between the tiles. In the silence that followed, she wondered if she could rewind the clock to the minute the taxi had taken her home, then she could have stayed inside and told the driver to take her somewhere else... anywhere where she didn't have to face this nightmare. She stepped across the mess on the floor and using the breakfast bar for support, she reached the stool and climbed onto it.

'Not what you expected to hear, eh?'

'No.' It was the only word she could find. She lifted a hand to wipe her eyes and held it there, pressing her fingers into the sockets as she gulped back the tears. Nathan reached over, pulled her hand away and held it in his, looking at her across the breakfast bar with such sorrow in his eyes. This man that she loved, a man she'd known forever. 'You wouldn't hurt a fly, Nate. I don't understand.'

He kept her hand in his, rubbing it gently. 'It was one of those jobs we did as a sub-contractor. For DS Construction. Remember them?'

Keri frowned, then nodded slowly as she remembered. 'Run by Dexter Sylvester. A bit of a shady guy, we stopped doing business with them a long time ago.'

'We weren't so fussy in the early days.' Nathan wiped his nose with the back of his hand. 'They were doing renovation works on a manor house and needed a specialist stonemason to repair a Gothic window that had been damaged. It was the kind of thing we wanted to specialise in so I was delighted even though...'

'Even though?' Keri encouraged when the silence continued.

'I'd heard the company had a poor safety record. They cut corners and took risks to maximise profit. I didn't think it mattered, I knew I could keep myself safe.'

Keri couldn't remember the job Nathan was talking about, there were so many small ones in the early days. But if it was for a company with a poor safety record, it had to have been before they'd developed their business philosophy about twenty-three years before.

'The manor house was a 12th century sandstone construct,' Nathan said. 'A delivery lorry packed with scaffolding had reversed into the Gothic window and the poles had hit it dead centre, breaking the tracery and cracking one of the supporting columns. The driver, instead of leaving the lorry where it was and going for help, decided to pull away and the poles dragged some of the tracery with it.'

Keri had picked up enough knowledge over the years to know that the tracery he was referring to was the thin stone frame that supported the small panels of glass in the window. 'I assume the lorry belonged to DS Construction. No wonder they wanted it fixed as quickly as possible.'

'The driver shouldn't have been there, he was taking a shortcut. The window was a mess with bits of the tracery everywhere. I needed to do a lot of sanding down to effect a repair. Because of the intricate design of the window, it was a fiddly job. I told them it was going to take time.' Then softly, he repeated, 'I told them.' He pressed his lips together. When he was able to continue his voice was thick with tears. 'The company wanted the job done in a hurry, I think they were afraid the owners would find out and sue. They sent a young apprentice to help me and speed up the job.' He looked at her with tear-filled reddened eyes. 'Sandstone, Keri.'

A chill swept over her. Sandstone was one of the more dangerous of the stones they worked with. It contained seventy per cent silica and the wearing of a proper respirator was essential. Otherwise, silica dust could enter the lungs and cause inflammation and scarring... silicosis... it was a hideous progressive disease. 'I'm guessing the apprentice didn't have a respirator.'

'He didn't have a mask of any kind. I should have refused to allow him to work but–' Nathan shook his head slowly. '–they offered me a bonus if I got the job done quickly and having him help me made that doable. I thought since it was for such a short time, that he'd be okay.

'But it was an incredibly difficult job requiring a lot of sanding down between mortar applications. Usually, I'd have used masonry clamps to hold the pieces of tracery in place but they were unusually fine and ornate which made using clamps awkward and slow.' Nathan took another drink. 'To speed up the process and get the bonus we desperately needed at the time, I asked the lad to hold each piece while I sanded. It didn't take long before his face and hair were coated in white. I remember he laughed and brushed it off with his hand.' Nathan gulped. 'He thought it was funny, and all I could think about was the bonus I was going to get for having the work done quickly.'

Keri pictured the young man, white silica dust on his face, in his hair, in his lungs and racked her brain for all she had read about silicosis. As far as she could remember it could take up to thirty years after exposure to develop. Was that it? Perhaps the man had died recently and the family was looking for someone to blame. 'DS Construction should be held accountable. They should have ensured he had the proper safety equipment. He wasn't your employee, after all.'

Nathan clenched his hand into a fist and thumped it on the counter. 'I was the expert!' He released his fist, slid his hand across the counter and grabbed her hand. 'He was only an apprentice, a boy. Sixteen, maybe. It's funny how clearly I remember his face. He smiled a lot, was so enthusiastic and watched everything I did, taking it all in, determined to make the most of every opportunity. I remember thinking that he'd go far, that maybe he would work for us one day.'

Keri watched emotions twist Nathan's face. 'Did he die recently, is that it?'

'Recently? No, no that's not it. He died over twenty years ago, a few months after the job.'

She squeezed her eyes shut and shook her head trying to understand. 'Then he didn't get silicosis–'

'No, he did.'

Her eyes flew open. She saw Nathan's tear-streaked face, the guilt that dragged it down and she knew. 'Oh God!' Acute silicosis, a form so rare Keri had almost forgotten about it. It could occur after one exposure, leading to death after only months. *Sixteen.* 'How did I not hear about this? There must have been a huge scandal.'

Nathan chewed his lip and shook his head. 'Twenty-three years ago, it was easier to get away with things. I didn't hear about it until a couple of weeks after the boy died. I bumped into someone who used to work for the company and he filled me in on the gossip over a pint. The apprentice became sick within weeks. Nobody considered acute silicosis. Why would they, he wasn't a stonemason and his couple of days helping me out weren't even considered. It seems it wasn't until the post-mortem that they realised the cause.'

'But they must have known then what had happened.'

'The guy I was talking to didn't know any more. I expected to hear from the company, maybe even from the police. I was pretty edgy at the time, I was afraid you'd ask me what was wrong–'

'I remember you being fed up with all the going-nowhere jobs we'd been picking up and you moaning about the dodgy practices of some of the companies. That was when we decided we were doing well enough to concentrate on better quality work and we drew up our business philosophy.' She glared at him. 'I don't understand why you didn't tell me.'

'Because...' He spread his hands out. 'We were only married a couple of years at that stage, and you'd already put up with so much, skimping and trying to make ends meet. I didn't want to cause you more grief.'

She saw the lie in his eyes and heard it in his voice. He'd been afraid to tell her because he knew she wouldn't have let it go. Not even to save Metcalfe Conservation. Not over the death of a boy. She would have insisted on holding DS Construction to account. The apprentice should never have been assigned to Nathan without the proper protective equipment.

But she hadn't known. 'What happened then?'

'I decided to speak to the CEO of DS Construction.' Nathan got to his feet. 'I need a beer.' He grabbed one from the fridge, opened it and drank from the bottle downing half before retaking his seat. 'I don't think you've ever met Dexter Sylvester, have you?' When Keri shook her head, he continued. 'He was a big, tough, straight-talking man. Like us, he'd started small, worked hard and built DS Construction into a successful company.' Nathan took another swig of beer. 'He was also known to bribe whoever it took to get what he wanted, use the cheapest material he could get away with for his builds, and the cheapest labour he could find.

'When I called into his office, he was friendly at first but when I asked him about the apprentice his manner changed. He said he didn't know anything about the lad working with me and insisted he'd been doing nixers for other companies and that's when he must have been exposed. He said if I tried to say anything else, he'd destroy me and my "poxy little excuse for a company".' Nathan drained the bottle, got to his feet, and took another from the fridge. 'There's wine open, you want a glass?'

Keri shook her head absently, still trying to absorb all he'd told her. 'You obviously did as he wanted, and let it drop. So–' She tilted her head, puzzled. '–if this all happened over twenty years ago, what's going on now?' Nathan stayed on his feet sucking from the beer bottle until she wanted to get up and pull it from his hands. 'Nate, it's been a tough few days, please, no puzzles, tell me straight what the hell is going on.'

He tipped the neck of the bottle towards where his mobile sat on the breakfast bar. 'Remember last Wednesday I had a message, and I told you it was nothing important? I lied.'

Keri would have punched the air if there'd been anything exciting in proving she was right about Nathan lying to her. Now she was going to find out why.

He glugged more beer before wiping a hand over his mouth. 'It said, *remember JC.*'

31

Keri stared at Nathan, puzzled. 'JC?' Keri had been a Catholic, way back when. JC would always be Jesus Christ in her head but she doubted if that were who Nathan was referring to.

'JC. Jim Cody. That was the apprentice's name.'

'Okay,' Keri said, although nothing felt any clearer. 'I still don't understand. Where have you been for the last few days?' *When she needed him here with her, dealing with what was happening now, not something that had happened over twenty years before.*

'I went to Stevenage–'

'Stevenage? What on earth for?'

'If you'd let me finish!' He glared at her. 'That's where DS Construction has their office. I went to speak to Dexter Sylvester. To see if he'd had a similar message, to see if perhaps he'd heard from Cody's family. If maybe they were threatening him... or something.' Nathan ran a hand through his hair. 'I don't know why really, but the message had rattled me. I couldn't tell you. You'd want to know why, and I suppose I never wanted to tell you a story that cast me in such bad light.'

Keri suddenly understood. 'You've been harbouring guilt all of these years. You should have talked to me, I can't believe you kept this a secret. It must have been eating away at you.'

A smile lit Nathan's face, chasing away the shadows. 'You're crediting me with the kind of good virtues you have. You were always a much more honest person than me. No, I haven't been feeling guilty all these years.' The smile faded and he shrugged. 'Maybe a little when Daniel was sixteen. He had the same kind of innocent enthusiasm I remember seeing in the apprentice. But although I didn't always feel guilty, I never forgot, and when I got that message, I knew...'

'What?' She was still lost.

He looked at her. 'That someone else hadn't forgotten.' He got to his feet and paced the room. 'I decided to go to Stevenage that afternoon but when I got there I found the office shut. I thought maybe they'd closed down, although I would have thought we'd have heard–'

'We would have done,' Keri interrupted. 'Sylvester is one of the rotten apples of the building trade. There's been rumours of bribery and intimidation going back for as many years as I can remember.'

'Nothing's ever been proven,' Nathan said, settling back on the stool. 'Anyway, I looked around for a bit, then rattled the gateway till a Doberman came galloping towards me, teeth bared. I stepped back, but the dog stayed snarling at me until a security man came over. He wasn't particularly friendly until I mentioned I knew Sylvester, then he was happy to lock the dog away and come back for a natter.'

'And?' Keri wanted to shake him till all the information poured out. Like any nasty infection, only when all the pus was gone did any healing take place.

'Dexter Sylvester had been found dead at home the previous

week.' Nathan looked at her, eyes wide, his mouth opening and closing as he tried to get the words out. 'He'd been murdered.'

32

'That's awful,' Keri said, feeling her way. She still wasn't sure why Nathan was so upset. The death of anyone was sad, but Sylvester, by all accounts, wasn't a particularly nice guy. There were rumours of gangland associates. Mixing with the wrong people inevitably brought bad news. 'It's terrible, but I don't understand why you're so upset over a man you barely knew.'

'It's not because he's dead, it's why.'

'There've been rumours about him for years.' She held up a hand. 'Yes I know, nothing has been proven, but everyone knew he was on the take and there was all the talk about gangland connections. Maybe he ended up pissing off the wrong people.'

'I think it was something to do with Jim Cody, and that message I got.'

No wonder he looked so terrified. Keri went to Nathan, put an arm around his neck and pulled him close. 'You daft thing,' she said softly. 'You're taking huge leaps linking one to the other. You don't even know if that message you got was relating to this Jim Cody. Maybe JC is a supplier or customer, someone you promised to do work for or to send a quote to.'

'You think?' Nathan wrapped an arm around her waist.

'I do. Maybe you were rattled because of Roy's death.' She pushed him away to look into his eyes. 'I think you're fooling yourself too, I think you do feel some guilt for that boy's death even after all this time, so I think, when everything with Roy dies down, you should go and speak to a counsellor.'

She left him thinking about that idea and went to the fridge for the glass of wine she richly deserved and was pleased to see he was looking a little less tense when she returned.

He picked up his beer and tipped it against her glass. 'I don't know what I'd do without you.'

Fall apart or more likely find another woman to take care of him, Keri thought with few illusions. But there wasn't another woman now. One worry off her mind.

Nathan slurped noisily from the bottle before putting it down. 'Sylvester had obviously made an enemy somewhere.'

'I bet it's gang-related.'

'You might be right. The security man said that a couple of days before Sylvester was murdered, a wreath had been delivered to the office with RIP on the card. Then the following day, animal entrails were left outside the main gate. Sheep entrails, the police said, as if it mattered.'

Keri had been sipping her wine, listening as Nathan spoke. It was good to watch him talk through it and unwind. She was still annoyed he'd abandoned her but was starting to relax now she knew the reason. His words were drifting over her head until *wreath* dragged her abruptly back.

Her fingers tightened on the glass and her eyes narrowed. A wreath and animal entrails left outside the Stevenage premises, a wreath and mangled rat left outside their home. *Dear Lord, she'd been wrong.* She'd been blinded by her guilt over that tawdry affair into thinking Barry had been to blame. A lump of painful truth was suddenly lodged in her throat and she swallowed convulsively.

She'd been wrong, too, in trying to convince Nathan that there was no link between the message he'd received and what had happened to Sylvester.

Sylvester who had been murdered.

Nathan was still talking, she tuned back in.

'I think I was simply stressed out over what happened to Roy and let that blind my judgement. JC is, as you suggested, probably a supplier or someone. I'll check my records when we go into the office tomorrow.'

Keri saw relief sweep across his face, his colour already brightening, the look of terror gone from his eyes. It would have been easier to leave it, to let him live in ignorance, but Keri, unlike Nathan, never took the easy option.

A frightening thought slammed home. If Sylvester was killed by someone because of Jim Cody then Nathan was at risk. Not only did she need to tell him, but they also needed to inform the police. Their dirty secrets were going to be discovered.

'No,' she said, abruptly startling him. 'There's something you don't know.' She'd barely touched her wine, she picked up the glass and swallowed a mouthful. 'Sunday before last, someone left a wreath on the doorstep. There was a card with it that said, RIP. The florists who delivered it said they were given this address. They were told to leave it on the step outside the door without ringing the bell.'

Nathan had lifted the beer bottle to his mouth but took it away without drinking. 'What? How come I'm only hearing about this now?'

Because she thought they were from the man she'd been having an affair with. 'You were watching the football and I knew you had those two new contracts coming up, so I didn't want to worry you.' She shrugged. 'Anyway, I thought it was a mistake. The florist came and took it away. Then a couple of days later there was the horrible mangled rat. I never connected the two.'

A lie. She had but she'd made the wrong connection.

33

When Nathan headed to the fridge again and took out another bottle of beer, Keri smacked her hand on the counter. 'Getting plastered isn't the answer.'

'You're the one who always has an answer for everything, the great fixer, I'll leave it to you to find the answer to this conundrum.' He popped the lid off the bottle and slurped the foam that oozed up.

'We have to ring the police.'

'And say what exactly? That twenty-three years ago, I was culpable in the death of a sixteen-year-old.'

'You don't know that you were. Maybe the lad *was* working elsewhere and got exposed that way.'

'I know I'm right.' Nathan sat back on the stool nursing his beer. 'I don't want to be but I can still see him wiping that dust from his face. Sandstone dust. Sixty per cent silica.'

'Seventy.' She held a hand up when he frowned. 'Yes, I know I'm being pedantic. You're right, of course, there's little doubt about where the poor lad was exposed. And someone, after all this time, is looking for revenge.'

'It must be a relative. If I could find them, I could pay them off.'

She looked at him guzzling his beer and thought, not for the first time in all the years they were together, that he wasn't that bright. 'If they'd wanted money, Nate, they could have blackmailed us. You'd have paid any amount of money to keep this quiet, and I have no doubt Dexter Sylvester would have done the same rather than paying with his life.'

'What are you saying?'

She groaned and shut her eyes. It had been an impossible day. She was so tired she wasn't sure of anything anymore. When she felt Nathan's hand curl around hers, she opened her eyes again and met his sad, worried brown ones.

Stupid, foolish man. But she loved him. Always did, always would.

She turned her hand to clasp his and for a minute they stayed like that, saying nothing. Her voice was soft when she finally spoke. 'I'm saying they don't want money, Nathan. They want revenge. Good old-fashioned biblical revenge. *Eye for eye, tooth for tooth, hand for hand, foot for foot.*

'Someone. A member of his family, or maybe a friend, wants someone to pay for that young boy's death.' She pulled her hand away and stood. 'He didn't mention anything about his family when he was with you, I suppose?'

'Not that I remember.'

'And you didn't make any enquiries after you heard about his death?' She wasn't surprised when he looked away. Of course he hadn't asked about the family, he'd felt guilt for his part in the boy's death but not enough to do anything effective. Like ensuring that companies like DS Construction were held accountable.

She thought best on the move and paced the length of the room, turning at the far wall to cross the floor again, and again.

'I don't understand why they waited all this time? Twenty-three years.' She rubbed a hand over her face, then reached for her mobile phone.

'You're ringing the police?'

She should, of course. The wreaths, the animal remains. Too much of a coincidence. But she needed time to think. Involving the police would mean secrets coming out, his and hers. If she could avoid that... 'No, at least not yet.' She wanted to believe that Nathan wasn't in any danger but she wasn't sure. The inner workings of the mind of someone seeking vengeance was beyond her experience. 'To be on the safe side, though, I'm going to ask Abbie and Daniel to stay with their friends. If there's a problem, I don't want them involved.' She tapped her mobile against her palm. 'I'll tell them there have been reporters hanging around and we don't want them to be hassled.'

She sent a message, asking them to ring her as soon as possible. It was Daniel who was first to reply. He agreed to stay with friends until he heard from her. 'Much better idea, I'd probably throw a punch at reporters if they stuck a mic in my face.'

Keri smiled at the thought of her gentle son coming to blows with anyone. 'I'll throw some stuff in a bag for you and leave it at the university admin office tomorrow, okay?'

'Sure,' he said, laid-back as ever.

Abbie was more like her mother, instantly suspicious. 'Reporters! I can handle them, don't worry. I'd prefer to be home with you, to help keep your chin up.'

Mini-me, Keri thought with affection. 'No, honestly, I'd be happier with you safely out of the way. It would be one less thing to worry about. I'll pack some stuff in a bag for you and drop it off at the university. If you need anything else, pop it on your credit card and I'll make sure I top it up with funds to cover.' It was giving Abbie carte blanche to shop, but it would also stop her worrying about Keri.

'Oh wow, great. Okay, I'll stay away till you tell me the reporters have buggered off.'

'Good, chat soon, love you.' Keri put the mobile down and looked at Nathan. 'They'll stay where they are until they hear from us.'

'Right, so what now?'

'I'm starving, it's time for something to eat.' She didn't feel the slightest bit hungry but doing something was better than sitting staring into Nathan's helpless face. The freezer was well stocked with frozen dinners, she took out two and slipped them into the microwave.

What now? She'd absolutely no idea.

34

Keri insisted they go to the office the following day. 'We need to keep our wits about us a little more than usual but otherwise, we get on with life. Our contracts need to be fulfilled, our employees depend on us, as do our suppliers.'

'Business as normal.' Nathan looked at her with a raised eyebrow. 'How can you be so calm and cool about this? I barely slept last night for worrying.'

Because one of them had to keep it together and as usual, it was left to her. She'd never resented it over the years, she was made of far tougher stuff than he. A rod of steel ran down her backbone, marshmallow down his. It had been a good partnership but sometimes, like now, she wished the burden didn't feel so heavy.

She'd packed a holdall each for Abbie and Daniel earlier that morning. A taxi had picked the bags up and Keri had given the driver a generous tip to deliver them to the administration office where they'd be safe till they were collected. A quick message to Abbie and Daniel to remind them and she could put her children out of her mind for the moment.

The journey to the office was uneventful as usual but Keri

noticed she was looking closely at every face, her eyes flitting from one commuter to the other trying to keep them all under observation. She regretted not getting a taxi when she felt close to tears as commuters crowded around. Nathan, on the other hand, shut his eyes as he always did and she had to shake him awake when they got to their stop.

Luke was in reception, looking as if he'd always been there. Despite the recent revelations about Roy, Keri missed him desperately. He'd have known what to do for the best.

Annoyingly, because she craved solitude, Nathan followed her into her office, flopping into the spare chair as she slipped off her jacket. She hung it up and sat behind her desk resisting the temptation to tell him to go to his own office and leave her in peace.

'There has to be a connection to what happened to Roy.'

Keri was staring through the glass to where Luke stood, wondering how many times she'd come through reception without remembering that awful final sight of Roy sitting in his chair covered in blood. She dragged herself back from the memory and looked at Nathan, puzzled. 'What do you mean?'

'Roy. Dexter Sylvester. There has to be a connection.'

Keri shut her eyes and dropped her head back on the headrest.

'Don't you agree?' Nathan's voice urgent, agitated.

She had wondered about a connection between all the terrible things that were happening. All the liars and their lies. But that was before she'd heard Nathan's terrible secret, and about Dexter Sylvester's murder. Now, nothing made any sense. Worse, she was back to wondering if Barry Morgan had anything to do with Roy's murder. Okay, so he didn't send the wreath or the rat, but he'd lied about working next door. And he had threatened her. Maybe he'd come to the office on that Friday to have it out with her, and poor Roy got in the way. Was it possible? Or was she totally paranoid.

Nathan was staring at her waiting for an answer. 'No, I don't,' she said firmly, her eyes burning as tears fought for a way out. She searched in her pocket for a tissue and pressed it against them, one at a time.

'There has to be a connection,' he insisted, rolling his chair closer to the desk.

She was tempted to get up and run over to his office, lock the door, and hide. Except how could she, with those damn glass walls? 'Even considering Roy's secret past, what possible connection could there be between him and the corrupt Sylvester? Don't forget, Roy wasn't even working for us when you did that job in Stevenage.'

Nathan had that sulky expression he wore when he was convinced he was right about something. Usually, she'd put herself out to placate him, agreeing with whatever ridiculous plan or idea he had to re-establish the status quo. She'd pacify him, wait, then do whatever it was she'd planned in the first place and he was never any the wiser, assuming she'd done things his way.

But with Roy's bloody body sliding full colour into her brain, the terrifying thought that Barry may have been involved in his death, and the gut-churning worry that someone was intent on revenge for something that happened years before, she didn't have the energy for games. She thought about the wreaths that had been left, the entrails and the dead rat. Whoever was out for vengeance had a twisted mind.

'Let's talk about it later,' she said, shutting her eyes and resting her head back again. When she didn't hear him leave, she opened them and sighed. He was still wearing his sullen, sulky expression like a martyr. 'I really don't think what happened to Roy had anything to do with Sylvester.' She was using her pacifying voice and it irked her that she needed to. 'But the items left outside the Stevenage premises and our home... the wreaths, the rat, and entrails... they definitely connect us. We'll have to think about what we're going to tell that detective...' She searched for his name and failed. 'The one with the terrible ties.'

'Elliot.' Nathan pushed the chair away from the desk and folded his arms across his chest. 'I think we should give it a few days. Maybe I'm wrong about Roy, but maybe whoever is responsible has done all they're going to. You know, a life for a life. Dexter Sylvester's life for Jim Cody. The wreath and rat might have been left to let us know they knew about our part in Jim's death. Or something,' he added when he saw a sceptical light in her eyes.

'Maybe,' Keri said without agreeing. Someone had gone to a great deal of trouble to organise the wreaths and the macabre bloody offerings. Plus, by all accounts, Sylvester was a big man who was used to dealing with the seedier element of society, yet someone had managed to gain access to his home and kill him. She acknowledged the truth that was rattling around her skull. If it hadn't been for her own guilty secret, she wouldn't have thought twice about ringing the police. But that detective was no fool... he'd ask why she hadn't told Nathan about the wreath when it was delivered.

She conjured up a smile. 'Okay, let's leave it a couple of days and see what happens, but we need to be careful and stick together. A taxi between home and here. No disappearing on your own, okay?'

He got to his feet then, came around the desk and planted a kiss on her lips. 'Sensible as ever.'

Remembering his criticism of her tendency to want to fix

everything, she wasn't sure if he was being sarcastic. But his mulish expression had vanished, so she decided to take it as a compliment.

When he left, she put her head back and shut her eyes. She'd liked to have gone home, but after her argument that they stay together for safety, it wasn't an option.

She was amused at how remarkably calm she was being but there was a sense of unreality about it all. Ordinary people like them didn't get involved in murderous plots.

No, they just lied and cheated.

Keri looked across to her husband's office. The police still had Roy's computer but Nathan had brought in an old one from home and was probably going through the outstanding contracts and quotations. It was what she should be doing. Instead, she drummed her fingers on the desk before reaching for her keyboard to tap 'Jim Cody' into the search engine. Maybe if she could locate the boy's family, it would be a start. Hundreds of results appeared. She added his age to narrow down the search, surprised when there were no details, no reference to the sixteen-year-old Jim or James Cody who had died so many years before. With no idea where the boy had lived it was impossible to narrow down the search for his family.

Not a great start. She decided, instead, to pinpoint exactly when they'd worked on the window of that manor house. It had been Roy who'd insisted every job they'd ever done should be computerised. He'd spent several weekends sorting through the handwritten records and inputting them into a programme of his making. So it was thanks to him that it only took a minute to find the job for DS Construction. She wrote the date down, then sat back with a laugh. What had she achieved? Absolutely nothing.

Nathan had been right. She was a fixer. Over the years, she'd managed to iron out so many creases in their business and personal lives but this was beyond her experience. It was also, and it was time to admit it to herself, slightly terrifying. They should go to the police with what they knew. It was the safest option but still she hesitated.

Nathan's part in the death of that boy would come out and Metcalfe Conservation might lose custom if it became public knowledge, but she guessed most people in the business would simply shrug and say how great it was that things had changed.

But if her secret came out... Nathan would never forgive her.

35

Nathan would never forgive Keri, how could he when she couldn't forgive herself for risking so much for so little. Needing to see his face, she looked across to his office, expecting to see him working away. Surprised not to see him sitting behind his desk, she got to her feet and craned her neck to see the further corners of his office. He wasn't there. It was possible he'd gone to speak to someone in accounts, or one of their surveyors. She pushed down the dart of anxiety, shook her head and started to answer the business emails that were waiting for her.

Some were urgent, many complicated. All kept her attention on the computer screen. Eventually, satisfied with what she'd achieved, she leaned back and stretched her hands over her head. There were some less pressing emails to answer but she'd done well. It was nearly eleven. In happier days, Roy would come through her door with her favourite Costa coffee. She'd have to settle for what was available in the tiny staffroom.

She looked across to Nathan's office surprised to see he'd not returned.

Worry slithered cold fingers over her skin.

She picked up her phone and ran the extension for accounts. 'Hi, is Nathan there?'

'No, but while I have you can I discuss an issue with invoices?' Their accountant proceeded to complain about an ongoing problem they had with a couple of their customers. One had asked for extra discount if they paid within two months. 'It's ridiculous, we should stop doing work for them.'

Keri wanted to snap that she had more on her plate than worrying about what was his job to sort out. 'They're one of our best customers. Offer them a one per cent reduction. Add it on to their invoice the next time we do work for them.' She hung up before he could think of something else to complain about and redialled the surveyors' office.

When Nathan wasn't there either, Keri hung up, got to her feet, and went out to reception.

'Luke, where's Nathan?' Her voice was tight with anxiety but if he noticed he didn't comment. Or maybe he hadn't noticed. He wasn't Roy, after all.

'He went out for coffee.' Luke twisted his wrist to look at his watch. 'About an hour ago. Costa must be unusually busy.'

The café was only a five-minute walk from the office. No matter how busy it might be, Nathan should have returned by now.

Keri walked to the glass frontage overlooking the street. Five minutes' walk. Nathan would have assumed he'd be safe. He should have been, but what if whoever was responsible for the wreath, the rat and the murder of Dexter Sylvester was waiting for the opportunity to get Nathan alone. Maybe they'd been stupidly foolish to assume one death was sufficient revenge for Jim Cody's death.

Conscious of Luke's quizzical stare, she turned, threw him a wavering smile, and headed back to her office. She tried Nathan's mobile, left a message when it wasn't answered then stood staring at the phone. It was time to ring the police. Time to tell them everything. Secrets and all.

Instead, she reached for her jacket, slipped it on and ignoring Luke's *what's going on?* hurried from the building.

It was only a short walk, but the café was two streets away. Keri walked briskly, pushing past people without apology, breaking into a half-run as she approached the corner of the second street. She came to such a sudden halt that a pedestrian behind walked into her and swore loudly before he moved off holding up his middle finger. Keri didn't hear the words or see the action, her eyes fixed on the flashing lights of police cars and an ambulance halfway down the street. Outside the café.

Shock sent blood rushing to prop up her major organs, leaving her feeling faint. Jerky steps on trembling legs took her to a barrier of crime-scene tape that deterred entry. It didn't stop the sightseers, the curious, the inherently nosy, all those who lived vicariously. Many had mobile phones held high, trying to film what they could of the tragedy that was unfolding before them.

Keri pushed her way through, stopped then by the flimsy tape and the stern-faced uniformed officer who was pacing back and forth as if he expected an intrusion any moment.

'Excuse me.' Keri held a hand up to stop him as he passed. His expression wasn't encouraging. 'My husband.' She swallowed. 'He left our office an hour ago to get coffee but hasn't returned. He's had threats. I'm worried that...' Her voice faded as the reality hit home. Nathan could be lying there injured, maybe dying. Or dead. He could be dead.

'His name is Nathan Metcalfe,' she said. 'Can you find out if he's involved in whatever is going on here? Please.' She was afraid he might brush her off but instead he stepped back, turned away and spoke in a muffled voice into his radio.

When he turned back to her, his expression had changed.

Keri swayed, held upright by the crowd that pressed from behind, desperate to be part of the drama. She would have given up her part in a heartbeat, would have happily traded places with any of the people she could feel breathing and muttering around her, people who'd be heading home later to their loved ones with a tale to tell. She'd have traded with any one of them.

The officer said nothing, merely putting a thumb under the tape in front of her and pulling it up. 'Come with me,' he said, waiting until she'd ducked under to stride away with her following behind.

A cordon of police cars and one ambulance formed a semicircle around the entrance to the café. The police officer stopped at a group of his colleagues who stood nearby. 'This is Nathan Metcalfe's wife.' With a nod to her, he turned away and went back to his position at the barrier.

Silent faces regarded Keri for a moment before one of the officers took a step forward. 'Mrs Metcalfe, I'm afraid your husband has been injured.'

Injured, not dead. Keri grabbed onto that thought and gulped a sob. 'Can I see him?'

The officer indicated the ambulance. 'The paramedics are stabilising him. They'll let us know when we can have a word.' He handed her the wallet he'd been holding. 'You might as well take this.'

She took it; had she been alone, she'd have held it to her nose to get Nathan's scent. She settled for pressing the leather between her fingers. 'What happened?'

The officer pursed his lips as if wondering how much to tell her.

'Please, I need to know. We've been having problems recently. Threats.'

'Right, not simply a random attack then, that makes it a different situation.'

It didn't make a huge difference to Keri, Nathan was still lying injured in the ambulance. 'Can you tell me what happened?'

'We're still trying to piece it all together but initial reports suggests he was attacked as he was leaving the café. He was carrying a tray of take-out coffee in one hand and a bag of pastries in the other. A witness said he was struggling to open the door when someone came to help him. It's not clear what happened but it appears this is when he was attacked. The person who helped open the door then fled and your husband collapsed.'

There were so many questions Keri wanted to ask, but only one seemed important. She looked over to the ambulance. 'Is he badly injured?'

'The attacker had a knife. I'm not sure what the extent of the injuries are but there was a lot of blood.'

Keri remembered the blood soaking Roy's chest and shivered.

One of the other officers stepped forward. 'Lots of blood isn't a reliable indicator of the seriousness of an injury. Superficial wounds can bleed quite extensively. Plus, your husband was lucky, a first responder was here within minutes of the call and had intravenous fluids going into your husband before the ambulance arrived. That would have made a huge difference.'

Keri was grateful to grab any positive remark to keep her from drowning in fear.

36

Anxious skin-crawling minutes passed before a paramedic jumped from the back of the ambulance and approached the group. He looked curiously at Keri.

One of the police officers hurried to say, 'This is the man's wife.'

'Okay.' The paramedic jerked a thumb towards the ambulance. 'Your husband was lucky. He's lost some blood but the injury doesn't appear serious. Not from want of trying by the attacker,' he said pointedly, addressing the remark to the officers. 'It was sheer luck. I'd guess the attacker was smaller than the victim.'

Keri winced and he looked back to her. 'Sorry... smaller than your husband.' He ran a finger across his neck. 'They cut here. From the direction of the cut, I'm guessing the knife initially hit the clavicle.' He tapped his collarbone. 'It probably threw the attacker, then he overcompensated and brought the knife upwards but managed to miss the carotid artery on either side. It's deep enough to need suturing so we're taking him to hospital now. He'll be left with an interesting scar, no doubt, but that should be it.'

'Can I come with you?' Keri wanted to see Nathan, wanted to see for herself that he was alive. To hold his hand, keep holding on to something she almost lost.

'Sure.'

She followed the paramedic back to the ambulance and climbed the steps, her eyes on the body she could see lying to one side, tears washing her eyes when she moved closer and saw Nathan's pale face. The second paramedic finished checking one of the monitors that beeped reassuringly and moved to let her sit beside Nathan.

'Nathan,' she whispered, laying her hand on his arm.

His eyes flicked open. 'Keri.' One word but filled with relief, his eyelids closing again.

'We've given him something for the pain,' the paramedic said. 'It's made him sleepy, don't worry. He's going to do fine.'

Almost immediately, the ambulance door was shut and it moved off.

'The Royal,' the paramedic said when Keri asked which hospital they were going to. She'd only a vague idea where that was, and no idea whether it was any good. But it was a hospital, Nathan would be looked after. She sat listening to the regular beep of the monitors and watching numbers she didn't understand, reassured by the calmness of the paramedic that all was as it should be.

It was only a short drive away, she was told, but it seemed a lifetime before the ambulance stopped and the doors were opened.

Later, when she was trying to tell Abbie and Daniel about what happened, she couldn't remember the period between arriving and being shown into the operating theatre waiting room. All she was left with was a hazy memory of long corridors and kindly faces asking questions, some of which she answered, some of which didn't make sense.

The waiting room was empty. There were multiple signs to say mobile phone use was prohibited. Keri, never a rule breaker, ignored them as soon as the door shut behind her and rang the office.

'Metcalfe Conservation, how may I help you?'

For a second, Keri was confused, then she squeezed her eyes shut. It was Luke, not Roy. 'Luke, it's Keri. Listen, there was an incident at the café. Nathan is in hospital. He's okay but he needs some minor surgery.' *That was all, wasn't it, the paramedics had told her the truth, hadn't they?*

Luke was understandably shocked and started to babble. 'But he's okay? He's not badly injured? Gosh, that's awful. You must be shocked. I'm so sor–'

Keri cut off his rambling words. 'Manage as best as you can, will you? Hopefully, if all goes well, I'll be back in tomorrow.' She hung up before he'd time to comment and sat tapping the mobile against her chin as she wondered who else she should ring.

There seemed to be no point in worrying Nathan's brother, or any of their friends and she had no intention of distressing their children. Time enough when Nathan was out of theatre and she knew for certain he'd be okay.

She alternated between sitting and staring at the door wishing it to open, and pacing the room worrying. The police would come but hopefully not until Nathan was safely back on a ward. They'd been naive to believe that Dexter Sylvester's death was going to be enough revenge for Jim Cody's. They had failed in their attempt to kill Nathan, but they'd try again. He needed police protection until they caught whoever was responsible.

They'd have questions, of course. The truth, with all its

secrets, would come out. Damage limitation. With Nathan temporarily out of the way, she could be honest without repercussions.

Couldn't she?

It was time to live up to her reputation.

She'd fix this and get their life back on track.

37

It was an hour before a doctor came into the waiting room and called her name.

'I'm Mr Winfield,' he said, sitting in the seat beside her. 'Your husband is doing well. There was no underlying damage to the tendons, nerves or arteries. His blood pressure was a little low due to a combination of blood loss prior to and during surgery. We gave him a unit of blood and he still has an intravenous line in situ. We'll keep a close eye on his pressure but I'm expecting that to right itself over the next few hours.' He looked at her through narrow spectacles. 'The wound was long however, and it took twenty sutures to close it but you're in luck, my interest is in cosmetic surgery so I was happy to spend time to make sure it would leave as little a scar as possible.'

Keri tried to look grateful for that but the truth was she wouldn't have cared if Nathan had been left with a scar a mile wide as long as he was safe. 'Thank you, he'll be pleased.' She gave a genuine smile then, realising that her husband would be. He was far more vain than she.

'I'll see Mr Metcalfe in the morning but if everything goes

according to plan I'm anticipating he'll be ready for discharge in a couple of days.'

Home. Keri felt her eyes fill. She snuffled, stood, and held out a hand. 'Thank you. That's so good to hear.'

'He was lucky,' the doctor said shaking her hand gently before getting to his feet. 'I hope they catch the person responsible. Right, you'll be anxious to see him for yourself. Come with me and I'll show you how to get to the ward.'

In a daze, Keri followed him to the door of the four-bedded unit where Nathan lay with his eyes closed, an intravenous infusion attached to one arm, a blood-pressure monitor on the other. No ECG machine. She took that as a good sign. The thick dressing across his neck was dry, no telltale line of blood to mar its pristine whiteness. Another good sign.

Mr Winfield took his leave after a few more words that Keri didn't hear. When he'd gone, she picked up a chair from a stack near the door and sat beside Nathan's bed.

For two hours she stayed staring at him, examining every line on his handsome face, every grey strand that had appeared in his dark hair over the last year. The cuff on his arm inflated every thirty minutes with a soft growl. She watched the numbers appear, then vanish. They meant nothing to her. Regular as clockwork, a nurse came. She checked the dressing on Nathan's neck, and peered at the intravenous infusion, pressed a button on the blood-pressure monitor, wrote something on a clipboard that hung on the end of the bed, then gave a satisfied smile and went away.

Reassured, Keri felt the tension in her shoulders and neck ease.

Once, Nathan's eyes opened, but he couldn't turn his head

because of the dressing and by the time she got to her feet so he could see her, he'd shut them again. She kept her fingers curled around his, calmed by the warmth of them.

In the early morning, exhausted, she bent her free arm on the bed, rested her head on it and drifted off to sleep.

Not for long, and certainly not long enough to clear the woolliness in her head.

At seven, two nurses came and asked if she'd wait outside while they looked after Nathan. She guessed it wasn't really a request and got to her feet. 'Is there somewhere I could get coffee?'

She was directed to a café on the ground floor near the entrance. Distracted, she got out of the lift on the wrong floor and trailed down seemingly endless corridors before realising her mistake. It was another five minutes before she saw a sign for the café. She'd walked to the counter, her eyes skimming the menu scrawled on the whiteboard behind when it hit her that she'd no money. It was this mundane lack that tipped her over into desolation.

With her head down, blinded by tears, she hurried back into the corridor. There was a ladies' toilet nearby. She went inside and locked herself into a cubicle. There, sitting hunched over on a toilet seat, she sobbed.

It was a cathartic cry. Afterwards she felt, not better precisely, but more in control. It cleared her head too. She had Nathan's wallet in her pocket.

The café was busy, the coffee and breakfast roll she purchased at the counter surprisingly good. She took her time and went back for a second coffee when she'd finished the first. The combination of food, caffeine and rest did her good and she felt stronger and more capable of dealing with whatever that day threw at her as she headed back to the second-floor ward.

Nathan was sitting more upright. His eyes were still closed

but he was looking a little less scarily pale. The nurses had changed the dressing on his neck, replacing the thick padding with a thinner one. Yet another good sign, another hole released in her stress belt. She was standing beside the bed staring at him when his eyes flicked open.

Blank eyes stared at her and a jolt of fear shot through her. Had they lied, was he more seriously injured than she'd been led to believe?

38

'Nate,' Keri whispered, moving closer to slide her hand into his.

He squeezed his eyes shut and when he opened them again, they were focused. 'Hi.' His voice was raspy.

'Hi yourself. How're you feeling?'

'Like someone tried to take my head off with a rusty tin-opener.' His fingers curled around hers and squeezed gently. 'But I'm alive.'

She kept her hand in his, hooked her foot around the leg of the chair to bring it closer and sat. Trying to keep her voice steady, she said, 'I was scared I was going to lose you.'

He managed a ragged laugh. 'You're not getting rid of me that easily.'

She leaned forward to hide her tears, bending to press her lips to his hand. 'I may never leave your side again.'

'Sounds good to me.' His eyes flickered and closed. Several minutes later, he opened them again looking more alert. 'Hi. Sorry, I didn't mean to fall asleep.'

'All part of the healing process.' She dropped her eyes to their clasped hands. 'Can you remember what happened?'

'Not really. I'd bought the coffee and buns and was on my way out of the café, but what happened then is a blur of light and noise.'

'You don't remember someone opening the door for you?'

He turned his head a little to look at her and frowned, trying to remember. 'No, I don't. Was that when I was stabbed? It's all a blank. The next thing I remember is opening my eyes in the ambulance and feeling your hand in mine. I knew I was safe then, that you'd never let me go.'

'Never.' She squeezed his hand gently. 'I spoke to the police at the café after it happened and told them you'd had threats made against you. I'm sure they'll be in with questions. We need to tell them everything, then they can catch whoever did this to you.' She felt his fingers tighten and looked up. 'It'll be all right, sweetheart, I promise.'

'You always fix things, Keri.' He pulled her hand to his mouth and planted a dry kiss on her knuckles. 'I'm sorry for using that as criticism, I didn't mean it. The tough choices, the hard jobs, I've left them to you over the years because you're much stronger than I am, much better at making those difficult decisions. Don't think I haven't noticed and loved you for it.'

Keri stood again, leaned down and kissed him gently on the lips. 'We're a team, remember.' For a little while, she'd forgotten. She'd not forget again. 'We've been working too hard recently. When everything is sorted, let's take some time away together.'

'I'd like that.'

'Back to Italy, maybe.' Keri sat again feeling more positive about everything. The police would catch whatever maniac tried to kill Nathan, she'd forget about her moment of madness, and everything would be as it had been before. No, it wouldn't, it would be better.

'Italy would be good. Venice. Get a photo taken in a gondola for Abbie to use in a poster for our next anniversary. Make that a yearly tradition.' He laughed softly, then his grip on her hand loosened, his eyes fluttered once and closed.

Keri took her hand away, sat back and smiled slightly. She wasn't sure of the yearly tradition idea, but Venice sounded good.

When the police came, she'd insist Nathan was too weak to speak to them. She could tell them everything they needed to know... more than Nathan knew. She didn't know if Barry had any involvement in anything that had gone on, but it was time to be completely honest. Nathan's life might depend on it.

She regretted not having her handbag with her. She'd put that detective's card into it, she could have rung him rather than having to wait for someone to turn up. There was something trustworthy about him; she felt she could ask... beg... that the information about her affair be kept quiet unless absolutely necessary.

The four-bedded unit had a half-glass partition that separated it from the corridor outside. Shortly after nine, a figure she recognised passed by. DI Elliot stopped in the open doorway, looked her direction, and gave a slight nod. Perhaps he'd have come to the bed but Keri held her hand up to stop him.

Nathan was still asleep. She stood and pressed a light kiss on his forehead. He didn't wake, not even when she laid her hand gently against his cheek. 'Back in a few minutes.'

'Let's go somewhere to talk,' she said when she joined the detective. Without waiting for an answer, she crossed to the nurses' station. 'I need somewhere to speak to the police about the assault on my husband, is there a room we could use?'

She was directed to a small visitors' room. That early it was empty. Once she and the detective were inside, Keri kicked the doorstop away and let the door swing shut. 'Detective Inspector Elliot, I'm glad you're here.' She was also relieved he was alone.

Her tale would be easier to tell without the critical eyes of that other detective boring into her.

She crossed to a seat in the corner of the room and sat. It was a comfortable chair, she'd liked to have curled up on it and gone to sleep. *Hide away*. The thought almost made her smile. The time for hiding was gone.

'Your husband is doing okay, I gather.' Elliot took the seat opposite. 'I also understand from the reports I've read that he was incredibly lucky.'

'Someone tried to kill him.'

'Cut his throat, the same as Roy Sheppard.' Elliot sat forward, his clasped hands dangling between his knees. 'It looks like someone has it in for Metcalfe Conservation.'

Keri blinked, her thoughts spinning. She hadn't connected the attack on Nathan to Roy's death. She should have done. Nathan would be pleased to have been right. Barry Morgan's stupid threats had blinded her. He wasn't involved. It gave her little consolation.

The detective's eyes had narrowed as if he were considering she'd taken too long to comment on what he'd said. Was he afraid she was going to lie? She wasn't, not really, there was no longer any reason to tell him about Barry, no reason to confess her infidelity. Small mercies. 'Not only Metcalfe Conservation, I'm afraid you don't know the full story.'

Elliot tilted his head, then sat back and folded his arms across his chest. 'You told an officer at the scene that someone had threatened you. Do you want to tell me about that?'

'It's a complicated tale,' she said, playing for time while she got her thoughts in order. For all his crazy ties, she'd be foolish to underestimate this detective. His eyes were sharp and probably missed nothing.

'The sooner you tell me–' He gave a slight smile. '–the sooner it'll be finished.'

'Right.' Keri took a breath, then started her story, backtracking at times when she'd left a detail out. 'And that's it.'

The frown on Elliot's forehead had deepened as she spoke. 'Okay, let me see if I have this straight. Your husband was somehow involved in the death of a sixteen-year-old boy twenty-three years ago. He had a message recently which said 'remember JC' after which he went to see Dexter Sylvester who also had a role to play in the boy's death and discovered he'd been murdered. Your husband was told that a wreath with a card saying RIP had been delivered to Sylvester's business and the entrails of an animal left outside. Since there had been a wreath delivered and a rat left at your home, he was worried that whoever had killed Sylvester was now after him.' His frown didn't ease as he took up his previous pose, clasped hands dangling between his knees, garish tie swinging forward.

Keri spread her hands out. 'That's pretty much it.'

'When were the wreath and rat left at your house?'

Her timeline had been deliberately vague. She should have guessed he'd want to pin it down. 'The wreath was left Sunday before last, the rat on the following Wednesday.'

'Yet you didn't mention any of this either on the Friday or Saturday when I spoke to you.' He looked at her closely as if trying to figure out why they'd have neglected to tell him something so important.

She squirmed on her seat. *What a tangled web she'd woven, perhaps she should tell him about Barry and her fear that he'd sent both items.* 'It didn't seem necessary,' she said finally. 'Roy hadn't worked for us when we did that job on the manor house. He'd no involvement in the boy's death. Plus, we hadn't known about Sylvester at that stage, not until this week when Nathan went to Stevenage.'

'And he went to find out if Mr Sylvester had received a similar message regarding this Jim Cody, is that correct?'

'Yes.'

Elliot sat back, his hands resting on the arms of the chair, fingers tapping. He was looking at Keri as if he didn't believe a word she said.

It wasn't a good feeling especially since she'd been almost completely honest. Telling him about Barry Morgan would simply have muddied the waters. 'Now you know everything.' She leaned towards Elliot. 'Nathan isn't safe until you get whoever is seeking revenge for the death of Jim Cody.'

'I'm not involved in the investigation into the murder of Mr Sylvester,' Elliot said slowly. 'However, I know the details of the case and there's something you should probably be aware of. He was killed in his home.' He waited a beat then gave a sigh as if deciding to go ahead. 'His throat was cut, Mrs Metcalfe. It does indicate a link between the deaths of Roy Sheppard and Dexter Sylvester and the attack on your husband but if, as you say, Mr Sheppard wasn't in any way involved in the death of the boy, I'm struggling to see why he would have been targeted.'

39

Keri was trying to absorb the information that Sylvester's throat had been cut. Once again, she realised how lucky Nathan had been.

'I have no idea why Roy was targeted,' she said, when Elliot raised an eyebrow in a silent question. 'I thought his death was something to do with that woman, Tracy.' *Or Barry Morgan, but she'd keep that one to herself.* 'What now?'

'The investigations are all at their early stages. Perhaps if we'd had the information about the wreath and the rat last week, we'd have connected it to the murder of Dexter Sylvester and might be a little further forward.' It seemed to be a statement of fact rather than a criticism.

'I'm sorry.' She might have said more but footsteps rushing past on the corridor outside distracted her.

They caught Elliot's attention too. He got to his feet, opened the door, and peered down the corridor. 'Some emergency happening.' When he turned, his eyes were shuttered. 'Maybe we should go–'

'Nathan?' Keri jumped to her feet and brushed past Elliot to hurry back to the ward. Nathan's bed, the first inside the open doorway, was surrounded by staff. They were all intent on the person in the bed and didn't notice her arrival.

It was Elliot who held her back when she cried out and tried to rush forward to the blood-slicked body in the bed, who pulled her away, whispering in her ear to let the staff do their job. Keri was pulled, resisting, down the corridor, her cries fading to a low sob as the detective continued to hold her.

Nathan's bed was wheeled out surrounded by staff. Loud voices gave directions. The nurse Keri had seen earlier joined her. 'They're taking him back to theatre for emergency surgery.' A shout took her away. The bed and its attendant satellites disappeared into the lift. Then there was silence broken only by Keri's sobs into Elliot's shoulder.

He stayed with her in the operating theatre waiting room, sitting while she paced the floor. An hour into their wait, he disappeared, returning with two disposable mugs of coffee, one of which he pressed into her hands. 'Sit and drink it.'

She did sit for a while, sipping the coffee he'd laced with sugar. He was being kind, she drank a little then put it down and got to her feet. She'd done one length of the small room before the door opened.

Keri didn't recognise the woman who came into the room. Her face was lined with experience and shaded with sadness. She wore pale-blue scrubs with one single blood spot over her chest as if her heart were leaking. Keri's eyes fixed on it as the woman approached her.

'Mrs Metcalfe?'

Keri felt Elliot coming to stand beside her but she couldn't lift her eyes from that spot on the woman's chest. Was it Nathan's blood? Would he be missing it?

'Mrs Metcalfe?' The voice again, softer, kinder.

'Yes.' Keri finally looked up. She felt Elliot's arm slide around her shoulder and wondered why.

'My name is Tina Bailey, I'm a vascular surgeon.'

'Yes.' Keri couldn't think of another word to say.

'I'm sorry. We did our best, but I'm afraid he's gone.'

'Gone?' Keri stared blankly, then turned to look at Elliot. 'Gone where? What's she talking about?'

'Perhaps we should sit down,' he said.

Keri shook off his arm. 'I don't want to sit. I want to know what you're talking about. Where has Nathan gone? To another hospital, is that it?'

'Mrs Metcalfe, your husband is dead. It happened suddenly. An arterial bleed. By the time the staff were alerted, he'd already lost too much blood. We did the best we could in theatre but we couldn't stabilise him.'

No, this wasn't right. This couldn't be. Keri backed away, her hands clasped under her chin. 'But...' She shook her head. 'Nathan looked well, he was talking to me, we were making plans...' Her voice faded. She turned to look at Elliot. 'He's really dead?'

Elliot looked stunned. 'I'm so sorry, Keri.'

She stumbled backward, accepting the detective's help when he put a hand out to guide her to the seat.

'I need to go,' the surgeon said. 'Stay here for as long as you need.'

'Can I see Nathan?' *Maybe they'd made a mistake. She'd go in and find him sitting up, laughing at all the fuss.*

'They'll be bringing him back to the ward, probably into a private room, you can ask at the nurses' station.'

It was Elliot who replied. 'Yes, that's fine, I'll bring Mrs Metcalfe down to the ward and stay with her for as long as needed.'

Keri sat motionless. She heard the detective make phone call after phone call, but didn't hear any of the words. All she could hear was Nathan's voice. *You always fix things, Keri.* Not everything. She wouldn't be fixing this.

40

K eri left the talking to Detective Inspector Elliot when they reached the ward and followed him and the nurse to a small side room. Hiding Nathan and his death away as if it were something to be ashamed of.

She was being unfair. It was to give her privacy, of course, so that she could wail like a banshee for her loss. Instead, she stood in the doorway of the room and stared across to where the man she had loved for so long lay. He'd always looked serene in sleep. He looked like he did every morning. Every morning for the last twenty-five years since they married and the years they were together before that.

'He doesn't look dead,' she said.

Elliot, standing behind her, said nothing.

Keri didn't want to go closer. Didn't want to put her hand on Nathan's cheek and feel the chill of death, didn't want that final confirmation. 'What am I going to do without you?' She hadn't realised she'd said the words out loud. They floated on the air before fading into silence.

'You need to say goodbye, Keri,' Elliot said quietly. 'Then you need to contact your children and your family. They'll want to come in to say their farewells too.'

Of course. All the things she'd need to do. There'd be time for tears. A whole empty future stretching ahead for her to fill. Time for regrets and recriminations. For the guilt of her infidelity to seep into the memories and sour them.

A few short steps took her to the bedside. She reached under the sheet for his hand. It was already cold and stiff. Taking her hand from under the sheet, she placed it on his cheek. There was a little warmth left there. She brushed the pad of her thumb over his lips. Warm. She leaned down and pressed hers to them. Wishing she were the prince in *Sleeping Beauty* with the power to restore life with such a simple act.

'It's not sinking in,' she said, glancing back at Elliot who hovered inside the doorway.

'Sudden death is always more difficult to accept.'

'I need to ring Abbie and Daniel but what do I say to them?' She cried then, hot tears that came and wouldn't stop.

Elliot hesitated before stepping in as he'd done earlier and putting an arm around her. 'I'll help where I can.'

'Thank you,' she said, pulling back. 'You've been so kind.' She reached into her pocket for her phone, then looked blankly at it. 'What do I say?'

'Tell them that there's been an accident, Nathan has been hurt, and that a car will pick them up and bring them here.' He took out his mobile. 'Tell me a location and I'll arrange it.'

She gave him the name of the university. 'There's an administration office in the main building. That would be the easiest place. Wait until I contact them though, it isn't always that easy.' She looked at Nathan and shook her head. 'I can't ring from here.' It was illogical, she knew it was, but she couldn't bear to talk about him being dead while he lay there.

Elliot opened the door. 'We can go back to the visitors' room.'

When they were inside, he shut the door. There was no lock on the inside, he improvised and leaned against it. 'I can wait outside, if you'd prefer.'

Keri shook her head. 'No, thank you, that's not necessary. She rang Abbie and Daniel and was in luck. Between lectures, they answered immediately, sounding so normal, so cheerful. Soon that would change. 'Your dad's been in an accident. You need to come to the hospital.' Each of them responded with disbelief and shock and asked the question Keri dreaded to hear.

'Is he badly hurt?'

She held her hand over the phone as she took a shuddering breath and let it out slowly. 'Yes. You need to get here as soon as you can. There's a car on its way to pick you up from outside the admin office. I'll see you when you get here.' She cut the connection both times before they'd time to ask more questions.

It was tempting to tap out *Nathan's dead* and send it to all her contacts, informing the world in two words. Instead, she made call after call. Nathan's brother was stunned but recovered quickly to say he'd be in as soon as he could get there. Friends were shocked and quick to offer support.

The last call she made was to the office. 'Luke, hi, it's Keri. Will you tell everyone that there's been an accident, that Nathan...' It was strange that this final call was the one she couldn't finish. She handed the phone to Elliot. 'Tell him please.'

'Luke, this is Detective Inspector Elliot. Unfortunately, Nathan Metcalfe passed away a little while ago. Can you tell everyone who needs to be told–'

'Tell him everyone is to go home and shut the office.'

Elliot repeated her message, hung up and handed the mobile back.

She took it and sank onto a chair. 'Nate and I wondered how we were going to cope without Roy, but we had each other. How am I going to cope now?'

Elliot said nothing, his silence strangely comforting. Over the next few hours and days, she'd hear the usual platitudes, *time was a healer, she was lucky to have had him for so long, she'd get through it, her children would keep her going,* she was glad he hadn't resorted to using them. 'I suppose you get used to dealing with grieving people and their loss.'

'No. It's not something I've ever got used to.' He sat in the chair opposite. 'It helps keep me focused on my job though, makes me work harder to get justice for people like your husband.'

The tears came and Keri let them fall.

Soon she'd need to be strong for Abbie and Daniel.

41

DI Elliot stayed with Keri as she negotiated the minefield of telling her two children that their father was dead.

'There was an incident in a café, your dad was stabbed. The hospital did what they could but he didn't make it.' In case the euphemism confused them, as she had been confused, she added, 'He's dead.'

Blood rushed from Daniel's face and he dropped to the ground in a faint. Abbie cried out, then stood with her hands clamped over her mouth, her eyes wide in shocked disbelief. Elliot turned the unconscious boy on his side while Keri pulled Abbie into her arms, holding her while she sobbed.

Daniel came to as fast as he'd gone out and sat up looking confused and embarrassed. 'Slowly,' Elliot said, reaching a hand to help when Daniel struggled to get to his feet.

'I'm okay.' He stood and brushed a hand over his shirt, looking at Elliot blankly before turning to look at the entwined mother and daughter. 'It's true? Dad's dead?'

'Yes.' Keri's voice trembled on the one word. She took a breath. 'We can go and see him in a minute. You can say goodbye.' She looked across to Elliot. 'I'm sure you need to go, we'll be fine. Thank you for everything, you've been extraordinarily kind. Now go and do what you promised me.'

Daniel was still brushing a hand over his clothes as if by doing so he'd be able to restore order. He looked at Elliot in surprise. 'I thought you were a doctor or something. Who are you?'

'Detective Inspector Elliot. I'm in charge of the investigation into Roy Sheppard's death, and now your father's too.'

Abbie pushed away from Keri's arms and glared at him. 'What?' She looked from the detective to Keri in confusion. 'There can't be a connection between the two. Roy was a paedophile.' Her eyes grew round. 'You're not saying–'

Keri grabbed her arm. 'No! Of course not, that's not it at all. We think your father was killed because of a job he did years ago. I'll explain, but not now.' She prayed her daughter would settle for that, she couldn't have gone through the twisted tale without breaking down. 'Now, it's time to say goodbye to your dad.' She looked back to Elliot. 'Thank you.'

He looked as if he wanted to say something but realised there was nothing to say and left without a word.

Only the need to be strong for her children stopped Keri falling apart when she brought them to say goodbye to Nathan. She stayed dry-eyed with one arm around each as they sobbed. It was easier when her brother-in-law arrived with his wife and daughter. Philip looked pale and shocked. Eva, his daughter, was a year older than Abbie and Daniel and they'd always been close. She joined in the huddle, arms stretching to enfold her cousins.

Keri stepped back and found herself pulled into a hug by her sister-in-law. 'I'm so sorry. I'll be here for you. For whatever you need,' Louisa said quietly. No platitudes there either. The simple promise of support. It would get them through the hours, days and weeks that loomed ahead.

The worst part was leaving Nathan behind when, eventually, they had to depart. Louisa took the sobbing Abbie while Eva put her arm around Daniel.

'Leave me a minute,' Keri said to Philip. She put a hand on his arm. 'I'm okay, I'll be right behind you.' She waited till he'd gone before approaching the bed to stand and stare down at the only man she'd ever loved. Then, because she needed to, because she'd never be able to do it again, she kicked off her shoes and lay down beside him, her head on his shoulder, her arm across his chest.

He was cold and the chill seeped through her. She'd never feel warm again. 'Oh, Nathan, I will miss you forever.' It was time to go. She swung her feet to the floor, slipped on her shoes and stood, her eyes on the door. She needed to go. But how could she leave him? How could she go on without him?

She sat on the side of the bed, and leaned over to press her lips to his, her hand on his cheek. What wouldn't she give for one more hour with him? 'What am I going to do, Nathan?'

You always fix things, Keri.

The words so clear she was startled and looked at him more closely, hope stupidly rising at the thought they'd made a mistake, that he wasn't dead. Of course, he wasn't dead. He couldn't be.

But there was no warmth under her hand, no heat in his lips when she pressed hers against them.

You're much stronger than I am, much better at making those difficult decisions. Don't think I haven't noticed and loved you for it.

Memories. Not words. Keri got to her feet. Nathan was dead.

But he'd been right. She was much stronger than he was.

Always had been. She'd need that strength to get through without him.

She had to leave.

A final kiss before she walked slowly backwards from the bed. She reached for the door handle, holding onto it tightly as she took one last lingering look at the man she loved, wanting desperately to return to his side, knowing she had to leave. She pushed down the handle, and slipped through the doorway.

'Ready?' Philip's quiet voice, his hand reaching for hers.

'How could I be?' She squeezed his hand. 'I have the children to think of. They'll get me through.'

It almost amused her that she was the first to use a platitude.

42

Philip insisted that he, Louisa, and Eva stayed at Northampton Park that night. 'And we're happy to stay for as long as you need us.'

Keri was grateful for their company, for the extra work required to make up the spare beds, for Philip's insistence that he'd organise the funeral when Nathan's body was released. 'It'll be a couple of weeks,' he said. 'Because he'd been...' His voice faded.

'Because he'd been murdered. You can say the word. If I hear it often enough, it might eventually sink in.'

Louisa looked after the practicalities and, after checking the cupboards, fridge and freezer, made a list and ordered a mountain of food from Waitrose.

Friends of Abbie and Daniel's arrived to offer condolences and support, but after a few minutes when everyone spoke together, an awkward uncomfortable silence fell. 'Why don't you get some beers and take your friends upstairs?' Keri whispered to Daniel. The attic room had been converted years before. At various times it had been the children's den, a gym, and a cinema room, but since Daniel and Abbie had started at

VALERIE KEOGH

university it was rarely used. It would be a good place for them to sit with their friends.

Daniel looked conflicted, wanting to stay with her, wanting to be with his friends. 'You sure you'll be okay?' She kissed his warm cheek, the heat bringing tears. 'Yes, of course, I'll be here with Philip and Louisa. No doubt we'll have more visitors.'

It was easier when they'd gone. She could let the strong woman mask slip a little without worrying about them.

'They're good kids.' Philip handed her a glass of wine.

She didn't really want it. No, that wasn't true. She'd have liked to have got blindingly stinking drunk and stayed that way, possibly forever. And maybe if she didn't have Abbie and Daniel she'd have taken that easy option.

Louisa put a plate of food in front of her, and a fork in her hand. 'You need to eat.'

Keri wanted to ask why. What was the point in eating to stay alive in a world without Nathan?

Instead, she did as she was bid, eating without tasting, swallowing each mouthful with difficulty, brushing away the tears that wouldn't stop falling. Neither Philip nor Louisa told her she should stop crying, neither offered any words of comfort. Because there weren't any. She was grateful to them for that, for letting her cry while she could, while the children were out of sight. For allowing her to be weak for a while. Before she'd have to face this strange new life on her own. Before she'd have to take on the burden of running Metcalfe Conservation without Nathan.

Especially before she had to face the terrifying truth. DI Elliot believed that the same person had killed Roy, Nathan, and Dexter Sylvester. If it was an act of revenge for that boy's death were they satisfied? And how on earth was Roy tied in with it?

There was another truth that simmered. If she hadn't had that affair, if she hadn't thought the wreath had come from

190

Barry, she'd have told Nathan about it the day it arrived. They'd have talked about it, and maybe they'd have called the police.

Perhaps then, the police would have made the connection with Sylvester's death. They might have looked in the right direction and found the person responsible.

And Nathan would still be alive.

43

K eri couldn't discuss her fears with her family so she did what she had to and hid behind her mask of sorrow.

A constant flow of people came and went, with long faces and words of condolence that she learned to accept with a simple *thank you.* Louisa made pots of tea and coffee, plates of sandwiches, set out cups and saucers, glasses for those who wanted something stronger.

Like it was a bloody party.

Keri looked around the room on Saturday evening. Friends had come, staff from Metcalfe Conservation, some of their suppliers and customers. Drinking, eating, and chatting. She wanted to sweep the glasses and cups from the table, wanted to throw the plates of food so carefully prepared by Louisa, wanted to scream at them and tell them all to get out.

Perhaps Keri would have done, but then Chris Dolan was at her side, genuine sadness in his eyes. 'I'm so sorry for your loss, Keri.' He fiddled with the glass he was holding. 'Nathan gave me my first break, you know, I'll be forever grateful for that. If there's anything I can do for you, all you need to do is say.'

'Oh, Chris.' She put her arms around him as her anger

faded. These people were here because they cared. She spent the rest of the evening chatting to as many as she could, swopping anecdotes about funny things Nathan had said and done. There were multiple promises of support that Keri knew were genuine. She thanked them all.

Sunday was quiet. Friends of Daniel and Abbie's had stayed over and with little encouragement they went out to brunch in a local pub.

Keri insisted on cooking breakfast for Louisa and Philip. 'I owe you so much, it's the least I can do.' She put three plates of food on the table and sat. 'I'm going to go into the office tomorrow.' The expression on Louisa's face was almost comical. 'I have obligations. There are things that only I can do.'

'But surely–'

'No, some things can't wait. The business has commitments that Nathan's death doesn't change. Anyway–' She pushed a hand through her hair, wondering when she'd brushed it last. '– it will do me good to get out of the house.'

'If you're sure.'

'I am. And also, that you should go home.' She saw surprise and a hint of doubt flicker on Louisa and Philip's faces and hurried to reassure them. 'I'm so grateful for you being here the last couple of days, it's made this horrendous time a little easier but I think it would be good to grab onto a bit of normality.'

'Okay, if you're sure. But if you change your mind, if you need us, we're at the end of the phone, okay?' Philip reached for her hand. 'You still happy to leave the funeral arrangements to me?'

'Oh absolutely. It's such a weight off to have you do that.'

'If there's anything we can do, you only need to ask,' Louisa said, taking Keri's other hand. 'We're here for you.'

They were there for her, but it wasn't them she wanted. Keri brushed away the thought and held on tightly to their hands.

It was early afternoon before Philip and Louisa left. Eva hadn't returned from brunch. 'She can make her own way home,' Louisa said, unconcerned. 'Or she might want to stay over, if that would be okay?'

'Yes, of course,' Keri said. 'She's welcome to stay for as long as she likes. It's good for Daniel and Abbie to have someone their own age to talk to.'

'Ring anytime,' Louisa said giving Keri a hug.

'I will.' Keri waited while they got into their car, then waved until they disappeared around a bend in the road.

And then she was alone.

She'd been alone before, of course, many times but not like this. Not this unending gaping hole of loneliness that stretched as far as she could see.

Keeping busy seemed to be the solution. She rang the employment agency. When she gave her name, the reaction was shocked silence followed by a babble of commiserations.

'Thank you,' Keri said interrupting her. 'I hope Luke is still available. Metcalfe Conservation will be opening the office as usual tomorrow.'

'Yes, yes, of course. I'll get on to him immediately.'

'Thank you.' Keri hung up and dropped the phone on the table. It would get less gut churning eventually. When every new conversation didn't elicit the same reaction.

Every member of the company's staff had called in to offer condolences over the last few days. Nobody mentioned the business, but she had no doubt they were concerned about its future. She sent a short message in the company WhatsApp group. *Metcalfe Conservation will be open as usual tomorrow.* It was too stark and impersonal. She added, *Nathan loved this business, it's not going to change,* and sent it.

Keri filled more time in rearranging the kitchen. Louisa had moved things around and put things in the wrong place. It was satisfying to restore the status quo here at least.

An hour later, when Keri had rearranged everything, even things that didn't need to be moved, when the silence of the house was becoming depressing, she heard the front door open. She heard the muted sounds of her children's voices with a relief that sent her heart sinking. She wasn't going to be one of those sad widows who clung onto their children to relieve their despair.

'Hi,' she said, almost too brightly as they came through the door. 'Did you have a good brunch?'

'The usual,' Abbie said, looking around with a frown. 'Where're Louisa and Philip?'

'They've gone home.' Keri turned to Eva. 'They weren't sure how long you were going to be so they said you could either make your own way home or stay here again. It's up to you, you're welcome to stay.'

'Oh, do.' Daniel went to the fridge, pulled it open and grabbed a couple of beers. He knocked the cap off both and handed one to Eva. 'Here you go. We can go upstairs and watch that movie I was telling you about if you'd like?'

Eva held the bottle and looked at Keri. 'If you're sure it's okay, I might stay another night. I've no lectures till late tomorrow.'

'Of course.' She did a shooing action with her hands. 'Go,

watch the movie.' She wasn't surprised when Abbie stayed behind. 'I was going to make a cup of tea, would you like one?'

'Please.'

It wasn't until they were sitting with a mug of tea before them that Abbie spoke. 'You'll be okay, won't you, Mum?'

'Eventually.'

Abbie sighed as if it were the answer she expected. 'What are you going to do about the company?'

Keri had picked up her tea. She held it to her mouth and took a sip before putting it down. 'Open tomorrow as usual. It's what your father would have wanted.'

'Tomorrow?' Abbie looked horrified. 'Isn't that a bit too soon?'

'I was the same age as you are now when your father and I married, but we'd known each other for years before that. I can't imagine him not being with me, can't believe I'll never hear his voice again. The thought of carrying on the business without him is so painful that I'm not sure I can bear it, but the thought of letting him down is even worse.' She reached for her daughter's hand. 'I need to go in tomorrow. To get that first awful step over with. If I didn't... if I left it for days, weeks... I'm not sure I'd ever go back. And your dad would be disappointed in me.'

Abbie brushed away tears. 'Okay, I understand. Why don't I go in with you? That would make it easier, wouldn't it?'

It would but it was just passing that difficult first step to another day.

Keri leaned over, kissed her daughter's cheek. 'What would make it easier for me, would be knowing that you and Daniel were getting on with your lives. I'll be okay.'

44

K eri took a taxi to the office on Monday. When it pulled up outside, panic gripped her. Could she really do this?

She stepped out and stood looking up at the sign across the front of the building. *Metcalfe Conservation.* So much hard work... so much fun... and what a success they'd made of it. She and Nathan should have had years yet to enjoy it all.

The automatic door swished open when she approached. She walked inside as nausea hit her making her swallow frantically and look around in panic. She needed to get out of there. The doors had shut behind her but if she moved back they'd open again. She could run away. Abbie was right, it was too soon.

Too soon, too late. Too bloody everything.

Luke must have seen her distress because suddenly he was there, a hand on her elbow guiding her to a chair. He left her, hurried away, and returned a moment later with a glass of water.

'Here you go.'

The glass was pressed into her hand. She would have liked to have thrown it, smashed it. Smashed all the damn glass in

VALERIE KEOGH

that ridiculous reception, those stupid walls which meant she'd be on view all day. The grieving widow.

She sipped the water she didn't need or want because what she did need, what she wanted so desperately, would never be available again, and because Luke was being kind and right at that moment she didn't know what else to do.

'Thank you.' She handed him the glass back and got to her feet. 'I'll be fine now.'

Luke, it appeared, could see a lie. He waited, walked with her to her office and didn't leave until she was sitting behind her desk.

Keri managed a smile for him before he left. Maybe he wasn't too unlike Roy after all. Perhaps she'd ask him if he wanted to stay with them. It would require a release fee to the agency but it would be worth it to have one less thing to worry about.

As she'd expected, all the staff who were in that day came to see her over the first few hours. Chris, saviour that he was, brought her a coffee. She was even more touched to see he'd not bought it in the café where Nathan had been killed.

She sipped it, looking out over reception, trying to stop her eyes drifting to the right to Nathan's office. It would be as he'd left it on Friday before he went out for those damn coffees. The thought sent a wave of anger through her and she threw the coffee, the almost-full container hitting the glass wall and releasing its contents in a splash of beige.

Luke turned a startled face her way as Keri gulped down a sob and dropped her face into her cupped hands. She didn't look up when she heard the door open or when she heard the footsteps, the distinct sound of sheets of paper being torn from a roll. Only when the door opened and shut minutes later did she straighten.

The mess had been cleaned up with only a smear on the glass proof of her temporary insanity.

She switched on her computer, read through and answered emails until the words blurred on the screen and her tear-filled eyes stung. When Chris called in at lunchtime to see if she wanted anything, she pushed the keyboard away. 'A mineral water, please.'

'You need to eat something, Keri.'

'I'm fine, honestly, just the water would be good.'

When he returned twenty minutes later, it was with a bottle of water and a sandwich. 'In case you get peckish,' he said putting it on the desk.

His simple kindness brought more tears that made him flush with embarrassment. 'Thank you,' she said. 'I might eat a little.' She picked it up when he'd gone. Egg and cress, he knew it was one of her favourites. She opened the package but the smell of egg sent a wave of nausea over her and she closed it again. Maybe later. She shoved it into a drawer out of the way.

She picked up her phone to make the call she'd been putting off. It took a while to get through the layers of administrators, secretaries and unnamed persons who answered as her call was transferred from A to B and on again.

Finally, she heard a voice she'd recognise forever. Tina Bailey, the vascular surgeon who'd operated on Nathan that last day. 'Thank you for taking my call,' Keri said. 'I've been worrying about something and needed to ask you.'

'I'll answer if I can, Mrs Metcalfe.'

'Mr Winfield, the surgeon who operated on my husband on Friday, said there were no underlying injuries, that it was soft tissue and would heal easily.'

'Yes.' A sigh came down the line. 'Your husband had lost quite a lot of blood prior to and during surgery and there was some indication he was dehydrated because his blood pressure was quite low. When we opened the wound, we identified damage to the carotid artery. Because your husband was dehydrated it was easy to miss during the initial surgery, but once he was well hydrated it looks as though it was unable to withstand the increase in pressure.

'You have our deepest commiserations for your husband's death, Mrs Metcalfe. I know it won't be any consolation but we will be doing an internal investigation as to why the original injury was missed.'

No consolation, how could it be. 'You said by the time the staff were alerted, he'd already lost too much blood but he had a blood pressure monitor on, why didn't that alarm?'

'It's something we will be asking.' The surgeon's voice was resigned rather than angry as if dealing with this kind of problem was an everyday occurrence. 'Your husband wasn't considered to be in any danger, it is possible that the alarm had been switched off.'

'But...' Keri swallowed the lump in her throat. She needed to ask this final question. Otherwise, it would haunt her. 'If I'd been there... if I'd not gone to talk with the detective, then I'd have noticed something was wrong, wouldn't I? He could have been saved then. Am I right? If I'd been with him...' She ended on a cry of despair.

The surgeon was clearly a pragmatic woman who believed in honesty especially when it was the easier option. 'If you'd been there, you'd probably have assumed your husband was asleep. You might have noticed blood on the dressing after a minute or two. You probably wouldn't have thought to ring the emergency bell, instead, you'd have gone in search of a nurse, and you might eventually have found one who was free to go back with you. To be frank, I think by that stage it was already too late.'

Keri heard noise on the line.

'I'm sorry, Mrs Metcalfe, I need to go. Once again, I'm so sorry for your loss but take my advice, stop beating yourself up. Nothing you did or didn't do that day was going to make any difference.'

45

Keri put the phone down and sat back. The tears had stopped. Too numb to cry. She didn't know why she'd bothered to make that call. Perhaps she'd been looking for someone to blame. The detective for pulling her away from Nathan's side, the surgeon, Winfield, who'd boasted of his sewing skills. Anyone.

Even that smiling enthusiastic boy whose death had started it all.

All she could do was wait for the police to catch the person who was really to blame for Nathan's death.

It was almost 2pm when she looked up from yet another email offering condolences to see DI Elliot at her office door. She sat back and waved him in. 'Hello. I wasn't expecting you. Have you news for me?' Would it make it easier to know they'd caught the person who'd taken Nathan from her? She wasn't sure, but it couldn't make it worse.

The detective was wearing yet another of his garish ties. It was an odd symbol of normality in her increasingly strange world.

Elliot pulled a chair closer to the desk and sat. 'No, I've no news, I'm afraid. Actually, I wasn't expecting to find the office open. I was interviewing staff in the café and decided to retrace your husband's steps.'

Keri bridled at what she took as criticism. She straightened in the chair, her hands gripping the armrests. 'The company meant a lot to Nathan, I wanted to make sure it didn't suffer.'

Elliot held a hand up. 'I intended no offence, Mrs Metcalfe. I've learned that people handle grief in a myriad of ways. Some jump straight back into their lives, some withdraw completely. Neither way is right or wrong.'

Annoyance vanished in a long sigh, her shoulders slumping, hands reaching for each other, fingers intertwining, holding on. 'It's been a tough weekend, but I'm lucky, I have family and friends to support me.'

'That makes a difference.'

'Yes,' she said with a slight smile. 'So did your kindness on Friday. I don't know if I thanked you, some of that day is a bit of a blur to be honest.'

'You did thank me, several times.' He shuffled in his chair. 'Do you think you're up to answering questions?'

Questions? Keri's eyes narrowed slightly. Elliot was a police officer not a friend. It might be a good idea to remember that. 'Sure. What do you need to know?'

'It seems pretty clear there is a connection between the attack on your husband and the murder of Dexter Sylvester. The wreath and the animal entrails left outside his business, you already know about, but we checked Mr Sylvester's phone and he, like your husband, had a message that said, *remember JC.*'

'Jim Cody. He was only sixteen.' Keri shook her head sadly. 'Nathan never told me, you know, kept it a secret all these years.

Twenty-three years ago, we were struggling to get by and he thought he was doing the right thing.' She saw Elliot shake his head. 'What?'

'Even twenty-three years ago, it was the wrong decision to make and from the little I know of you, I don't think you'd have let the boy's death slide. That's why he didn't tell you then, isn't it?'

He was right, of course, but Keri cringed at the image the detective appeared to have of her as this straight-thinking, truthful, virtuous woman. She had pushed to the back of her mind the idea that everything might have turned out differently if she'd told the police about the wreath in the very beginning. But it squirmed guiltily, jabbing her brain with a vicious sharpness.

Ignoring Elliot's question, she wrapped her arms around herself and dropped her chin on her chest. 'I wasn't completely honest with you. Or with Nathan. Perhaps if I had been...' She sighed and looked up then. 'I didn't tell Nathan about the wreath when it came, because I thought it came from someone I knew.' She lifted her chin. 'I'd had an affair. It didn't last long, a little more than a month, but it didn't end amicably. He was annoyed that I wouldn't meet him one night and it made me reconsider what I was doing, so I finished it. He said I'd regret ending our relationship so when the wreath came a couple of days later, and then the rat, I believed they were from him.'

'Okay,' Elliot said slowly. 'So, it wasn't until your husband told you about the wreath that had been sent to Sylvester that you realised your mistake?'

'Yes. I told Nathan about it then, explained that I hadn't bothered telling him because it had been delivered in error. He believed me, of course, he'd never have considered that I had a reason to lie.'

'He didn't know about your affair?'

'No, he didn't. I've never cheated on him before.' She saw a shade of doubt in the detective's eyes. 'I swear to you. I loved Nathan. It was... I dunno, I think I was feeling old, you know, wanted to know I was still attractive.' She ran a hand over her mouth. 'I think, too, I was envious of my daughter, the exciting life she leads, lots of boyfriends, romances, so much in front of her.' Keri sniffed. 'You must think me so pathetic.'

'I think you've been beating yourself up over this unnecessarily. You've been married how long?'

'Twenty-five years.'

'And you made one mistake. Sounds like you'd a pretty solid marriage to me.'

'But if...' She swallowed. Did she really want to know the answer to the question.

'If?' Elliot leaned forward. 'You may as well ask whatever it is otherwise it'll keep preying on your mind.'

'You should have been a priest.' A minute passed before Keri sighed. 'Okay. Tell me, if I had rung the police that day to say a wreath had been delivered with a card that said RIP, would it have been connected with the one that was delivered to Dexter Sylvester?'

Understanding lightened Elliot's expression. 'You're thinking that if you had reported it, that you might have prevented the attack on Nathan?'

Keri felt her lower lip quiver, knew that tears were once again close. 'Yes.'

'Did you contact the florist that sent the flowers?'

'Yes, they said it must have been a mistake and took it away.'

'If you'd never had an affair, wouldn't you have assumed that was the truth and simply forgotten about it rather than ringing the police?'

Of course, she would have done! The detective was right.

She'd have accepted the florist's word and put it out of her head. A smile wavered. 'Yes, you're right.'

'My wife says I often am, but I think she's usually being sarcastic.'

It made Keri laugh. She'd have to tell Nathan that one. The thought made her shut her eyes, the pain instant. 'I keep forgetting he's gone,' she said, opening her eyes to see Elliot looking concerned. 'He's been part of my life for what feels like forever.'

'We'll get who did this, Mrs Metcalfe.'

'Keri, please.'

He ran a hand down his garish tie. 'Okay, Keri, tell me about this man you had the affair with.'

46

DI Elliot must have seen the look of surprise on Keri's face because he shook his head. 'No, it's not spurious curiosity, believe me, everyone in your life is of interest to us. Especially people you have met only recently.'

Keri gave an awkward laugh. 'But he wouldn't have been involved with what happened to Nathan. That's all to do with someone wanting revenge for that boy.' Elliot's face told her nothing and a trickle of fear made her sit forward. 'Isn't it?'

'I find it best to keep an open mind at this stage in an investigation.' He shrugged slightly. 'It concerns me that you appear to be reluctant to talk about this ex-lover though, that makes me more than curious.'

'I'm not reluctant. Not as such.' She heaved a sigh. 'I didn't tell you everything.'

'People often leave things out they think aren't important. Problem is, they don't know what is or isn't crucial and sometimes we miss something.'

'Fine.' Her voice bristled with annoyance. Or maybe it was embarrassment at having to talk more about her sordid little affair. 'I met him outside the office block next door. He told me he was a solicitor there.'

'But he wasn't?'

'No. They'd never heard of him.'

Elliot frowned and reached into an inside pocket for a notebook and pen. 'What was his name?'

'He told me it was Barry Morgan.'

Elliot wrote it down. 'You doubt everything about him now which is understandable. Do you know where he lived?'

'He said he had an apartment in Hatch Lane but I never saw it.'

'Where did you—'

'Have our seedy assignations?'

His eyebrows rose. 'I was going to say 'meet'.'

'I'm sorry.' Keri sighed. 'It had seemed so romantic, so dangerous. How stupid I was.' She realised the detective was still waiting for an answer to his question. 'We met in a hotel near the train station. The Walthamstow Central.' *How very seedy it all sounded now.*

Elliot jotted the name down. 'Did he pay or did you?'

'He did. And, I remember, he used a card.' She could have gone back to the hotel, found out who Barry really was. She wondered if they'd have told her.

'Okay. What dates were you there?' Elliot made a note of the days and times she gave him. 'Right, I'll have a word with them, see who this guy is.' He put his notebook away. 'It concerns me a little that two people have come into your life recently and neither were who they were supposed to be.'

Keri's eyes widened, horrified she hadn't seen it. Of course, Tracy Wirick and Barry Morgan. Both had lied to her. 'Surely there isn't a connection between them.'

'Probably not,' Elliot said. 'But in a murder investigation, every stone gets turned over.' He pushed his chair back and stood. 'If you think of anything else, you have my card.'

'Yes, thank you but there's nothing else. I've told you everything.'

He smiled at that and left.

Keri stayed sitting behind her desk feeling more confused. There couldn't be any connection between Barry Morgan and Tracy Wirick, could there?

47

Keri rested her linked hands on the top of her head. *Tracy Wirick and Barry Morgan.* She couldn't in her wildest imagination think how they'd be connected.

Maybe Roy knew. She wondered if it would have altered the course of events if she'd stayed to listen to what he'd had to tell her that day.

She'd never know but she'd always wonder. There was always the possibility, of course, that during the investigation into his or Nathan's death the truth might come out. Maybe, but did she really want to know that if she'd stayed to listen, her husband's life might have been spared.

Could she bear to live with that truth?

There was another worry, one she'd not thought to discuss with Elliot. If all three deaths were linked – Sylvester, Roy, and Nathan – and all were in revenge for the death of that young boy so many years before, who was to say it was over?

Maybe their anger had grown over the years. The two companies, Metcalfe Conservation and DS Construction, were now industry leaders. Successful and powerful.

Jim Cody never had the chance to grow up and make something of himself.

Was that what this revenge was all about? Not simply for his death but for the future he was denied?

Keri reached for her keyboard. A few seconds later, she was staring at the worksheet for the job Nathan had done on that Gothic window all those years before. The forms had been simpler in those days. A description of the job, estimation of time required, estimate of costs involved. The name of the company they were doing the work for, DS Construction, the name of the stonemason doing the work, Nathan Metcalfe, and the name of the person accepting the job on behalf of Metcalfe Conservation. *Her name.*

She stared at the screen trying to think calmly. It would have been relatively easy to find out who did the work on the Gothic window of that manor house in Stevenage, but only people who had access to the Metcalfe Conservation computer files could have seen this report. Only a few people would know that Keri, too, had played a part in Jim Cody's death.

There wasn't a great turnover of staff within the company. Most were with them for years and the apprentice stonemasons who came and went with regularity had limited access to the company files.

Keri sat back with a frown creasing her brow, her eyes drifting through the glass to where Luke was speaking to someone. The reception desk had full access to the files in question. It made it easier when customers rang looking for details of a job done in the past.

Tracy Wirick. She'd been annoying Roy with all her questions. Had he given her access to the files simply to shut her up?

Tracy Wirick who had lied about her address and her references. Was she more than a liar?

Had she arrived early on Friday morning, smiled at Roy, slipped behind the unsuspecting man, and slit his throat?

Keri, who considered herself a good judge of people, thought back to the day Tracy had come into her office. Maybe the younger woman's air of defeat was designed to do exactly what it had done. Elicit sympathy. Persuade Keri to give her a chance. There was no indication Tracy was anything other than what she'd said, but in hindsight, hadn't she been a little too keen to please, a little too desperate? Maybe.

'Aaargh.' Keri swung around in her chair and got to her feet. She was driving herself crazy jumping from one conspiracy theory to the other. It achieved nothing except to fill her brain with white noise so she wouldn't think about Nathan.

She'd liked to have paced the floor but her goldfish bowl didn't give privacy for that. Her head was aching, possibly from all the thoughts rattling inside her skull, probably from lack of caffeine. Since she was on her feet, she went to the staffroom for coffee, relieved to find nobody there to force her into yet another stilted conversation.

She took the mug of instant back to her office and sat sipping it to wash down the lump of sadness that seemed to have taken possession of her throat.

That detective and the surgeon were probably right. Nothing she did or didn't do would have changed events. Life didn't work like that. Every action and inaction had consequences but not necessarily the ones that were wanted.

The mug was empty. She sat back and waited for the caffeine to kick in and provide clarity. But how could there be any in a world where Nathan wasn't around.

Coming to the office had been a mistake. She couldn't fix anything by being there and apart from answering unimportant emails, she'd done nothing of any significance. All she'd managed to achieve was to add another worry to the rest. There were three names on that worksheet and two of them were dead. Maybe she was next.

Did she care? If Tracy Wirick or whoever had been responsible suddenly appeared behind her with a sharp knife in her hand, it would be better if Keri stretched her neck to make it easier. One clean cut to end it. What, after all, did she have to live for without Nathan?

A twinge of guilt shot through her that she would so easily abandon the twins, but they'd get by without her, she wasn't so sure she could survive without Nathan.

But what if that didn't end it?

What if her death, along with those already claimed, wasn't enough to satisfy the person's quest for revenge? What if their aim was to destroy the two companies?

The caffeine suddenly hit home and with a surge of clarity Keri pulled her keyboard forward and brought up the emails she'd not answered. There was one from the president of the Stone Federation. Simon Nicholl was a man she didn't like so she hadn't rushed to read what she assumed would be his commiserations.

She opened it now with a sense of impending dread. If she was right...

48

Keri read the email from the president of the Stone Federation through twice before nodding. She was right. Whoever was seeking revenge, they weren't satisfied with destroying people. They wanted everything.

Some of her customers and suppliers might brush off Jim Cody's death as something that had happened before safety regulations had been tightened, but the president of the Stone Federation couldn't afford to be so dismissive. And it seemed that someone had acquainted Simon Nicoll with Metcalfe Conservation's part in the death of the young apprentice and he was taking the matter very seriously indeed.

Their membership of the Federation had been suspended with immediate effect until the situation was fully investigated.

Nicholl ended the email with one sentence of regret for the timing and commiserations on Nathan's death.

The suspension would have huge implications. These days there was no way to side-step health and safety regulations. The companies Metcalfe Conservation did work for would express regret and quickly move to one of their competitors. Their reputation would be cross-shredded. They'd lose contracts.

Their suppliers would take fright and demand payment. The gossip would build, whispers, innuendos and outright lies.

The company might recover... or go under.

Keri checked her contacts for DS Construction and rang. 'It's Keri Metcalfe, I'd like to speak to whoever's in charge, please.'

'Certainly, Ms Metcalfe, hold and I'll see if Mr Radstock is free.'

Radstock? Possibly Tom Radstock. If so she was in luck, she'd met him the previous year at a conference and got on well with him.

'Ms Metcalfe, how can I help you?'

If he'd heard about Nathan's death he wasn't rushing to offer commiserations for a man he'd never met. She wasn't sure whether to be relieved or annoyed at his lack of social etiquette but it made her job a little easier, she could do the same. 'It's Tom Radstock, isn't it? We met last year.'

'It is. It's good to talk to you again. I was sorry to hear about your husband.'

There it was, but thankfully brief. 'Thank you. Cutting to the point, I've had an email from Simon Nicholl. They've suspended us pending an investigation into the death of a young boy over twenty years ago, I need to know if you've had similar.' She heard a sharp indrawn breath. 'I take that as a 'yes'.'

'We did, it came through this morning. I've spent the last few hours searching for any reference to the boy's death but have come up empty-handed. What can you tell me?'

'You've found nothing?'

'Documentation pertaining to the renovation of the manor house but nothing else, no reference to an apprentice by that name working for the company.'

That bastard Dexter Sylvester had obviously tried to cover his tracks. Not well enough though. 'I think it's best if we meet,' Keri said. Face to face communication over sensitive matters was always better – so much could be missed during a phone call. If they met, she would be able to see if Tom were lying or hiding something.

'Okay,' he said slowly. 'I have to be in the city later, how about we meet near Victoria Station.'

'Perfect. Do you know Lester's?'

'I do, that would be ideal. I've a few things to do here so say I'll meet you there in two hours?'

'Yes, that suits.' She cut the connection and sat back tapping the phone against her chin. She'd been right. Whoever had killed the three men wasn't finished. They were also planning on destroying both companies.

Another more terrifying thought struck her. Maybe not only the companies. Keri had considered without much care that she might be a target for revenge... but what if they intended to go further, to destroy not only the Metcalfe company, but the Metcalfe family. Were Abbie and Daniel also targets?

She might not care whether she lived or died, but nobody was going to touch them.

49

Keri dropped her face into her cupped hands feeling suddenly overwhelmed. Was there a big conspiracy to destroy everything she'd ever loved, or was she simply trying to bury her grief. Perhaps it was easier to believe there was a big bad wolf out there waiting to gobble up her and her offspring rather than face the reality of life without Nathan.

Life without Nathan. The gaping emptiness seemed to be surrounding her. Soon it would have sucked her in and she'd be no more. She didn't seem to have the energy to care.

Her mobile buzzed. When it buzzed again, she peeled her hands from her tear-sodden face and glared at it. It was only when it buzzed for the third time that she picked it up. It was a message from Abbie.

Thinking about u, hope u get thru the day ok, wish u'd let me come with you. Love u.

Abbie had attached a big beating heart to the message. Keri ran her thumb over it. Her sad heart was still beating. It was time to stop wallowing. She couldn't fix Nathan's death but maybe she could try to fix whatever else was going on.

Metcalfe Conservation had been Nathan's pride and joy, she wasn't going to let it go down without a fight. The suspension from the Stone Federation was something tangible, something she could fix.

She could fix herself too. That nice detective had been right. One mistake in twenty-five years didn't make her a monster. The guilt mightn't have faded completely but she'd stop using it to whip herself.

Nathan was dead but she was alive. So were Abbie and Daniel. It was time to put them first. Time too to look at things with her business eye.

What were the facts? Nathan and Dexter Sylvester were killed by someone wanting revenge for what happened to Jim Cody. That woman, Tracy Wirick, had to be involved somehow. Perhaps she was a relative of some sort. Maybe Roy had discovered something about her and was killed as a result.

The email from the Stone Federation might be simply a coincidence. After all, the murder of two prominent businessmen would have set tongues wagging. There were plenty of people within the organisation who'd happily have dug deep in search for common ground. Jim Cody's death may not have caused a big furore when it happened but there was sure to be a reference to it somewhere in archived files.

Maybe the Federation authorities had decided that if someone was looking for revenge, it was time to give them justice and right the wrongs of the past. It would be the kind of thing she could imagine that prick Simon Nicholl saying.

A meeting with Tom Radstock was the first step to getting the suspension overturned. After all, her heart twisted as she considered using the argument, Nathan and Sylvester, the two men who could in any way be found culpable, were dead.

Keri looked through the glass walls. Luke was on the phone to someone. Otherwise, the reception was empty. She stood and went out, crossing to the glass frontage to look outside.

It would be faster to take a Tube to Victoria Station but as she watched the steady wave of passers-by on the footpath she imagined being among them and one of them creeping up behind to pull a knife across her throat. Suddenly, she realised how very much she wanted to live, because she wouldn't stretch her neck to make it easier for her attacker. She'd fight.

Back in her office, she called an Uber and twenty minutes later, crossed to the reception desk. 'I won't be back today, Luke. You can get me on my mobile if anyone needs me.'

'Have you a meeting?'

Keri hadn't realised how on edge she was until that moment, certainly hadn't realised she was staring at Luke wondering if, somehow, he were involved. 'Why are you asking me?' Her voice was sharp enough to bring colour to his cheeks.

'I'm sorry. It's only that I don't have a record of any meeting and I was worried I'd missed something.'

Did he look a bit shifty? Keri stared at him a moment longer. 'It was a spur-of-the-moment meeting,' she said and turned away. She waited until the taxi pulled up outside before moving closer to the door, waiting until it had fully opened before going outside and hurrying down the steps and across the footpath to pull open the taxi door and clamber inside. Maybe there was nothing to her idea that whoever wanted vengeance for Jim Cody hadn't finished. Maybe, but she couldn't shake the idea that she was right.

The taxi stopped immediately outside Lester's. The old-fashioned, decidedly untrendy pub was popular with people like her who wanted to have a drink and a chat without being bombarded with music. It had booths, too, where you could be almost guaranteed privacy.

Mid-afternoon, it was relatively quiet. There were a few empty seats including a booth separated from the others by a chimney breast on one side and a doorway on the other. It was also well positioned to give her a view of the rest of the pub, her eyes flitting from group to group. No woman bore any resemblance to Tracy Wirick, no man any likeness to Barry Morgan either.

What a tangle Keri's life had become. Leaving her jacket on the seat, she headed to the bar. She'd have liked a glass of wine but on a nearly empty stomach it might skew her judgement. Instead, she ordered a mineral water and a coffee.

Tucked into the corner of the booth, she sipped her cappuccino. She couldn't relax. Every time the door opened, she tensed and her heart thumped until the person came into view, then she slumped down again, until the next time.

By the time Tom Radstock arrived she was exhausted. She'd only met him that once, the year before, but she recognised him instantly. He was a tall, thin man with a thick mop of blond curly hair that like the year before, needed a cut. The shaggy hair was at odds with his conservative neat suit, white shirt, and dark tie. Strangely, it put Keri in mind of Roy's waistcoats and she liked Tom more for the reminder that it was good to be a little different.

He saw her immediately and crossed the room with an apologetic smile. 'So sorry I'm late, it's been one of those days.' He pointed to her empty cup. 'Would you like another coffee or something stronger perhaps?'

'Another coffee would be good, thank you. An espresso, please.' It would make her jittery but might help her focus.

'Here you go,' he said, returning with a tiny cup that looked lost in his big hands. He put it down in front of her, slid into the seat opposite and took a mouthful of his pint. 'I needed that.'

'That email from the Stone Federation causing you grief, is it?'

'That and other things.' He put his pint down, sat back and crossed his arms. 'I don't know how well you knew Dexter Sylvester.' He stared at her waiting for her answer.

'Not at all. I've seen him at the odd function but never spoken to him.'

'Would I be right in guessing you know the kind of person he was?' He smiled when she nodded agreement. 'He had his sticky fingers in all kinds of things, some of which were exceedingly dodgy.'

'There have always been rumours,' Keri admitted. 'But I thought he'd cleaned up his act, it's harder to get away with anything these days, regulations have become almost unbearably stringent.'

'People like Sylvester will always find a way.' He picked up his pint again and took a drink. 'I don't know if you're aware but there was some trouble last year. The company would have gone under if he hadn't managed to get some investors. It was they who persuaded me to take the reins when he was killed–'

'Murdered.'

'What?' Radstock looked confused.

'Sylvester, like my husband, was murdered. There was intention behind their deaths, it wasn't simply an accident.' Keri heard her voice rising as she got her point across but she was irritated at his casual mention of Sylvester's death.

Radstock held up a hand. 'It seems to be my day for apologies. I'm sorry, I didn't mean to be making light of his death, or your husband's. I'm very good at what I do, but I'd be the first to admit I'm the most socially awkward person you could hope to meet, and not knowing what to say about your husband's death I've chickened out by saying as little as possible.'

'That's okay,' Keri said with a faint smile. 'To be honest, I'm relieved not to have to listen to more commiserations. It's just–' She reached for her espresso and finished it in one mouthful. '– fucking hard at times.'

'I can't begin to understand what you're going through. This situation with the Stone Federation can't be helping.'

'It's better to have something to think about than my loss.' She waited a second before continuing. 'What did you manage to find out?'

'Nothing. The email referred to the death of a sixteen-year-old apprentice during the renovation of Stevenage Manor House twenty-three years ago. I've looked through all the paperwork we have pertaining to that job and there isn't one mention of an accident on-site resulting in death, or injury for that matter.'

Keri looked at him. He seemed trustworthy. Maybe it would be better to work together. 'Let me tell you what happened.'

50

Tom Radstock was a good listener. He didn't interrupt, didn't even add the usual encouraging mms and hmms that most people used. His only reaction to the story that Keri told him was a slight widening of his eyes.

'And that's it.' She reached for her water, wishing she'd ordered a glass of wine after all. 'Sylvester and Nathan were murdered in revenge for what happened. And probably Roy Sheppard too.'

'Roy Sheppard?'

'Our administrator, he was killed in the same way as the others almost a week before. The police aren't sure why, but I think he must have found out something damning about Tracy Wirick.' This time, Keri smiled at his confusion. 'The short version of that story is, she came into the office, asked to do work experience and started the following day. The next day, Roy was dead and she was missing. Turns out she wasn't who she said she was.'

Radstock picked up his pint and drained it. 'I definitely need another. Can I get you something?'

'A small white wine, please.' She deserved it at this stage.

But when he returned it was with a large glass of wine and a pint for himself. 'I've taken the liberty of ordering some food as well. You look like you haven't eaten–' He heaved a noisy sigh. '– since your husband was murdered.'

'I have, but not very much.' She lifted her glass. 'Thank you.'

He sipped his pint, keeping the glass to his lips, lost in thought. Finally, he looked at her. 'That is one hell of a story. It's hard to believe that someone would wait so long to take revenge.'

'Sylvester and my husband got messages sent to them saying *remember JC* plus the wreath and the dead animal or animal entrails.' She picked up the wine, then put it down again when the waiter arrived with the food.

'Here you go.' He placed the two plates on the table, dropped cutlery wrapped in paper serviettes beside them. 'Anything else?'

'No, that's fine, thanks.' Radstock turned to Keri. 'I guessed you'd say no if I asked, so I ordered steak and chicken hoping one of the two would appeal.' He looked at her with a raised eyebrow. 'Unless of course, you're vegetarian.'

'No, but I would prefer the chicken, if that's okay?'

'Of course.' He pushed it towards her.

Keri ate a few chips and a piece of the chicken then picked up her wine and took a sip. 'It is one hell of a story, as you say.' She looked at him. 'Tell me, why do you think the Stone Federation decided to investigate Jim Cody's death after all these years?'

'It might be that someone was suspicious of two members murdered in the same way within such a short time and decided to dig for some connection between them. Despite Sylvester sanitising DS Construction's files, there would have to be a report about the boy's death somewhere in the Federation's archives.'

'That's exactly what I was thinking.'

Radstock cut into the steak and speared a piece but held it on the fork without eating, looking at it meditatively. 'Simon Nicholl has a very astute brain. As president, he'd want to ensure that the Federation is seen to be taking the matter seriously.'

It all sounded so logical. Perhaps it was simple paranoia that was making Keri think her ordeal wasn't over, that there was more horror yet to come. She looked up from the chip she'd been nibbling and caught Radstock staring at her.

He smiled slightly. 'You've been gnawing on that one chip for a long time. Obviously, you've something else on your mind. Why don't you tell me what it is, I'm a good listener.'

She'd nothing left to lose, and she needed someone to talk to. 'What you said all sounds so logical, and it's much what I'd been thinking, but what if it was something more than someone putting two and two together. What if whoever killed Sylvester, Nathan and Roy isn't finished and it was they who sent the information to Simon Nicoll about Jim Cody's death. Both of our companies might come through this investigation okay, but we also might be destroyed. What if that's the plan? Not only death, but death and destruction.' She wanted to add her worry that she, Abbie, and Daniel might also be in danger, but she sounded paranoid enough.

Radstock frowned. 'Okay, no wonder you look concerned. Our first step then is to find out why they've suddenly decided to investigate.'

Keri felt inordinately grateful for the 'our'. 'How do we do that?'

He reached into the inside pocket of his jacket and pulled out his phone. 'Shouldn't be too difficult. Simon Nicholl and I are old friends. I was going to ring him this morning and ask him what was going on but then you rang so I left it. But I can call him now and ask.'

Keri picked up a chip and ate it while she listened to Radstock's side of the conversation. Since after the initial query this consisted of a series of yes, no, and um, it didn't tell her much. 'Well?' she said when he eventually put the mobile down on the table, tension tightening to see his grim expression.

Radstock picked up his pint and drank, then put it down and wiped his mouth with a hand. He was obviously finding it difficult to tell Keri whatever it was he'd heard.

'Not good news then?' she said, feeling sorry for him.

'I'm afraid not. It is, unfortunately, much as you'd feared. Simon had a letter yesterday accusing the Federation of a cover-up in the death of Jim Cody. It was signed simply, a relative, and it gave names, dates, the work involved and was accompanied by a copy of the death certificate of the apprentice listing acute silicosis as cause of death.'

'It didn't leave Simon much choice then, did it?'

'Didn't leave him any. The letter also stated that they'd go to the papers and the police if an investigation wasn't done.'

Keri picked up another chip and bit into it. It was cold. She dropped it on the plate. 'How bad is this going to be, do you think?'

Radstock shrugged. 'It would be impossible to prove, at this stage, where the boy was exposed. There's no paperwork in DS Construction to support their claim, and I assume there's none in Metcalfe Conservation either.'

He seemed to be waiting for her response so she shook her head slowly. 'The boy's name isn't on any of our paperwork.' There was no point in telling him that Nathan had admitted that Jim Cody had worked with him. Without the proper equipment on high-risk sandstone. No point in damaging Nathan's memory.

Radstock hadn't finished. 'My guess is they'll investigate, decide that errors had been made but that since more stringent rules are now in place, and since–' He held a hand up in apology. '–Sylvester and your husband are dead, there'd be no point in pursuing the case further.' He reached for his pint. 'There will be talk though, damaging talk that the two companies colluded to cover up the death of a sixteen-year-old. Our competitors will make sure the story grows wings. We'll lose contracts.'

'And our suppliers will start shouting for money owed and be wary about supplying in case they get caught in the crossfire.' She reached for her wine and gulped a large mouthful. 'We could go under, couldn't we?'

He lifted a hand and see-sawed it. 'It's certainly going to be bumpy for a while.'

Bumpy? Keri's fingers tightened on the stem of her glass. The man had no idea how bumpy it might get for her. Because it looked like she'd been right. Whoever was seeking vengeance for Jim Cody's death was far from finished.

Nathan, Sylvester, and Roy. The two companies.

Would that satisfy their need for vengeance?

Or were they going to continue until everything she and Nathan had accomplished was destroyed?

51

Keri pushed away her barely touched plate of food. There didn't seem to be any point in sitting mulling over what might or might not happen and with a final sip of the wine she gave an apologetic shake of her head. 'I'm sorry, I'm not feeling much like eating or drinking these days.' She gathered her jacket and bag. 'I'll leave you to finish your lunch in peace, thank you for meeting me.'

'You were obviously hoping the Federation's decision to investigate the apprentice's death had nothing to do with your husband's murder. I'm sorry I wasn't able to give you better news.' Radstock stretched a hand across the table. 'If there's anything I can do to help, please shout.'

His hand was big, bony and dry. Keri's was lost in it and for a moment it gave her comfort. 'You're very kind. I hope our companies survive this intact.' Withdrawing her hand, she shuffled along the seat and got to her feet.

Outside, a tiny finger of panic poked her. She should have rung for an Uber when she was inside. Now, it would necessitate taking her eyes from their continuous search of every passing face... looking for what? She didn't know. Maybe that woman

Tracy Wirick... maybe someone she'd never met... a knife-wielding monster who could blend in with the crowd.

It made sense to retreat inside but then Radstock would see her fear. Regardless of how nice a guy he appeared to be, in the business world showing fear wasn't an option.

Keri swallowed hard and edged to the inside of the footpath. There was a taxi rank outside Victoria Station. It wasn't far. Five minutes' walk, no more.

It felt like an eternity.

She hogged the inside of the pathway as much as possible, forcing oncoming pedestrians to swerve around her. The notion that her leather handbag might deflect a knife attack made her slip the handles over her head as she walked and carry it under her chin like a horse's nosebag. It garnered her strange looks but she didn't care.

There was a queue at the taxi rank. Keri assessed every face as she walked to join the end. Anxiously, she shifted her weight from foot to foot and looked over her shoulder. Once she spun around when she thought she saw someone familiar causing the elderly couple who were standing behind her to take a step backwards in alarm.

'Sorry,' she muttered, turning back. When she looked over her shoulder again seconds later, she noticed they'd taken a further step away as if fearful of her. She looked straight ahead with hot tears building. *Falling apart.* Maybe they were right to be afraid of her.

The queue moved quickly and five minutes later there was only one person ahead of her. A young woman with long hair in dreadlocks, multiple piercings to her lips, eyebrows, and ears. It was warm where they stood and she dragged off the heavy jacket she was wearing to expose bare arms.

Keri was immediately fixated by the striking tattoo of an eye on the woman's upper arm. It was staring at Keri, peering straight into her soul. Panic flooded her and she wanted to run. Away from the weird eye, from Victoria Station, her life, the appalling tragedy that it had become. All the sadness and guilt. Her overwhelming, catastrophic loss.

'You have this one,' the tattooed woman said softly to Keri as a taxi pulled up. 'You look like you're having a bad day and could do with some kindness.'

Keri stared at her and started to cry.

52

The kindness of the woman with her strange tattoo was almost Keri's undoing. She managed a mumbled, tear-choked 'thank you' before climbing gratefully into the taxi.

The driver tilted his head waiting for directions. He pulled away when she waved at him with one hand, the other clamped over her mouth to stop the sobs that were lining up to escape.

Perhaps the taxi driver had experienced a similar situation before. It was almost five minutes later before Keri was back in control. She unhooked her handbag from around her neck, dropped it on the seat beside her and sat back with a final snuffle.

The taxi was moving. She wasn't sure she cared where they were going. It took another five minutes for her to realise they weren't, in fact, going anywhere. The driver was doing the circle of Victoria Street, Lower Grosvenor Place, Bressenden Place, back onto Victoria Street and around again. Around and around.

Perhaps she should let him continue, put her head back and get some sleep. It was tempting. With a sigh, she sat forward. 'Thank you. Now, if we could go to Northampton Park.'

'Good. I was getting dizzy.'

Keri rested her head back and shut her eyes, not to sleep, that was a distant hope, but to try to get her thoughts in order. Once she was home, she'd ring DI Elliot and ask him to call around. Tell him about the Stone Federation investigation, the email they'd received. The detective could put it all together, maybe it would help him catch whatever maniac was out there still searching for revenge.

A maniac who knew where she lived.

She opened her bag to search for her mobile. It would be better if Abbie and Daniel stayed elsewhere but she knew they'd want to be with her, especially if they thought she was in any kind of danger. It would need clever planning. She rang Daniel's number first, grunting in annoyance when it went to voicemail. Rather than leaving a message, she tried Abbie's number. Something was going her way, it was answered on the first ring.

'Hi Mum, you doing okay?'

'I'm fine, Abs, how about you?'

'Up and down. You were right though, it was better to come back to lectures.' Her sigh was long and sad. 'People are being nice.'

Keri heard the pain in her daughter's voice and wished she could magic it away. She couldn't, but she could keep her safe. 'That's good. I'm on my way home. You were right, it was too soon to go into the office, but I don't want to hang around the house either so I'm going to stay with Philip and Louisa for a couple of days. They said you and Daniel are welcome to come too, but I wondered if you'd prefer to stay with your friends. You still have some of your belongings with them, don't you?'

'Yeeesss.' Abbie drew out the one word as she wondered if there was something behind what Keri was saying. Always wary. She and Abbie were so alike it was scary.

'Just for a few days.' Keri stopped herself saying more. Gilding the lily would make her daughter more suspicious.

'If you're sure.'

'I am. I can sit and chat to Louisa and Philip. You and Daniel sit and talk to your friends. It will help us all. In a couple of days, we can go back home and start adjusting.'

'Right.' It was obvious Abbie wasn't convinced.

'I've tried to get Daniel but he's not answering, can I leave it to you to talk to him?'

'Sure, I can get hold of him. He'll be okay, he's got good friends.'

'Okay.' Keri wanted to tell her daughter to stay safe, to avoid isolated places, to watch out for strangers. For monsters. 'I'll ring you tomorrow, make sure you're okay. Love you, darling daughter.'

'Love you too, adorable ma.'

Keri hung up and sat back with a smile. *Adorable ma*. The smile faded. How adorable would Abbie think if she knew Keri had cheated on Nathan.

At least Keri was going to be spared that horror. Nobody would ever need know about Barry Morgan.

The traffic was heavy and it was another twenty-five minutes before the taxi pulled up outside her home. 'Thank you,' she said, handing the driver the fare plus a healthy tip for his kindness. She was on the footpath, the car door shut behind her before she thought to ask the driver to wait until she was inside. Stupid fear. She hesitated too long and as she turned to make the request, the taxi pulled away.

The street was empty. Not a person in sight. But it didn't mean there wasn't someone hiding behind one of the gate pillars or garden walls, even hunkered down behind one of the many parked cars. Hiding and waiting for the right opportunity to pounce.

Inside, she'd be safer. The house looked as it always did: a family home that had been filled with love and happiness.

It looked the same but it was different. Abbie and Daniel would no doubt spend more nights at home for a few weeks, but they'd soon adjust to their new normal. Then, with the resilience for which youth is famed, they'd get on with their lives. Spend more time with their friends. Maybe they'd move into a place of their own. They would hesitate and she'd have to give them that final nudge, unwilling that they should sacrifice their futures for her past.

She opened the garden gate and climbed the steps to the front door, carefully avoiding the one where the wreath and rat had been left. By the time she'd reached the top step, she'd made a decision. The house needed a family, not a lonely woman rattling around the rooms. She'd sell up and buy an apartment. A penthouse maybe, with a view where she could sit, drink wine, and reminisce.

Maybe she'd get a cat. She'd always wanted one but Nathan was... had been... allergic.

She fished in her bag for her house keys. Two locks, two separate keys. Then she was pushing the door open into her big, lonely, silent house.

Silent?

It shouldn't be. There should be a beep beep from the alarm.

53

Keri had put the house alarm on, hadn't she?

She was religious about doing so. Nathan used to laugh that she'd put it on even when going to the local shops only ten minutes' walk away. *Always.*

But had she done so that morning with all that was on her mind? Maybe the combination of grief and guilt had impacted on her ability to think straight.

She shut the front door and tossed her handbag on the bottom step of the stairs. The silence of the house was almost overpowering, pressing down on her shoulders, making her feet heavy so that each step required a huge amount of concentration. In the living room, she flopped down on the sofa and dropped her head back, eyes gritty from too many tears.

Nathan. How was she going to live without him? What was the point? Whether she was rattling around in this big house or sitting in a fancy apartment looking out over a view she'd nobody to share with.

It would get easier. The pain would fade, the spiky edge of it filed down to a weary continual numbness. Was that preferable? A long slow decline rather than a sharp sudden descent. She shut her eyes, dislodging a hot tear. It trickled down her cheek and plopped onto the collar of her jacket.

A loud bang made her eyes fly open and stare unblinking at the ceiling. They'd lived in this house for almost twenty years. She knew every creak in the floorboards, every rattle of the plumbing, the low hum when the heating clicked on, the squeak of the antique wardrobe in the spare bedroom. Nothing made a loud bang.

Unless... had she left a window open? Or maybe Abbie or Daniel had. She was constantly warning them to shut them before they left their bedrooms but normally Keri would go to check. Just in case.

She hadn't that morning.

And had forgotten to put the alarm on.

Grief was making her stupidly forgetful, maybe she needed to start making lists.

Top of her mental to-do list was to ring DI Elliot to tell him about the email to the Stone Federation and her fears that she or her children or both might be next in someone's plan for vengeance.

She had reached into her pocket for her mobile when the bang came again. From where she sat, she could see the wind blowing through trees in the back garden, the branches swaying with alarming abandon. She'd better go to find what window was open and shut it before something got broken. With her mobile in one hand, she shuffled to the edge of the sofa and got to her feet.

The stairway of the old Victorian house ascended eight steps to a return where the main bathroom was situated, then it swung upward several more steps to the first floor. A separate spiral staircase led from the landing to the attic den.

Keri had started on the second set of steps when she heard a squeak.

You should squirt a bit of WD-40 on the bathroom door hinges. Was it only last week she'd said that to Nathan? He swore by the stuff, would walk around the house armed with it, squirting it willy-nilly.

But maybe he'd forgotten or got waylaid by something more important. Or maybe he'd run out of the damn stuff. 'How many tins of that do we go through?' she'd asked him once when she'd seen him with a can in hand. Critical, complaining. She wished she'd bought more. A gallon of it. Several gallons. She'd never get the chance now to make him happy.

It was seconds before fear broke through her sorrow. Why was the bathroom door squeaking? It only did so when it was being opened and it was shut when she'd passed it. She resisted the temptation to turn. Instead, she bounded up the last couple of steps and ran across the landing to her bedroom. She slammed the heavy pine door shut behind her and reached without stopping for the key to lock it top and bottom.

Fear was deafening, numbing, overwhelming. Keri could do nothing except slump to the floor and tremble.

She tried to think rationally. There had been no sign of a break-in. Perhaps the bathroom door hadn't been shut tightly and a breeze had squeezed through the big sash window to give it enough of a nudge to make it squeak.

It was possible, she wanted to believe it, but terror had her in its grip, reminding her that her death was probably the next step in a madman's plan for vengeance.

54

If there was someone on the other side of the door they were being quiet. Keri pressed her ear against it, but all she could hear was the wind swirling leaves against the bedroom window behind her. It whistled down the chimney too, an eerie sound that Nathan had said gave him the shivers. She used to laugh at him, but she wasn't laughing now as she stared over at the fireplace waiting for an intruder to slither down like an evil Santa Claus.

Fear and anger jostled for first place, anger winning by a small margin as she thought of all she'd been through in the last couple of weeks. She banged a fist on the door. 'Is there someone there? What do you want?'

There was no answer. Nothing to be heard. She rested her forehead against the smooth wood, frustration coursing through her. Perhaps she should face whoever was out there, take back control of something.

It was Abbie and Daniel that kept her strong. If Keri thought that her life would be the end of this crazed person's need for revenge she might have opened the door and got it over with.

She wasn't sure if she believed in life after death. But in death, she'd be in the same place as Nathan, and that had to be better than being here without him.

But she'd do anything to save her children.

She'd stay locked behind this door until the police arrived. Her mobile was in her hand, she lifted it to ring and looked in disbelief at the blank screen.

Irrationally, she blamed the intruder but then the truth hit her. She hadn't charged her phone recently.

Despair swallowed her, the darkness of it blinding her so that more precious time was lost before she remembered the rarely used landline. The phone was on her bedside table. She hurried across to it, picked up the handset and pressed 999. Her eyes never left the door as she waited for the call to connect. The house was old, the original doors heavy, the lock set in the top and bottom designed to make the door almost impenetrable.

Nathan insisted the house was impregnable. Front and back doors were double-locked. Every window had a lock, plus stops to prevent the sash windows from being opened more than two inches. *Impregnable.* So, how could someone have got inside?

Was she simply being paranoid?

She supposed she was allowed to be a little wary considering everything that had happened recently and she'd nearly reached the conclusion she was being silly when she realised her call hadn't been answered. Had she dialled? Swearing softly, she pressed 999 and held the phone to her ear. No dial tone. No nothing. She looked at it in horror. Tried again. Nothing.

The eerie ghost-story whistle of wind blowing down the bedroom fireplace startled her into dropping the useless handset on the bed and taking a step backward, then another until she was at the window. Turning, she stared out. Should she open the window the two inches allowed and shout for help?

But even if she could make her voice heard over the howling wind, there was nobody on the street to hear her.

Leaves were pirouetting along the middle of the road, branches of trees bowing in admiration. Dark clouds dropped a curtain of heavy rain, making the day unusually dark and adding to the dread that was seeping into her bones.

She tried to shake the feeling away. It was a storm. Maybe that was why her landline was dead and doors were banging and squeaking. It was nothing more menacing than British weather.

With a final look up and down the street in search of a saviour, she turned back to face the room. Her mobile charger was downstairs. She should go down. *Grab it, lock herself into the utility room and phone for help.*

Paranoid, stupid and pathetic. She sat on the corner of the bed, running a hand automatically over the silk bedcover she and Nathan had bought in a shop in India two years before. They had been dazzled by the colours and fabrics and found it impossible to choose between different patterns. Nathan had come up with the perfect solution. He'd insisted on buying one of each and had them shipped home.

'We'll have them forever,' he'd said when she'd remonstrated and frowned at the cost.

Forever. Wasn't it supposed to last more than two years?

She sank back onto the bed, spreading her arms out. The sound of the wind outside was louder, the whistle down the chimney a shrill, off-tone accompaniment. Keri shut her eyes and fanned her fingers over the silk of the bedcovering.

Memories came swirling back. That shop in India. The kaleidoscope of colours as the assistant shook each of the covers out and let them float down onto the pile that was building on the carpeted floor. The dry dusty smell. Nathan's dazzling smile. His sheer enjoyment in everything they did.

Life for him was a continuous adventure and if she baulked at something, he was there to grin and drag her onward.

He'd swing her around in his arms and insist they had to make the most of every minute.

Even in her dreams she wept for the minutes she'd not listened to him.

55

The room was in semi-darkness when Keri woke, her face slick with tears. Disorientated, she struggled to get back to sleep, to a dream where Nathan was still alive, but it faded away, as dreams do, and as it did fear slithered back. Unable to believe she'd fallen asleep, she lifted her head to look round the room. Had she imagined someone was in the house?

The curtains were open and the street lights illuminated the furniture but the edges and corners of the room were dark. The bedroom door was locked, she reminded herself. Impregnable. There was nobody waiting in the shadows.

No intruder waiting anywhere in the house.

But the alarm had been off.

She pushed that thought aside, reached out for the bedside lamp, and switched it on, flooding the room with light. And clarity. She'd been tired. The conversation with Tom Radstock had put her on edge and worry had done the rest, sending her into a spiral of paranoia. She lifted her wrist to check her watch, surprised to see she'd slept for two hours.

Maybe now she'd find it easier to get her thoughts together. First thing on her to-do list. Ring DI Elliot.

The storm appeared to have passed. With a lick of hope, she reached for the landline handset but it was still dead. That didn't mean anything, storm damage could take hours, even days to repair.

Everything was okay. She'd been stupid. This room, the house, they were impregnable.

'Almost a fortress.' She continued to reassure herself as she pressed her ear to the door for a long time before lifting a hand to undo one lock, then the other. She listened again before turning the door knob to open the door an inch, peering through, listening again. On high alert, all her senses intensified, she opened it fully.

The house was quiet.

Remembering the initial bangs that had startled her, she slipped along the landing to Daniel's room. Inside, she saw she'd been right, his window had been left open enough to have caused a draft. End of that mystery.

Keri managed a laugh when she thought of how frightened she'd been. How embarrassing it would have been had she managed to get through to the police. They'd have had to break down the front door to come to her rescue. With a shake of her head at how easily she'd been reduced to a trembling wreck, she picked up her dead mobile and went downstairs.

The hallway light had come on automatically but the kitchen and living room were in darkness when she pushed open the door. Her hand slid up the wall for the switch, the room flooding with light that made her blink.

In the seconds that took her eyes to readjust to the brightness her brain had taken in the sight of the person sitting at the breakfast bar holding a long sharp knife. Keri recognised it as one of a set she'd bought. They were viciously sharp.

Lethal, Nathan had called them when he'd sliced a finger the only time he'd used them.

Keri pictured it cutting through the skin of her neck, dissecting sinews, muscle, tendons, slicing across the artery. It was so sharp there would probably be little pain as her blood pumped. *Dead before she hit the floor.* Is that what her children would be told?

56

Keri thought about running to the front door but knew she wouldn't make it before feeling the knife in her back. Death didn't scare her, but she wasn't leaving her body there to be found by Abbie and Daniel. Leaving Abbie with a lifetime of guilt for not coming home when she knew something wasn't quite right.

Keri's eyes flicked to where the mobile phone charger sat on a shelf behind the sofa. Maybe with the element of surprise in her favour, she could grab it and race to the utility room. She discounted the idea when she saw the malicious gleam on the face of the pleasant, helpful agency temp. With a lethal blade in his hand, Luke didn't seem quite so like Tom Cruise anymore. Even with adrenaline pumping through her veins, she couldn't move fast enough to avoid being sliced into ribbons.

But she wasn't giving up yet. Playing stupid might give her time, and time would give her opportunity. 'Hi, were you trying to get hold of me? The storm seems to have knocked the phone out.'

'And your mobile's flat.'

Keri frowned. 'How did you kn–'

'Because I'm not thick!' Luke rammed the point of the knife into the door of the cupboard under the breakfast counter. 'I saw you run to your room with your mobile in your hand, if it had been working you'd have used it. I'd already sorted the landline so I knew you couldn't use that. I've been sitting here waiting for hours. If the police were going to come, they'd have been here by now.'

Keri edged towards the sofa. If she could get a little closer...

'Sit there.' The knife was pointed to the stool on the opposite side of the breakfast bar. 'It's time we got to know each other a bit more.'

'I don't think we know each other at all,' Keri said, moving to the indicated stool and perching on the side of the seat.

The laugh had a manic edge to it. 'Oh, I know far more than you think. How you and that husband of yours were so desperate to make a success of your shitty little business that you were willing to do anything... including murder a boy.'

'It wasn't murder.' Maybe it was the wrong time to be pedantic, but Nathan hadn't murdered anyone. 'Jim Cody's death was an accident.'

'An accident! He was exposed to high levels of crystalline silica while your damn husband breathed through his respirator. He didn't see the lethal dust that covered Jim's face, he just saw pound signs.'

'You can't know that: you weren't there.' As arguments went, it was pretty futile and she saw the face opposite tighten in anger.

'No, I wasn't, but Jim told my mother. She said he'd been so excited at working with such a well-known stonemason. Jim told her about being covered in white dust while he worked and how he'd spent a long time brushing it off before he caught the bus home. She said he was still brushing it from his hair that night.'

'Your mother?'

'She was sixteen and pregnant, but she didn't know and by the time she did, Jim, my father, was already sick.'

'I'm so sorry.' What more could she say? Impossible to turn back the clock and protect the enthusiastic young man, to tell Nathan that the money was never that important, that they'd have made it without taking such hideous risks with such catastrophic results. To turn the clock back and save Nathan so they could have that future they'd planned.

'She never wanted to talk about my father. I only knew that he'd died before I was born, then a year ago I got into a bit of trouble so she sat me down and told me everything.' Confusion slipped across Luke's face. 'I think she thought if she told me, it would make me consider how lucky I was to have a future, that I wouldn't waste it getting into stupid fights.' He waved the knife. 'She was right. I wasn't going to waste it anymore. I discovered I had a mission. To get revenge for my father. It didn't take me long to find out all about you and Metcalfe Conservation and that gangster Dexter Sylvester and his company.'

'You murdered Sylvester and Nathan.' *This was the monster who had destroyed her life.* 'I assume you were also responsible for Roy. What did he ever do to you, he wasn't even working for us when your father died?'

'That was all his damn fault, the stupid little man.' Luke waved the knife around. 'I had it all so carefully planned. I needed the paperwork to prove what your company did to my father so I found out which employment agency you used.' He smirked in satisfaction. 'Roy gave me the answer to that question when I rang Metcalfe Conservation. I said I worked for a company in the building next door and wondered if he could recommend an agency.'

Keri could imagine Roy wanting to be helpful. She'd liked to have reached over and smacked the smug expression from Luke's face.

'It was simple after that. I had enough IT skills to apply for a job with the agency, then I waited for the opportunity to arise. I wasn't in a hurry. It took two months before one day's work at Metcalfe Conservation came up and I jumped at it.'

Keri's head was buzzing. A thought managed to fight its way through the confusion. 'Why didn't you get what you wanted then? Why did you have to kill Roy?'

So quickly she didn't have time to pull away, Luke reached across with the knife and nicked the skin on her cheek. 'So beautiful but so fucking stupid.' He sat back and wiped the bloody tip of the knife on the sleeve of his shirt before sliding the blade back and forth across the granite counter. Sharpening the already lethal edge. 'It should have gone according to plan. Get the paperwork I needed. Get a close-up view of the couple who'd murdered my father through those fucking stupid glass walls.' He laughed. 'Seriously, whose poncy idea were they?'

Keri didn't think he really wanted to start a conversation about interior design but keeping him talking seemed to be a good idea. 'A company called Walthamstow Detail, they're very modern, very styl–'

The knife was jabbed towards her, shutting her up. 'I don't give a toss about the damn designer, you stupid cow. Getting a look at the two of you was only part of what I'd hoped to achieve that day. The most important part was to get the damn paperwork, but I didn't get it because the stupid suspicious man only gave me limited access to the files. In the note he left, he said to leave any queries for him to deal with the following day.'

Anger distorted Luke's face. 'I should have killed him then but I hoped Tracy would be able to g–'

'Tracy Wirick?' Keri shook her head, it was all falling together. 'She was working for you. I thought maybe she was the person responsible for Roy's death.'

Luke laughed at that. 'Tracy? She wouldn't hurt a fly.' He

waved the knife. 'She'd do anything for me though. I thought she'd be able to work on Roy and get a look at the files, but he was cagey about what he showed her.'

He tapped the point of the knife on the granite, an almost melodic tink tink tink that was loud in the silence, then remained as background music when he spoke. 'I thought Tracy would be able to wind him around her fingers and get what I wanted but she blew it by asking the wrong damn questions. She said he'd started watching her carefully and asking her pointed questions. I guessed he knew she was up to something, so I had to act.'

That was what Roy was going to tell her. Keri wished once again that she'd given him the time to do so. Not that it would have altered the course of events. Had he passed on his concerns about Tracy, she'd simply have given the woman her marching orders. It wouldn't have saved any lives, not Roy's, not Nathan's.

The point of the knife was hitting the granite harder, the sound discordant, grating. 'Roy was such a trusting fuck when I called in that morning. I told him I'd lost an earring the day I'd worked there and wondered if it had rolled under the desk. He laughed and told me to search away.

'He was still laughing when I dropped the knife I was hiding up my sleeve into my hand and cut his throat.'

57

Anger bubbled. Keri wanted to grab the knife and wipe the grin from Luke's face.

He must have seen her expression tighten. He pointed the knife at her. 'I wouldn't try anything if I were you.'

Keri slumped back on the stool, despair defeating her. The cut to her cheek stung and she felt blood trickle from it but she refused to lift a hand to wipe it away. Refused to acknowledge any action of the monster sitting opposite. With his malevolent grin and soulless eyes this was the real Luke. His disguise had been good.

'My mother said my father was clever, I like to think I take after him. I'd made sure to tell the agency how much I'd enjoyed working for Metcalfe Conservation, then made sure I was free when you rang for someone to take over when Roy had–' He jerked his thumb downward. '–departed for elsewhere. Of course, you gave me full access to all the files then.' He sliced through the air. 'Success! All so beautifully organised, if I do say so myself.'

He seemed to lose himself in self-congratulation. Keri looked across to where her charger sat. So close, so far away.

That wasn't going to be her answer. She needed to think of a plan B.

Luke tapped the knife on the granite again. He was looking at Keri as if trying to decide exactly where to stab her.

'So, Roy had simply been in the way. The destruction of Metcalfe Conservation and DS Construction and the killing of Nathan and Sylvester was your plan for avenging your father's death?' Keri expected the answer to be *yes*, her question was simply meant to keep him talking in the hope that the longer he did, the more chance her brain would have to come up with options. She expected him to say *yes*, so she was thrown when he said *no*.

Luke laughed, a long belly laugh that stopped as quickly as it started. 'That caught you out, didn't it?'

'Yes.'

A smile hovered on his lips as he stared at her. There was a smug satisfied glint in his cold eyes and if Keri had any doubt that he was going to kill her it was gone in that moment. Whatever his reason for what he was doing, she knew that pleasure played a big part. He enjoyed killing. The power trip. The blood thirst.

'Actually,' he said, with a swirl of the knife, 'I'm not being quite honest. When my mother told me about my father, I was angry that the two companies had got away with their part in his death. But my original plan was simple. Get enough proof to destroy both. Roy was... what's that wonderful expression they use?' Luke's eyes gleamed. 'Ah yes, *collateral damage*.'

Anger shot through her, dispelling the desperate dismay that had been weighing her down. 'But then you got the taste for killing, did you?'

His expression registered puzzlement. 'A taste for it? No, you're wrong. That wasn't what changed my strategy. It was that damn poster. When I saw it, I knew my idea for revenge wasn't good enough.'

Keri stared at him blankly for a second before it dawned on her what he was talking about. The photograph of her and Nathan that Abbie had blown up for their anniversary. Had that only been a couple of weeks before? Keri hadn't been happy with the poster, too afraid that Barry might see it, that it might spoil her illicit affair. That stupid pointless affair.

Now it seemed there was another reason to be unhappy about it.

Luke pointed the knife at her. 'That photograph of the two of you staring into one another's eyes, your future stretching ahead of you, a future you stole from my father. Twenty-five years of wedded bliss, the poster said. Almost all the years you took from him. That's when it hit me that the mere destruction of the two companies wasn't enough.'

'So, you decided to murder Nathan and Sylvester as well as Roy. Three deaths for one.'

'Only three? Oh no, you're wrong there.' The knife was held up and tilted to catch the light from the overhead bulb. 'It's going to take a lot more than that to make up for what you denied my father. The business he could have built, the children he could have had. The sisters and brothers I should have had. It seems only fair that I should deprive you of what you deprived him.'

Keri saw the truth in his eyes, heard it in his self-justifying words. He didn't care about a father he'd never known, didn't need an excuse for what he did. The reality was, she, Nathan and Roy had been unlucky. Their lives had intersected with that of a psychopath. Steel slid up her spine. She couldn't bring Nathan or Roy back. But she could stop this monster killing her children. Even if she had to die in the process.

She needed him to make one mistake. Just one and she'd make her move. 'You keep telling yourself that you're doing it for your father, keep lying about the real reason. That you're a monster who doesn't really care who he kills. Admit it. Go on, admit it, you know you want to,' she taunted, letting her eyes slide over him, her lips curling in a sneer. 'You enjoy killing. I bet you've fantasised about it for years. Your father's history simply gave you the perfect excuse.'

'It's revenge,' he snarled. 'I'm going to wait until your brats get home, then I'm going to kill you all.'

Keri laughed then. It startled him, making him loosen his grip on the knife. It fell to the counter with a clatter. Too far away for Keri to reach, but she was getting to him. She had to keep needling him.

'I don't think you did it on your own. I think Tracy or someone else helped you.' Keri folded her arms across her chest and frowned as she realised she had to be right. The morning Nathan was killed, Luke was in the reception when she left. She'd caught him out, maybe this was her opportunity. 'Who is it, Luke? Who does the dirty work that you take credit for, who makes you feel like a man?'

'I don't need any–'

'Liar!' She leaned across the counter. A drop of blood from the cut on her cheek fell and landed in a shimmering circle on the grey granite. 'You were in reception when I went to look for Nathan the morning he was murdered. Not even your colossal ego can put you in two places at the same time.'

A smile appeared. It was a nasty, foul tilt of his lips. He reached a free hand across the counter. She reared back making his smile grow wider. Then he ran his thumb through the drop of blood on the counter, brought it to his mouth and sucked it. It was a shockingly lascivious act. Suddenly Keri felt very afraid. There were, after all, worse things than death.

He withdrew his thumb slightly and circled it with his tongue.

Keri vowed she'd cut her own throat before she'd let him touch her. She was going to die anyway, she'd prefer to do so with the memory of Nathan's body in her mind, not this monster.

'You think you're so clever.' Luke wiped his thumb down the front of his shirt and sat back. 'You and your stupid, pretentious glass office. What did the designer tell you? That it indicated how transparent the company was in its business dealings, was that it?'

Keri wasn't going to admit that it was exactly what the designer had said. 'It was to let plenty of light in actually.'

'I bet you felt like a fucking goldfish in your office.'

'Not particularly,' she lied.

'I bet you thought you saw everything that was going on. Bet you thought you had your finger on the fucking pulse of everything.'

If his language was anything to go by, he was losing control. It was what Keri wanted but she still had no idea what she was going to do.

'Do you have any idea how pathetically stupid you are.' He laughed. A shrill demonic sound that seemed to echo around the room. 'You didn't even notice I was missing that morning when I left to follow your moronic husband to the café.'

Keri was stunned. He was right. She did think she saw everything. How could she not have noticed Luke had left reception? 'But you were there when I went to look for Nathan...'

Luke's smile was smug, self-satisfied. 'It was close. I had to be careful on my way back to avoid CCTV cameras so I only got back minutes before you came out of your office. Then I noticed blood on my shirtsleeve so I had to hurriedly pull on my jacket.'

He folded his arms, the knife resting along his upper arm, the point near his neck.

Keri stared at it. If she could reach across and push his elbow hard, drive that point into his carotid. Have him die in the same way as he'd killed Nathan.

'One of the coffees he bought was for me, can you believe that?'

'Nathan was a very thoughtful man. He'd never have gone for coffee without getting one for you.'

'So generous. Coffee and buns for everyone. It meant his hands were full though and he struggled to open the door. He was surprised but pleased to see me and so grateful when I opened it for him.' Luke lifted the knife and rested the blade against his neck. 'He wasn't so grateful when I slit his throat though.'

'But you messed that up, didn't you?'

She saw his eyes darken in anger. Maybe now she'd have a chance.

58

Keri braced herself. If Luke put the knife down or showed the slightest weakness she'd make a move. Adrenaline had diluted the fear a little, desperation to stop this monster harming Abbie or Daniel had done the rest. She'd become the clichéd mother hen defending her chicks.

Her shoulders slumped when she saw the anger on his face fade away and the smile reappear. 'I must admit, I was taken aback when you rang to say Nathan had been injured, not killed.' He shook his head. 'Roy and Dexter Sylvester had been sitting down and I hadn't made allowance for the height discrepancy. I was worried for a time, but when flashing blue lights and sirens didn't arrive at the door of the office I guessed I'd done enough damage to stop him giving the game away. You can imagine my relief the next day when you rang to say Nathan had died.' He wiped a hand across his brow. 'Phew!'

Bitter hatred shot through Keri. That Nathan should have died at the hands of such an evil man made his death all the more monstrous.

'So, no, I don't think I messed up, plus–' He waved a hand around the room. '–how do you think I got in here?' There was a maniacal lilt to his laugh as he lifted the knife and made an imaginary slice through the air. 'While I was cutting his throat, I was feeling in his jacket pocket for his keys. Then I simply waited for the right opportunity.' He laughed louder at her horrified expression. 'And as for your security alarm. Seriously! The year of your children's birth. Have you no imagination?'

Keri ignored him. She was imagining Nathan, his hands full of takeaway coffees and sticky buns, smiling at Luke as he went through the door. She was glad her wonderful husband hadn't remembered that betrayal. 'Right,' she said now, suddenly weary. 'You're going to kill me, get it over with. I'm getting tired and bored with this.'

His smile slipped away and for a second he looked unsure of his next step, then he stuck out his tongue and flicked it. 'I might have some fun with you first.'

She bared her teeth. 'Try it.' Her voice was a ragged snarl. 'I swear, I will chew you to pieces. I might die in the process but I won't go easily.'

Stalemate. They faced each other across the breakfast bar. Keri's breath came in noisy gusts, as he continued to wave his foul tongue. Spittle formed on the corners of his mouth. She would rather die than have him touch her.

He sucked his tongue back inside and wiped his mouth with his hand. 'We'll wait till your son and daughter get here. I've seen her photograph, she's pretty. I wonder what she'd do for me to save her mother.'

Abbie... Keri knew she'd do anything for her mother, but her daughter was safe. 'They're not coming home, they're staying with friends.'

The bottom of the knife handle crashed on the granite. 'Stop underestimating me. I've seen your eyes wandering towards your phone charger.' He curled his lip at her surprise. 'You think I hadn't noticed? Fucking stupid bitch. I bet your mobile is in your pocket. I'm going to plug it in, slice your PIN number out of you, then send your precious son and daughter a message telling them to come home.' He mimicked a high-pitched voice, 'I need you.' He banged the counter again. 'How long do you think before they come barrelling through the door to be with their darling mother?'

Not long. He was right, they'd ring first and when they didn't get a reply, they'd come home immediately. Abbie would be frantic and insist on taking a taxi. Keri looked at the monster sitting opposite. He was right, Abbie would do anything if she thought it would mean saving her mother. She'd never understand there was no way out for any of them.

Keri looked straight into Luke's eyes. 'I'd kill you first.'

What he might have said in return she didn't know because a sound from the hallway startled them.

59

Keri and Luke stared towards the open door to the hallway but it took one word to restart the action.

One word. 'Mum.' Daniel was home.

Keri turned back to Luke. He was looking confused as he tried to adjust his plans. It worked for her. She jumped to her feet, grabbed the stool she'd been sitting on and swung it with adrenaline-fuelled strength. It hit him but she didn't wait to see what damage she'd done, taking off at speed for the door and flying through it.

Daniel was kicking off his trainers and looked up in surprise when she appeared. 'Hi, I thought–'

Keri saw he'd put the safety chain on the front door and groaned. Of all the times he'd chosen to do what he was supposed to. Footsteps were thumping behind her. 'Run, Daniel!' She shoved him through the door into the small front sitting room and slammed the door behind them. Luke pushed it from the other side and almost succeeded in opening it before Daniel had recovered enough from the shock to turn and help her. They shut it, but there was no lock on this door.

'Put your weight against it,' she said and looked around the room for something to use as a barricade. The elegant sofa, the small side tables, all designed to look pretty in a room they never used, all absolutely useless for her need.

'Shit!'

Keri turned to see Daniel looking at his side. Luke had shoved the knife through the panelled door and caught him.

'Daniel, be careful,' she yelled, seeing the door move.

He put his shoulder against it again and shut it. 'Get the bookcase.'

The bookcase. The only solid piece of furniture in the room. Keri tried to move it but the tall mahogany unit had been in the same spot for years, its base embedded into the deep pile of the carpet. She ignored the cries from Daniel and the snarls and threats coming through the door and swept books, ornaments, and photo frames from the shelves, sending them flying. Once empty, she rocked the unit and freed it. 'It's coming, Daniel. Hold on.'

She toppled it over onto its side, then got behind and pushed. Blood was running down Daniel's arms, his face pale as he kept his shoulder against the door. The tip of the knife came through missing him by an inch. Keri manoeuvred the bookcase back on its feet and tried to slide it across the door, but the knife came through again, further this time, more anger and savagery behind it. When it was withdrawn, she shoved the bookcase into place before Luke could try again.

She and Daniel leaned against it, panting. 'You okay?' Keri asked.

'I think so. Who *is* that?'

'His name is Luke, he's the man who killed your dad and Roy.'

A loud bang on the door made them jump. 'He's trying to get through. Ring the police, quick.'

'It's in my bag, Mum,' Daniel whispered, colour rushing

from his face, horror creeping into his eyes. 'My phone. It's outside in my bag.'

Keri turned to look at her handsome son, his unusually serious face looking so like Nathan's she wanted to cry and drag him into her arms, protect him like she'd not been able to do with her husband. Blood was seeping through Daniel's shirt and dripping from his fingers. One spot was directly over his heart, like the spot of Nathan's blood she'd seen on the surgeon's hospital scrubs. So much blood, too much loss. She'd lost enough. It was time to get clever. 'Okay,' she said. 'Luke doesn't know you don't have your phone with you. Pretend to ring the police, raise your voice.'

He turned to face the door. 'Hello. Police. We have an intruder in our house armed with a knife.' He gave their address. 'We've locked ourselves in a room, please hurry.'

There was silence from the other side, then another louder bang that made the door and bookcase shudder. 'He doesn't believe us,' Daniel said.

'He's guessing it will take them several minutes to get here.' Keri pushed panic out of her head. She needed to stay calm. Think. If they only had something to defend themselves with but looking around the room there was nothing. They never used the fire so there wasn't even a convenient poker. But something did catch her eye. A bowl she'd swept from the bookshelf had scattered its contents and among them was something she recognised. The keys to the locks on the sash window.

She looked back to Daniel. 'We're getting out of here! I need you to stay strong for another few minutes.' She ran for the keys, grabbed them, and hurried to the windows.

Two locks. She slotted the key in place, damp fingers slipping on the metal. The first lock opened easily, the second was tight. She rubbed her sweaty hand down her blouse and tried again, ignoring the shouts of anger coming through the door, Daniel's cries of alarm.

The locks were open, but she still needed to remove the stops on each side that prevented the window from opening more than a couple of inches. They came away easily. She flung them to the floor and put the heel of her hand on the cross bar to push it open. It didn't budge.

'Shit! Daniel, it's stuck, you try.'

She took his place pressed against the door and watched while he attempted to lever the window upwards.

He stopped, wiped his bloody hands on his jeans and pushed again, grunting with the effort. 'It's not budging.' He peered closer, then rested his forehead against the glass. 'Remember when you had them painted last year.'

'It's painted shut?'

'Yes.'

A louder bang was followed by the distinct sound of wood splintering. It sounded like Luke had found something to use as a battering ram. They didn't have long. 'Quick. Try the top sash. It might be free.' Something had to work in their favour.

Daniel stood on the window seat to reach the top sash and put his finger through the loop to pull. The window moved smoothly down.

But success came too late. With a loud crack, the door gave way and the bookcase was pushed forward trapping Keri underneath when it fell.

60

Keri was stunned, the weight of the bookcase pressing her into the carpet, pain making it hard to focus. She would have shut her eyes and given in to the creeping darkness if she hadn't heard Daniel's cry. Her big gentle boy crying out in fear and pain.

Her right arm was useless. From the searing pain, she guessed it was broken. She tried to push upward to move the bookshelf but it wouldn't budge or maybe she was simply too weak and useless. *Ms Fix-it.* She couldn't save her son.

More yells and shouts came from a distance. Daniel's voice. He was alive. She still had a chance to save him.

She wasted precious minutes trying to push the unit off her. It wasn't moving so she tried to shuffle sideways to slide out from underneath. The pain was excruciating but she kept going, fighting off the nausea and the constant desire to shut her eyes and fade out. Then her hand was free. Almost there. Another few inches.

Then she was out. Her face was still pressed to the carpet. Grimacing in pain, she pushed to her knees.

It was the silence that struck her first.

The room was empty. A breeze blowing through the open sash window, the curtains fluttering almost merrily. Nothing merry about the smashed door or the blood that was splattered around, drops on the floor, a spray across the wall.

'Daniel.' Her voice was a broken whisper, her breath catching as she struggled to her feet. Her right arm was hanging uselessly, and a grating sensation as she breathed told her that she'd cracked some ribs. Carefully, she stepped over the smashed door, reaching for the door frame when the pain sent her swaying. She couldn't pass out; she had to find Daniel.

The silence was almost overwhelming. The stink of blood and fear catching in her throat, nausea making her weak. Daniel's bag lay slumped on the bottom stair, his phone sticking from the top. She grabbed it and slipped it into her pocket, then slid a hand along the wall and followed the blood trail to the kitchen. The breakfast bar stools were strewn about, the kitchen window shattered.

Keri staggered into the room and gasped when she saw her son slouched on the living-room sofa. 'Daniel!'

His open eyes were unblinking, his T-shirt blood-sodden.

A cry was wrenched from Keri's heart. Not Daniel. This was too much loss, how could she survive this? Sorrow bent her over, physical pain lost in a deeper soul-destroying agony that would never heal. Still doubled over, she staggered past the breakfast bar, stopping with a cry when the full scene was exposed.

The heavy glass coffee table that sat in front of the sofa had been Nathan's idea. To justify its frankly ridiculous price, he'd insisted it would be an investment.

It wouldn't be now. It lay in pieces.

But perhaps it had been an investment because the body that lay across it, was most definitely dead.

61

Keri gazed from Luke's body to her son's. Nathan, now Daniel. How could she possibly endure such pain, such loss. Such catastrophic sorrow. The knife... it was on the floor, a few feet from Luke's body. It was tempting to pick it up, to remove herself from the pain, but her daughter would need her. Keri dropped to her knees and sobbed at the thought of having to tell Abbie her twin was dead.

Then she saw Daniel blink.

The police arrived not long after Keri's call. She'd stressed the need to inform DI Elliot and was relieved to see him come through the door on the heels of grim-faced uniformed constables.

She was sitting on the bloodstained sofa, her arm around Daniel who looked stunned and shocked. He'd barely spoken a word since she'd sat and pulled him into her arms.

Elliot had a word with one of the constables before crossing the room to her. 'An ambulance is on its way.' He looked at the body lying prone on the broken table, a piece of glass jutting through its back, blood pooling underneath.

'It's supposed to be unbreakable,' Keri said, indicating the table. 'Looks like they lied.'

'You were lucky they did.' Elliot hunched down to try to see the man's face. A frown creased his brow when he straightened and turned back to Keri. 'You know who he is?'

'Yes, Luke Crocker. Jim Cody's son. He said he was trying to get revenge for his father's death.' She remembered the evil, malevolent face. 'I think he was a psychopath. A monster. He killed Nathan, Roy and Sylvester. He got what he deserved.'

Daniel lifted his head from Keri's shoulder. 'He was coming at me. I don't think he saw the table and fell forward.' He pointed to the bloodstained knife that lay on the floor a few inches away. 'I think he cracked it with the butt first, then the weight of his body, I suppose finished the job.' His voice trembled. 'I stood looking at him for a long time, waiting for him to get up and come at me again.'

Elliot eyed the blade: it looked lethal. He cocked his head as the sound of a siren grew louder. 'That sounds like your transport. If it's okay with you, Keri, we'll be in to take statements when you're feeling up to it.'

'That's fine.' She looked down at her arm. 'It's broken, so I'll probably be in plaster. Daniel has some nasty gashes that will likely need stitches.'

'You won't be able to come back here for a while.'

Keri looked around the room. It had been filled with so many memories but it was time to move on. 'I don't think we'll ever want to come back. I've phoned my brother-in-law, Philip, we'll be able to stay with him until we get sorted.'

'What about your daughter? You were lucky she wasn't here.'

Keri hugged Daniel closer. 'Neither were supposed to be here. Daniel came home to pick up a book he needed.'

'Lucky for you he did.'

'It seemed like nothing was working for me at one stage but maybe when it came down to it, the good guys won.'

'It's important to know they often do.' Elliot looked back to where the body lay. 'He was a nasty piece of work.'

'He lived by the sword and died by the sword,' Daniel said. 'Seems fitting.'

The paramedics put paid to further conversation. Soon Keri and Daniel were strapped on gurneys heading from the house into the back of two ambulances that blocked the road.

The paramedic gave Keri something for the pain and before they arrived at the hospital she was asleep. It wasn't until she was transferred to a trolley that she woke and then it was only a brief opening of the eyes, before drifting off.

When she woke again, she was in a small quiet room and her arm was in plaster.

'Hey.'

She turned her head to see the worried face of her brother-in-law. 'Hi.'

There were tears in his eyes. He bent and pressed a kiss to her cheek. 'We could have lost you and Daniel. Doesn't bear thinking about.'

'We were lucky. That monster was going to kill us all. I'm not sure where he was going to stop.' She sniffed and shook her head. 'Have you seen Daniel?'

Philip pointed to the door, tilting his hand to the right. 'He's two rooms down. He's okay, a couple of stitches to the deeper lacerations but nothing broken. He's pretty shook up but Abbie is in with him, making him talk. He'll do okay.'

'Abbie must have got a shock when you called her.'

'She's pretty pissed with you for trying to deceive them. She was here for a while but when you didn't wake, she thought she'd be better sitting with Daniel.'

'She'll be good for him. But I'll get him professional help–'

'And you too,' Philip interrupted. 'You've not had a chance to grieve for Nathan and now all this on top of it.'

'That man talked about getting revenge for something that happened over twenty years ago, but I didn't believe a word of it. He was simply an evil monster who enjoyed causing pain and chaos.'

'But now the monster has been slain and you can grieve for Nathan, then get on with your life.' Philip squeezed her hand. 'I'm making that sound simplistic but I know it won't be easy. Nathan was special. Together, we'll get through it.'

Together. Without Nathan.

But if she'd learned anything that day, it was that she could survive whatever was thrown at her.

62

A week after Nathan's funeral, Keri walked back into the offices of Metcalfe Conservation. A woman she didn't know stood at the reception desk. The employment agency had been suitably horrified to learn the truth about Luke and had reassured her they'd make up for it by sending the best they had. According to the other staff, they'd lived up to their promise.

'It's Gina, isn't it?'

'Yes, Mrs Metcalfe.'

'Keri is fine. Everything okay?'

'It only took me a couple of hours to get sorted. Roy was good at what he did, everything was efficiently organised so it was easy.'

Keri left her to it and with a glance towards Nathan's office headed for her own. She'd have to stop thinking of it as Nathan's office. Especially now that someone else was sitting in it. She sat behind her desk and dropped her head back.

The funeral had almost broken her, grief overwhelming, loss an exquisite pain. The sadness of others, her children, his brother, their friends was unbearable. The constant need to be polite, to put on a brave face, to listen to the anecdotes. It had all been too much.

The crematorium couldn't cope with the crowd who wanted to pay their respects and she was told that many had stood outside listening to the service. And afterwards, each of those who came had pressed her hand and offered sympathy. As if they could share her grief. As if they'd ever know how she felt. As if they ever could.

Now it was over.

An almost empty box of tissues sat on the corner of the desk. She pulled one out and blew her nose. The clear glass of her office walls had been frosted. She'd delayed returning till they were done, unable to face being on view while she was there.

There was a mirror in her desk drawer, she pulled it out to check her face. Thanking Chanel for its waterproof mascara, she put the mirror away again and got to her feet. No point in putting it off.

She left her office and crossed to Nathan's... the other office she corrected herself... her steps slowing as she neared the door, her heart beating faster, head thumping. If she could only turn the clock back.

Her knuckles hovered before hitting the glass door, in a firm rat-a-tat-tat.

'Come in.'

'I thought I should come and say hello,' she said, peering around the edge of the door with a feeling of dread that quickly faded.

Tom Radstock got to his feet and came round his desk with a hand outstretched. 'I wasn't sure you'd be in.'

'I said I would, didn't I? You'll learn I mean what I say.'

He waved to a chair. 'Have a seat.'

She sat and looked round with a raised eyebrow. 'You've changed everything.' He had. Different furniture. The back wall that had been pale grey was now aubergine. Huge pot plants were dotted here and there to soften the hard edges. Keri guessed they would grow too big and start to encroach on the workspace and would eventually need to go. But that was in the future.

'I thought it was best.'

It was. And she was grateful for his thoughtfulness. There was no hint of Nathan in the room. Keri's sadness was painted over with the consolation she wouldn't see him every time she walked through the door.

She sat on the comfortable spare chair. 'Everything on schedule for the merger?'

'Yes. Should all be signed off by the end of the week.'

It had been Radstock's idea. He'd rung and asked to meet her two days after Nathan's funeral and offered what Keri instantly recognised as an interesting proposition. A merger of Metcalfe Conservation and DS Construction. When Radstock had reassured her that his company would adopt Metcalfe's work philosophy, it was a done deal.

'Good.' This was going to work. She wasn't sure if she could have kept going alone.

'How's the arm?'

'I was lucky it was my left one. It's healing well and the plaster will be coming off in another couple of weeks.' She wriggled her fingers. 'I've learned to adapt.'

'With my lack of social skills, I'm almost tempted to say you were lucky.' He smiled and waggled his eyebrows.

Keri laughed. 'Lots of people have done, then looked aghast when they remembered about Nathan.' She got to her feet. 'I'm in for a few hours then I have an appointment so I'll be leaving early.'

'Fine. Maybe later in the week we could have a lunch meeting.'

'Sounds good.'

Back in her office, she sat and worked through the hundreds of emails that had come over the last few weeks. She answered each one, kept going even when tears ran down her cheeks.

~

Mid-morning, she raised her eyes when there was a knock on the door. Gina came through, a takeaway coffee in her hand. 'I found Roy's daily schedule. There was a note in it, saying you liked a cappuccino mid-morning.' She put it down with a smile that wavered when she saw Keri's face. 'I got it in a new café that's recently opened.'

Keri took a breath. 'Thank you, that was kind.'

When the door shut, she gripped the disposable cup too tightly, the contents lapping over the top to run down the side. She mopped the mess with a handful of tissues, tossed the plastic lid in the bin and sipped the hot coffee.

It was almost one when the desk phone rang. 'A Detective Inspector Elliot would like a word if it's convenient,' Gina said.

'Yes, put him through, thanks.' Keri owed the detective so much. She'd seen him at Nathan's funeral but hadn't had the opportunity to speak to him. 'Detective, good to hear from you.'

'I was told you'd be back today. I had hoped to call in but something's come up.' Voices in the background interrupted him. 'Sorry,' he said coming back to her. 'I thought I'd put your mind to rest about a couple of things. Firstly, Barry Morgan. He *is* a solicitor, works for a private practice. One of their clients is a graphic designer who has an office in that building next door to you. Morgan's name should have been on their emergency list. I had a brief word with him.' Elliot sighed. 'It appears he was quite smitten with you and aggrieved you cast him aside so easily but he's moved on now and doesn't hold any ill will.'

'It was guilt over my affair that made me suspicious of him,' Keri said.

'Perhaps now, you can put it behind *you*.'

'Eventually. Thank you for letting me know. What was the second thing?'

'I thought you might like to know that Roy Sheppard's computers were clean. He had an unhealthy obsession with the best way of growing vegetables, but nothing more sinister than that.'

It brought a smile to Keri's face. 'He did love his allotment. I'm so relieved to hear that, thank you, detective.'

'Stay safe, Keri.'

She put the phone down and sat back. It didn't change anything, wouldn't have done had she known weeks ago. But somehow, knowing that Barry hadn't been a con man made it easier to let go. As Elliot had suggested when she'd first told him about it, she'd stop beating herself over one mistake.

It was good news about Roy, too, although she'd never doubted him. Abbie and Daniel might find it easier to forgive him for one mistake. As they would if they knew about hers.

63

At 2.50pm, Keri left to keep her appointment with her general practitioner. Nathan would be smiling. Even when he'd gone, Keri was still listening to him. HRT. It was time she faced reality that she needed help to get her through the menopause.

Dr Grace Andrews had rooms in a multi-disciplinary private medical complex a mere five-minute walk from the office. She had looked after the Metcalfe family for as long as Keri could remember and had become a valued family friend. At Nathan's funeral, her grief obvious but restrained, the doctor had slipped a business card discreetly into Keri's hand, given her a hug and walked away. It was only later that Keri had looked at it and saw the details of a grief counsellor.

The doctor had a suite of rooms on the ground floor of the complex. They were, like the doctor herself, elegant and welcoming. It had been a while since Keri had needed to attend and she didn't recognise the receptionist.

'Keri Metcalfe. I have an appointment.'

The receptionist checked her computer screen. 'Yes, Mrs

Metcalfe, if you'd like to take a seat in the waiting room, she's a minute or two behind.'

It was almost ten minutes before Keri was called. She'd spent her time restlessly flicking through magazines and wondering if she should pop into the room labelled *Facilities* for a quick wee before acknowledging that she was nervous. That she had no reason to be didn't make her any less anxious.

'The doctor will see you now.'

The receptionist said the words as though Keri had a treat in store. It amused her and took away a little of the anxiety.

Dr Andrews met her at the office door and enveloped her in a brief hug before retreating to the far side of the desk. 'I won't ask how you're doing but I hope you've started the grief counselling I recommended.'

'Not yet,' Keri admitted with a smile. 'But Daniel has, and is finding it helpful.'

'He'll do well. He's a good lad. It would do you good too, you know, but I'm not going to nag.' Dr Andrews steepled her fingers on the desk and smiled gently. 'What can I help you with today?'

Keri relaxed under the sympathetic scrutiny. 'The menopause. My period had always been regular, then earlier this year it became erratic before stopping altogether almost four months back. I was hoping to manage without any help but...' She shrugged. 'Now, I think it would be best to start HRT.'

'With all you've gone through recently, that makes perfect sense. Right, let me take some details and do some observations.' She took Keri's blood pressure, pulse, and temperature, and tapped them into her record. 'That's all fine.' She searched in a drawer for a sample bottle. 'Can you manage a drop?'

Keri took the bottle. 'I'll try.' She went out to the toilet, grateful she hadn't visited earlier. The plaster on her arm made everything more awkward, but with patience and the assistance of a running tap, she managed.

Back in the doctor's office, she handed it over. 'Here you go.'

'Thank you. Give me a second to test this, then we'll discuss the best form of hormone replacement therapy for you.'

The doctor was, in fact, gone for so long that Keri was tapping her foot impatiently, a worm of worry slithering into her brain. When the door opened, and she saw the doctor's expression, the worm developed tentacles. 'Is everything okay?'

Dr Andrews sat and pressed her lips together. 'Have you had any unusual symptoms recently? Nausea maybe?'

Keri had, but she'd put it down to stress, the guilt over her affair, then the snowballing trauma that had followed. 'Yes, but it was only now and then, I didn't think much of it.' She looked at the concerned expression on the doctor's face and wondered if, yet again, the world was going to vanish beneath her feet. 'I'm sick, am I?'

'No.' The GP shook her head. 'Not sick, as such.' She reached for Keri's hand and held it tightly. 'You're pregnant.'

64

Keri laughed. Then she shook her head and started to cry. Great big heaving sobs. Emotions swirled. Guilt, joy, sorrow, sadness. She couldn't hold onto one before the next came pushing in.

'Keri.' Dr Andrews squeezed her hand. 'It'll be okay.'

Would it? Keri swallowed a sob, then hiccupped. 'How far?'

'Only an ultrasound could confirm that.' The doctor released her hand and reached for her phone. 'I might be able to expedite that.' She pursed her lips as she waited. 'Hi Jo, I have a favour to ask. An urgent ultrasound.' A smile appeared. 'You can? Yes, she's sitting right here. I'll bring her up straight away.' She hung up and got to her feet. 'My colleague is going to fit you in between bookings.'

～

Fifteen minutes later, Keri was lying on an examination couch having gel squeezed onto her belly. *Her flat belly. It had to be a mistake, she couldn't be pregnant.*

'Right, now let's see what we have here.' The sonographer

slid the transducer through the gel and over her abdomen, then looked at the monitor. 'There we are.'

Keri's hands were pressed together, the tips of her fingers resting against her lips, much as she'd held them when, as a child, she'd pray for something she wanted. 'How far gone am I?'

'Based on what I'm seeing here, about four months.'

Nathan's child. *Nathan's.* Not the man whose name was already fading from her memory and would now vanish completely. She was having Nathan's child. On the monitor, she saw the baby move, the perfect hands, the feet. And then, clear as could be. Proof it was a boy.

Keri's eyes rounded in wonder. 'He's perfect.'

'Yes.' The sonographer smiled. 'If you give me your mobile number, I'll send the recording to you so you can show it to your family.'

'Thank you, that would be fantastic.'

Dr Andrews bent and kissed her cheek. 'You going to be okay? I have to go.'

'Yes,' Keri said, looking up at her face. 'I can't thank you enough.'

'In return, get that counselling appointment.' Dr Andrews laughed. 'See, now you're making me nag.'

A short while later, Keri was walking slowly back to Walthamstow train station feeling a little numb after the earlier emotional cascade. Despite having seen the evidence, she still couldn't quite believe she was pregnant. After the twins were born, she and Nathan had planned to wait a couple of years before having any more but then, when it didn't happen, they decided to be grateful for what they had.

And now. When she thought it was all over, here she was,

pregnant. *Nathan's baby*. He would have been so happy. Her lips curved in a smile as she imagined his face.

The smile faded and her footsteps slowed, then stopped. In the middle of the pavement, the crowd parting and weaving around her.

It had been the first time she'd walked to the station for a long time.

Their photograph was still a poster on the side of the bus shelter. She remembered Nathan's laugh when he'd seen it, could almost feel his warm hand tightening around hers as they'd stood and stared.

Had the company known about his murder and left it there as a tribute? She moved closer, forming a strange triumvirate with the couple in the photograph. She let herself drift back to that day in the train station. It had been so hot, dust swirling along the platform, the smell of coffee drifting from a nearby café. For a precious moment, she remembered the feel of Nathan's skin, the heat of his hands on the small of her back. As they'd stood, so much in love they didn't notice the world whirling around them, they thought they had forever.

She laid her palm against his face on the poster. So cold. Twenty-five years. Not enough, never enough.

Blowing up the photograph to life-size had blurred their faces. Keri felt a tremble in her lower lip as her eyes filled. Was that the way he'd go in her mind too... blurring a little more as the months passed? She caressed the cold, smooth cheek with one hand and rested the other on her belly. Twenty-five years married, years before that as lovers and friends.

It was more than most people had.

It was hard to take her hand away and break that surreal triad... the couple they had been, the woman she was. Difficult to leave, but with a final glance at the couple in the photograph, people she'd known a lifetime ago, she pressed her lips together and moved away.

But as she walked to the station, she kept a hand on her belly.

Nathan's child.

THE END

ACKNOWLEDGMENTS

As ever, grateful thanks to all in Bloodhound Books especially Betsy Reavley, Fred Freeman, Tara Lyons, Heather Fitt, Morgen Bailey, Ian Skewis and Maria Slocombe.

When you work so hard on a story you want people to read it – so a huge thanks to all the bloggers who get the word out. Thanks to all who review – always such a relief to see when people enjoy what you wrote. And a big thanks to all who contact me to tell me they love my writing – that never gets tired.

The support from the writing community is always fantastic and an author's world would be a lonelier place without it – so a big thanks to all my fellow Bloodhound authors and a special thanks to the writers Jenny O'Brien and Leslie Bratspis whose almost daily communication keeps me relatively sane.

A reader, Tracy Wirick, wanted her name in a book – I hope I've done her justice.

Thanks to my husband, Robert, my sisters, brothers, extended family, and my friends for always being there for me.

I love to hear from readers – you can find me here:

Facebook: www.facebook.com/valeriekeoghnovels

Twitter: www.twitter.com/ValerieKeogh1

Instagram: www.instagram.com/valeriekeogh2

A NOTE FROM THE PUBLISHER

Thank you for reading this book. If you enjoyed it please do consider leaving a review on Amazon to help others find it too.

We hate typos. All of our books have been rigorously edited and proofread, but sometimes mistakes do slip through. If you have spotted a typo, please do let us know and we can get it amended within hours.

info@bloodhoundbooks.com

Made in the USA
Coppell, TX
07 October 2021

63655732R00173